The impulse to show ~~her what their could~~ **be was almost overpowering. All he had to do was dip his head, let his lips touch hers and kiss her as he wanted to, as she clearly wanted him to also.**

"I don't *know* what we are now, Cristin," he said instead, his voice shaking as his breath evaded him. "But here is not the place, and now is not the time, to try to find out. Best we return to the castle. The day is fading fast."

The day wasn't fading at all, but if they remained here, she so warm and close, with the sunlight in her hair and promise in her eyes, he would never want it to end. Danger may be lurking, but the greatest peril was the longing inside himself to disregard everything else. The yearning to accept that call of her eyes, the promise in her lips, a beguilement so strong he could almost taste it.

Author Note

In the first book of The Warriors of Wales series, *The Warrior's Reluctant Wife*, Rhianon watches her new husband, Peredur, ride out to war. She notes, with relief, that her beloved brother Llywelyn is not riding with him, not because he's too young, but because their father thinks him a coward. I knew then that this sensitive and pious boy had to have his own story. A chapter later, in a snow-swept castle bailey, Llywelyn, bound for home, bids his sister a sad farewell. But he doesn't say goodbye to her maid, Cristin, standing silently at her mistress's side. In fact, he barely looks at her, and I realized I'd found my heroine—and his nemesis! I hope you enjoy their story.

THE WARRIOR'S
FORBIDDEN MAIDEN

LISSA MORGAN

Harlequin
HISTORICAL

Harlequin®
HISTORICAL

ISBN-13: 978-1-335-59623-9

The Warrior's Forbidden Maiden

Copyright © 2024 by Lissa Morgan

Harlequin Enterprises ULC
22 Adelaide St. West, 41st Floor
Toronto, Ontario M5H 4E3, Canada
www.Harlequin.com

Printed in U.S.A.

Lissa Morgan hails from Wales but has traveled far and wide over the years, usually in search of the next new job, and always pursuing her love of the past along the way. A history graduate and former archivist, she now works in website design and academia. Lissa lives between the mountains and the sea in rugged North West Wales, surrounded by medieval castles that provide the perfect inspiration for her writing—the best job of all! Visit her at lissamorgan.com, Facebook.com/lissamorganhistoricalromance and Twitter.com/lissamorganauth.

Books by Lissa Morgan

Harlequin Historical

The Warriors of Wales
The Warrior's Reluctant Wife

The Welsh Lord's Convenient Bride
An Alliance with His Enemy Princess

Visit the Author Profile page
at Harlequin.com.

For Sallyann

For the crown of flowers on the
crug and so much more.

Prologue

***

'God keep you, Rhianon…and Cristin also.'

The blessing, said *for* her, but not *to* her, was nothing more than an afterthought. The first flakes of snow began to fall from a leaden sky and Cristin pulled the hood of her cloak up over her head. An icy wind brought water to her eyes, hiding the tears that welled and threatened to fall, thicker even than the snow.

Why couldn't she look away, for it was bold indeed of her to stare at them? She was a servant and not of noble birth like they were, though she had something in common with them now, on this grey morning of parting.

Her mistress, Lady Rhianon, was bound for the castle of Abereinion with her new husband, Lord Peredur, and she would go with them. Llywelyn, Rhianon's brother, would ride south, homeward to Ystrad Meurig, the castle that had once been *her* home too.

But it would be bolder still to speak up and announce that she suffered as they did. So Cristin stood, mute and invisible, her heart frozen not by cold but by pain, as Llywelyn kissed his sister goodbye.

Then his gaze met hers at last, distant behind long black lashes. He still didn't speak *to* her, though for a moment she almost thought he would. And she *couldn't* speak, for it wasn't her place. But as he looked at her in silence, with the snow falling around them, oh, how she wanted to!

Servant or not, she wanted to demand where the man of two nights ago had gone. The man who had stared intently from his seat at the high table, the potent gaze as blue as summer speedwell calling to her where she sat, much farther down the hall of Castell Llanbadarn.

The man who, after the evening meal was over, had slipped out of the shadows of a dimly lit corridor, taken her hand and led her out into the chill of the winter's night and into the warmth of a stable. The man who had loved her with his body as ardently as she'd loved him with her whole soul for as long as she could remember.

Afterwards, they'd lain in the straw, deep in each other's arms. His lips soft against her hair, he'd told her that he'd never lie with, or love, any other woman but her. And then he'd told her that they could never be together because he'd given his life to God.

The following morning, the news of his elder brother's death at the battle of Ystrad Meurig had come. Now, Llywelyn would become a warrior, not a monk, and devote his life to ruling the lordship instead of giving it to God. But it made no difference. Even though they'd known and loved each other since childhood, the barrier of status between them was as high and as unassailable as ever.

Cristin blinked as the tears gathered faster behind her eyes. He blinked, too, and, although his eyes were dry, his face was grim as he turned back to his sister.

'If you ever need me, Rhianon, you only have to send word and I will come.'

Anger closed in icy fingers around her throat, squeezing so tightly that, even if she'd *had* licence to speak, she couldn't have. What of *her* needs? What if *she* were to send him word? Would he come for *her*?

No, of course he wouldn't. Llywelyn ap Cadwgan was a lord and she was naught but a bondsman's daughter. And, even if they had joined together, passionately and with a desperate hunger that had transcended their difference in status, it had been nothing more than a stolen moment of time, a fleeting visit to a world that didn't exist.

No doubt, he'd soon forget all about her. Perhaps, on occasion, he might recall the closeness of their childhood friendship. Perhaps even think about the stable at Llanbadarn, as the place where he'd lost his virginity with his sister's maid. But she would remember forever.

Already, he was going, heedless of the fact that he was dragging her heart in his wake, like mud clinging to his boots. Bidding their host, Eilyr ap Bleddyn, farewell, he turned and strode over to where his mother, Lady Tangwystl, waited, already mounted, and swung himself gracefully up into the saddle.

The party moved off, the gates opening before them to reveal snow-covered hills stretching to eternity. At the last moment, as they passed out under the archway, he looked back. Snowflakes glistened on his raven-black hair, and his eyes, no longer the speedwell blue of summer, raged like a storm in a winter sky.

And then he was gone and Cristin was left to weather that winter alone.

Chapter One

〜〜〜〜〜

Llywelyn stood in the shadow of the church—the old church but with a new Norman tower now—and gnawed his lip. Twilight was falling over the landscape, shrouding everything in shadows of blue and black. A brilliant line of silver hung on the crests of the hills between heaven and earth, and nearer, from the castle, lights began to glow, gold spearing through arrow slits and wooden shutters.

He'd been waiting here, where the old village had been—before the Normans has burned it, leaving only this church—for an hour, perhaps more. His body was stiff, his legs ached and his bones had frozen despite the warmth of the evening. The scent of the fields—or at least the few still being tilled—was thick and heady, recalling long-lost memories.

In his boyhood he'd worked those fields alongside his father's bond tenants for the sheer joy of it, and had earned himself a taste of Cadwgan's belt as a reward. He'd gone on toiling, nevertheless, only stopping when his father punished his tenants instead.

Those years of harvests and hard work were long gone. Cadwgan ab Ieuaf was dead, his corpse lost amid the carnage and confusion of the battlefield. But his soul was surely rotting in hell, paying the penalty for his lifetime of violence and cruelty. *He* was lord now—albeit dispossessed—made his father's heir when his brother Rhodri had been killed in battle seven years ago.

The time in between seemed even longer than that, years of war and strategy, of treaties and the breaking of them, of advancing and then retreating before the Norman enemy, of hiding in woods and caves, renegades all, even their prince, the Lord Rhys. But now the time had come for the Welsh of Deheubarth to strike back.

The bell from the Cistercian Abbey of Ystrad Fflur, little more than a league distant, started to ring for Vespers, and Llywelyn's scalp began to prickle. The reverent notes carried clearly on the air and wrapped around him like the mist that was rising from the river to drown the meadows.

The candles would be lit now in the chapel and the monks would shuffle in and sing the plainsong, though their voices wouldn't carry so far as the bell did. Llywelyn's lips began to move instinctively, in silent proclamation, with only the rooks gathering in the treetops for the nightly roost to accompany him.

'Deus in adiutorium meum intende. Domine, ad adiuvandum me festina. Glória Patri, et Fílio, et Spirítui Sancto.'

If fate had been otherwise, he'd be enclosed with the *mynaich* of Ystrad Fflur, too, shut away from the world in peaceful cloisters and not waging a war at all. But fate had been contrary, and, instead of a monk he was a warrior.

The moments dragged out and, still, the road remained empty. Llywelyn went on praying, in a whisper so low that not even the rooks would hear. At the intercessional psalm for the souls of the departed, when he should have said a prayer for his father, he fell silent.

There were no words in his heart, only thoughts of hate for the man who'd sired him and made him what he'd become. For Cadwgan had triumphed in the end, though it had been the Normans that had caused the religious vocation he'd chosen in boyhood to be postponed, not the beatings he'd borne, as had Rhodri—their father's way of making them into men!

The next instant both words and thoughts vanished, as Cristin *ferch* Ifor came into sight at last. A bundle in her arms, she was walking quickly along the track that led from the castle to the new village that had been built some distance away. Llywelyn pressed himself back into the shadows and the psalm died on his lips.

He couldn't see her face, hidden beneath the hood of her cloak, but he didn't need to. He knew well enough the curve of her cheek, the curves of her body, too, stamped on his soul, never to be purged, that night they'd lost their innocence together, to each other. It felt like a lifetime ago now. It *was* a lifetime ago.

He waited until she drew abreast of where he stood and then called her name, quietly. 'Cristin!'

She stopped and whirled around. 'Who's there?'

Her voice was the same, soft and low, though now it held a sharp ring of alarm. Llywelyn's gut hollowed, as if a mailed hand had reached inside him and wrenched his soul clean out of him. He hadn't expected to feel *nothing* at seeing her again, even after all these years, but neither had he been prepared for the jolt that shook him from head to foot.

When he made no reply, she took a wary step forward

and peered through the dusk. 'Who are you and why are you hiding there? Speak up, *y cnaf*!'

The trickle of the stream nearby became a roar in his ears and, from the bank, came the squeak of a water rat, followed by a splash. Then, through the dark, he saw the glint of a blade. The weapon was only a small kitchen knife, however, and it wavered in her hand as she pointed it at him.

'I said who are you? And what are you about? Answer me, *y 'sglyfaeth*!'

Despite the threat, Llywelyn smiled. He'd never heard her use such coarse insults, not once, in the old days…but a lot had happened since then. She must have changed in so many ways, as had he, during the years of war that had ravaged their homeland.

Drawing a deep breath, he stepped out in plain view. All at once the scent of the fields, even the stench of the village *carthbwll*, rancid from a quarter league away, ceased to exist as a vague floral essence drifted through his memory and stirred his senses.

'*Henffych*, Cristin Gwalltcoch,' he said, quietly. 'It has been a long time.'

Cristin gasped and the earth seemed to shake under her feet. The figure took another step forward and, as if the sky had opened with a flash of lightning, seven long years vanished. She blinked, peered again. It wasn't possible— it *couldn't* be possible—but he was there, real, and right in front of her.

Llywelyn ap Cadwgan, her former lord…her former lover…her *only* lover.

Despite the gloom, despite the humble woollen cloak he wore with the hood low over his forehead, his features were cruelly familiar. Every sharp bone, every deep hollow, the sensitive line of his mouth, was exactly as she remembered them. Even the slight bump in his nose, where his father had broken it so many years before, was painfully visible.

His form, too, was different and yet the same. Tall and straight of limb, the slightness of his youth had become a lean hardness, the boyish grace turned to manly strength. Dressed as he was, he looked more like a serf than a nobleman, but she would have known him anywhere, with a knowledge that went beyond sight.

'Wh—why have you come back?' she demanded, finding her voice at last. 'Why now?'

He took another pace forward and swept his hood back from his head, revealing his face. 'I came to speak to you.'

Cristin grasped her weapon tighter. If he wanted to speak to her, why was he loitering in the dark like a common cutpurse? And what would he *need* to speak to her about? She might still be a servant but she wasn't *his* servant anymore. His lands, his castle, the village and its people, belonged to another master now.

Not even Lord Cadwgan had been strong enough to resist the Normans, who'd swept into Uwch Aeron six years ago. He'd retreated, sent his wife into exile, then fled with the few men left to him into the forests and high grounds. From there, they'd harried the enemy as fleas harried a dog, and the common people were left to the mercy of their *new* lord, which had no mercy about it at all.

She levelled her knife, not with intent but in a defence she would never have needed before. For there was a presence about Llywelyn now that he hadn't had in his youth, a formidable and relentless presence that came at her like a storm sweeping down a mountainside.

'Don't come any closer!' Cristin moved back a step, the

change in him frightening her where a moment ago she'd been merely stunned. 'Stay where you are!'

His brows drew together but he stopped in his tracks. 'I mean you no harm.'

Oh, easy words! Had he forgotten the injury he'd done her seven years ago? When he'd taken her body and her heart for his own and left her with nothing but an aching chasm of loss that no one else could ever fill.

'Or perhaps you have forgotten me, Cristin Gwalltcoch?'

The childhood name was one she hadn't heard in a long time. *Cristin of the red hair.* A name that, as they'd grown up over endless summers, was said less in jest, more in earnest. And with a promise in it that had made her believe the differences in their status hadn't mattered. But as for forgetting...no, never!

'Nothing is forgotten, Lord Llywelyn.'

As she spoke, a light appeared farther along the track, then a footfall sounded, coming from the village. The next instant Llywelyn's hand closed around her wrist and she was pulled out of the road and around to the back of the church.

He flattened them both against the wall, pressing her beneath him, his forefinger over her lips. His body touched hers all the way down, and the wild mountain scent of him—heather and oak, rain and earth—swamped her senses.

'Don't make a sound,' he whispered, so close his breath caressed her face.

Cristin couldn't have uttered a sound even if she'd wanted to. The bundle she carried fell noiselessly from her grasp, her knife with it. Squeezing her eyes shut, she welcomed him, just as she had that night in the stable. He might have changed, as *she* had changed, but one thing was still the same.

She still loved him with every bone of her body, every drop of her blood, with her whole soul.

The truth of that made her gasp out loud. As her lips parted, she tasted him on her breath, and another gasp rose up in the wake of the first.

'Ust!'

At his warning, Cristin opened her eyes to see the light bobbing closer. Then the footsteps shuffled past and faded away, darkness closing in once more. Llywelyn's gaze was locked on hers, gleaming like hoarfrost under a midnight moon.

'Who was that? And where is he bound at this hour?'

'It was Owain Dafad, the shepherd, going to check the lambing pens,' she whispered, tasting him on her lips again. 'This is the lambing time,' she added, unable to stop herself wanting to taste more.

He nodded. 'Of course, I'd forgotten…'

His gaze lingered a moment longer, then he turned his head to look up and down the road, before his eyes met hers again. 'It's quiet now, no one else abroad. I don't think he saw us.'

She said nothing and he smiled but his voice was tentative, uncertain. 'But I never expected to see *you* again, Cristin. Have you nothing to say to me?'

It was that motion of his lips, a smile and yet not one, that unsealed her own lips at last. 'No,' she retorted. 'I have not.'

A shadow crossed his face. 'I suppose it *is* too much to expect after so long.' He drew a breath, let it out. 'I, however, have much to say to you, but we can't talk here. Take me to your house.'

Cristin pressed herself back against the wall, her eyes

darting to the village, dark in the distance. 'No,' she said, quickly. 'We can't go there.'

'Would your father bar me entry?' The question held both disgust and disappointment. 'Has *he*, like so many others, accepted Norman rule so readily?'

'We had no choice in the matter!' She glared up at him, anger biting as he condemned them without knowledge or cause. 'We are bond tenants of a *new* master now and a cruel one at that.'

'But not for much longer. The Lord Rhys has taken to the field at last.'

'What is that to us?' He spoke like a warrior and not like the man she'd once known. The man who'd abhorred and rejected violence and all those who waged it, but now he was changed in *that*, too, it seemed. 'In war, we peasants matter little to one side or the other at the end of the day.'

'You were never a peasant, Cristin, not to me.' His brow furrowed. 'Nor were *any* of my family's bondspeople…or have you forgotten *that* too?'

Cristin's heart trembled. Part of her longed to tell him that she remembered every single moment they'd shared, the other part fearing to reveal anything at all.

'Since the Normans came, the folk here have forgotten the old days,' she said. 'Now we strive only to stay alive.'

'Are the villagers not to be trusted, none of them?'

'Most are still loyal,' she replied. 'But there are others that cannot be trusted at all.'

He sighed, shook his head. 'Well, this won't be the first village to turn coat and betray its countrymen to the enemy, and it won't be the last.'

Cristin couldn't deny it. She'd witnessed with shame and with sadness how living under the new lord of Ystrad Meurig had split families and communities. How fear and greed had made traitors of men until everyone kept their own counsel, lived in secrecy instead of openly and in trust with their neighbours as before.

And she herself lived with the greatest secret of all.

'Who here has turned traitor?' There was urgency in his tone now. 'I need their names.'

'The shepherd that passed by just now is one who would betray you without hesitation.' She answered with care, choosing her words, keeping back others, in order to protect the innocent. 'But most of the villagers are still faithful to the house of Cadwgan.'

'Including Ifor, your father?'

'My father is dead…my mother too,' she said bluntly, for how else could it be said? She had no tears left to convey the grief, or the loss, or the aloneness, so she didn't try. 'They died of the sickness two years since.'

There was a pause before he nodded, slowly, a heavy motion. 'Yes, I had heard of the pestilence in these parts. Is that why the Normans burned the village, to contain it, and stop it spreading to the castle?'

'There *was* no pestilence in the village before they came.' Cristin let her anger flow at that injustice. 'It was *they* who brought it here! But they destroyed our homes all the same, and ordered us to rebuild further from the castle.'

Even in the gloom, she saw the expression of disgust that crossed Llywelyn's face, and the soft curse on his breath was clearer still. 'And what of your brother?'

'Idris was killed at Llanymyddfri fighting for the Lord Rhys.'

An owl shrieked overhead and somewhere a dog barked, as the night crept closer. 'It grieves me sorely to hear about your family, Cristin. God keep their souls.'

The sorrow in the words was real. Llywelyn had known

her family well, had liked them, and they had liked him. Her jovial father had shown him that not all fathers were the same, and her mother had given him the affection that his own mother had withheld.

Of course he would feel their loss as keenly as she did. How could someone so gentle, so sensitive, *not* feel it? The piety of his youth that he'd adopted almost as a shield of defiance against his *impious* father had been one of the reasons she'd loved him.

That he spoke to her and only her about his fears, showed her and only her the wounds he hid from everyone else, had made him brave in her eyes, not weak, as his sire thought him. And the differences in their status hadn't seemed important as they'd grown up together—and grown closer.

It had been cruelly ironic that his faith, even more than his noble birth, had driven them apart. Crueller still to learn, on her return to the village—only a week after they'd parted at Llanbadarn—that Llywelyn had abandoned his religious calling so completely and taken up the sword with a zeal she would never have believed of him. And it was the soldier now, not the erstwhile monk, who addressed her as if there had never been any closeness between them at all.

'But now I need information from you, and quickly. How many men garrison the castle?'

Cristin answered at once, a lifetime of servitude to his family behind her prompt reply, only *she* aware of the hurt inside. 'Near fifty, though not all are soldiers. There are masons and craftsmen among them, too, and some of the villagers serve there in some capacity or another, as do I.'

He chewed his lip for a moment and looked away, his gaze sweeping towards the castle, looming darkly on its mound. 'What is your role there?'

'I wash and mend garments.' She spoke in whispers still,

as he did, just as they had that night in the stable. Then they'd not been soldier and serf, lord and minion, but simply man and woman, for a short while at least. 'Sometimes, if I'm needed, I help in the kitchen and serve at the tables.'

He was silent a moment, as if thinking hard, and Cristin studied him as well as she could in the gathering gloom. Why was he here, in the midst of his enemies, dressed like a peasant, his sword hidden beneath his cloak?

'Maelgwn ab Eilyr is still in command?'

She nodded, and shivered, her flesh suddenly chilled as realisation dawned. This wasn't the man she had loved. Like his religious vocation, that man had gone, and it was a stranger now who stared down at her with hard and unremitting eyes.

'Yes,' she said, 'though the Normans under his command fear him almost as much as we do.'

'That I don't doubt, even though he is my kin by marriage.' He shook his head. 'It is a blessing that Eilyr ap Bleddyn is dead and spared the shame of knowing his son fights for the enemy.'

Cristin had seen Maelgwn long before he'd become lord here in Uwch Aeron. He was the brother of Peredur ab Eilyr, husband to her former mistress, Rhianon. He'd never recognised her, of course, even though she'd been at the wedding feast at Llanbadarn seven years earlier. But why would he recognise a mere bondswoman, after all?

'And at night, how many guard the gates?'

Llywelyn's relentless questions pounded like hammers in Cristin's ears, battering her with the knowledge of how little she must mean to him now, or rather to the man he'd now become. Yet, there was a time when she'd thought she'd meant everything to him, as he had to her.

'I don't know,' she said, hiding her hurt behind a shrug

of her shoulders. 'I return home before dusk. But during the daytime, there are two on the main gate and one at the postern.'

'Why do you return to the village each evening?'

Cristin hesitated. 'Why would I *not* return?' she said, hoping he didn't hear the evasion in her voice. 'They have no need of me at the castle once my duties are done, and I have…domestic chores to fulfil at home.'

He walked away a few paces and stared along the road at the dark village, where lights were beginning to show, thinly, through poorly made doors and windows.

'So, you have a husband that you return to? Children, too, perhaps?'

Cristin almost laughed. A husband! How could she ever take any other man under her roof, to her bed, into her heart? Even if she'd wanted to, even if she *should* do if she were sensible, she'd lost her bride's worth that night when she'd given him her maidenhead.

'No, I have no husband, my lord.' She lifted her chin but her cheeks flamed. How foolish she had been. She wasn't the first minion to let a nobleman rob her of her most valuable possession, and she wouldn't be the last.

'And now, if you have done with me, may I have leave to go?'

Cristin pushed herself away from the church wall and rearranged her clothing, disarrayed when he'd leaned so close. As he'd left *her* in disarray by stirring up memories that didn't exist for him but were torture for her.

She picked up the bundle that had fallen to the ground, and the knife, which she tucked into her girdle. Then she paused. She was still a servant and couldn't go without his leave so, clearing her throat, she stepped forward.

'I asked you if I may go now, Lord Llywelyn.'

* * *

'Stop calling me that.'

The words were out before Llywelyn could prevent them. Yet, what else was she supposed to call him, after all? Not the endearments she'd uttered that night in the stable, shyly at first, uncertain, and then bolder, with feeling and with passion.

Endearments he'd returned, meaning every word, even though he'd no right to say them, nor to embrace that passion, that need, that had eclipsed everything else. But because he'd known he'd never see Cristin again, he'd yielded to his love for her—desperately, with total abandon.

Her chin tilted upwards. 'So, what *should* I call you?'

Llywelyn could well imagine what she'd *like* to call him. He'd called himself worse over the years since they'd parted. Yet, he'd always told her, even when they were children together, that the only way to avoid becoming the man his father expected him to be, the only way to avoid fighting and killing—the destiny of all lords—was to take the vows of a monk.

'Llywelyn,' he said, with a stab of guilt as sharp as it had been that night, for those vows, though delayed, still stood as firm as when he'd given them as the reason that they must part, forever. 'You called me so once upon a time, did you not?'

Her eyes held his, boldly through the growing darkness. Not that he needed either daylight or torchlight to know their colour. They were hazel with a hint of green below the surface. Beautiful eyes with hidden depths, which had always seen deeply.

'That was a long time ago.' She turned her head away with a sharp little jerk. 'Things are different now.'

Her hood fell back a little, revealing the coif below that

hid her hair. Like that of her eyes, the colour of it was branded on his soul, too, like a fire that had burned quietly inside him all down the years.

'Cristin Gwalltcoch.' Instinctively, Llywelyn's fingers twitched at the memory of how he'd loosened her braid that long-ago night and let those glorious locks tumble down into his hands. 'Is it still as fiery as ever it was?'

She met his eyes again, her own suddenly cool, defensive and, at the same time, accusing. 'Is it the lord…or the monk who asks?'

Those eyes had looked at him like that, too, in the bailey of Castell Llanbadarn, on that morning of departure, as the snow had fallen over him, burying him in shame. With people around them—his sister and her husband, a host of others—he'd had no opportunity to speak what he should have spoken.

'I am not a monk,' he said, the statement like a penance waiting to be paid. And one day he would have to make amends for putting down his prayer book and taking up the sword instead. Just as he would have to ask forgiveness for cursing his dead brother, time and again, for dying and leaving the mantle of lordly responsibility on *his* shoulders. 'Not now.'

'No… I know you have chosen a different path.' Her tone was withering. 'But neither should a lord think on the hair of a bondswoman, whether she be *his* bondswoman or another's.'

'You are right, Cristin,' Llywelyn moved a step closer, breathed once more the aroma of meadow flowers, feeling a memory stir. 'A lord should not have such thoughts any more than a monk should, and I am here on matters of war, not of faith,' he said. 'In two days' time, an attempt will be made to retake the *cantref* of Ceredigion, and all its castles—the Lord Rhys upon Castell Llanbadarn, Peredur ab Eilyr upon the castle of Abereinion, and I here upon Ystrad Meurig.'

In the growing dusk, her face went pale. 'A battle…?'

He nodded. 'The three castles must be taken quickly and all at once, but I would prefer stealth to slaughter, and to take the castle by surprise, with as little bloodshed as possible.'

Reaching out, he touched her arm. 'Ystrad Meurig's walls are of timber, so could be fired if necessary, but it has a new tower of stone. If the enemy barricade themselves in there, it would mean a siege that might last weeks.'

Cristin's eyes searched his, intently and with alarm, as if she expected a *coup de grace* to fall from his lips. Llywelyn steeled himself to give it and, at the same time, cursed this war that was about to commence. And, most bitterly of all, he cursed himself for his part in it. For to wage it now, during the Holy Easter Feast, was nothing less than sacrilege, yet another sin to stain his soul.

'You have access, you come and go freely, you know the routine of the garrison. So, tomorrow night after sunset, when the Easter Vigil begins, I need you to open the gates for me.'

Chapter Two

~~~~~~~~~~~

The bundle Cristin held almost slipped from her grasp all over again. She fumbled with it, managed to stop it falling to the ground, but she wasn't quick enough to prevent it from coming undone. And as the cloth parted, its contents tumbled out to land with little thuds at her feet.

Her face burning, she bent to retrieve them. 'Leave be! I'll do it!'

But Llywelyn was already helping to gather the paltry and betraying items—a chunk of bread, half a dozen oat-cakes, a hard lump of cheese and the ends of two burned-out candles. She felt him watching her as she piled them into the cloth and tied the bundle into a knot. And, when they had both risen to their feet, the inevitable question came.

'You are stealing food from the castle?'

'Yes, and whatever else I can steal too!' Cristin lifted her chin. 'What of it?'

'Has it been so hard for you these last years, then?'

Did he think all this food was for *her*? Glancing down at herself, she felt her cheeks burn hotter still. Of course, he must, how could he not? She had grown so thin, *every-*

one had, except those treacherous few who crept up to the enemy's table and begged like dogs.

'It has been hard for us *all*,' she replied, her shame complete. 'At least those who are left alive.'

'So hard that you have to *steal*?'

She glared up at him. 'Why should the villagers starve while the Normans gorge themselves? We can't survive on the scraps they leave us after they take our corn and our livestock! Why, their horses eat better than we do! Even your parents—'

Biting her lip, she swallowed back the rest of the words. She must be careful what she said, even to Llywelyn… *especially* to Llywelyn.

'Even my parents what?'

'Couldn't save us since they couldn't even save themselves,' she replied. 'They suffered and starved along with their bondspeople.'

'I know. And I wasn't here.'

'No, you *weren't* here,' she accused, unheeding of the fact that a servant should not accuse a *lord* of anything. 'You don't know how it has been here since *they* came.'

There was a long silence and Cristin wished she could swallow the words back. How *could* he have returned, when the Normans had captured every castle in Ceredigion, when all the Welsh were either bondspeople like her, or dead, or in hiding, or dispossessed, or traitors.

Even the Lord Rhys, the mighty Prince of Deheubarth, had gone as prisoner of Henry of England for a while, so she'd heard, his sons also, powerless against the king and his marcher lords. If Llywelyn *had* come back, he, too, would have lost his life or his liberty in a futile cause. At least in exile, he was alive and free.

Whether he saw the contrition on her face, she wasn't

sure, but when he spoke again, the words were not a request but a command. 'Then tell me.'

Cristin looked away, toward the miserable cluster of houses in the distance. Half of them were empty now, in ill repair, their surviving inhabitants living in hardship. It hadn't been like that once. The old village had been a community, a place of belonging, its people bond tenants of Llywelyn's family for twenty years and more, until all had fallen to the enemy. He *deserved* to know.

'It wasn't too bad at first,' she began. 'But after the pestilence came, and our houses were burned, and people died, and animals starved and crops failed...terrible things happened. Neighbour turned on neighbour, friendship turned to hate, everyone living in fear.'

Cristin drew a steadying breath, forced herself to go on, reliving all the horror of those years. 'I've seen a man kill another over a mouldy piece of bread! No one laughs now, children—the few that are left—are afraid to play out of doors.' Her voice broke then. 'Nobody is safe, or happy anymore...'

As her words faded, Llywelyn cursed and moved past her to lean against the church door. Folding his arms, he stood in silence for a long moment, his gaze cast down to the ground. Cristin waited, her heart thumping, clutching her bundle to her breast, as if that would muffle the sound.

'I should have returned before now,' he said.

The remark was said quietly but remorse lay below it, like a terrible and irrefutable echo.

'If you had, it wouldn't have made any difference.' She shook her head, knowing it to be true. 'You would have been killed, or suffered an even worse fate, like your father...'

'Cadwgan?' With the name, the remorse was gone and

his words came with bitterness now. 'Some might say my father's fate was a just punishment.'

Cristin shivered, not at the words themselves but at the way they'd been said. She might be low born but she wasn't ignorant. She'd lived in Cadwgan's household for a while, as maid to his daughter, Lady Rhianon, and knew full well what had gone on within those walls.

She'd heard the shouts, the curses, the tears, the lashings of belts and thumping of fists. When it happened, afterwards she'd tend to her mistress, treating cuts and bruises, but she never administered to the eldest boy, Rhodri, when he fell afoul of his father's temper. It wasn't her place, and anyway she was afraid of him, since he grew up to be cruel and violent too.

But Llywelyn…somehow, wherever she was in the castle, she always knew when it was *he* at the end of his father's rage. She felt his pain, as keenly as if the rod fell upon her, breaking *her* skin, shattering *her* bones. And, dropping her duties, she would wait for him…and he always came, sooner or later, into her arms.

'Do *you* say so also?' she asked.

'He received in death only that which he had dealt during his life.'

A taste of pity filled Cristin's mouth, though whether for the father or the son, she wasn't sure. Perhaps both. Llywelyn had just cause to hate his father, yes, but there was more he didn't know, more that she couldn't tell him, not until she was sure of him.

'Lord Cadwgan's cruel whims were nothing compared to those of our new lord at the castle.' Suddenly, the comparison made her afraid. 'You shouldn't have come back at all, not now, not alone! It isn't safe for *you* either…'

'I'm not alone. My men are camped in the forest of Mynydd Bach to the north.'

Of course. The battle. That was why he was here, to seek a war, not safety. To embroil them all once more in conflict and, if that battle were lost, nothing would change. It might become even worse.

'I am a soldier and so nothing in life is safe, but you...' His gaze found hers, darker than the falling twilight. 'Is that why you carry a weapon, Cristin? To protect yourself?'

'Only a fool ventures out without a weapon now,' she replied, since it was true. 'Everyone here must see to their own defence since no one else will.'

'I am here now.' Llywelyn pushed himself away from the wall and in two strides was standing in front of her. 'And, in a few days' time, *no one* will have cause to fear ever again.'

'You seem very sure of that. But what if you lose the battle?'

'We won't.' His conviction was as terrifying as that impending battle. 'Roger de Clare's hand in the murder of Einion ab Anarawd, nephew to the Lord Rhys, has opened the floodgates. Rhys is out for revenge and means to drive the invaders out of Deheubarth for good.'

'But the Normans are too many,' Cristin argued. 'They are too strong...'

He shook his head. 'The Princes of Gwynedd and Powys are of one mind with Rhys. None have done homage to Henry of England, as he demanded last year at Woodstock. Instead, all are determined that Wales will be free, with God's help...and with *your* help.'

Cristin didn't understand his words. She didn't know what Woodstock was and Einion ab Anarawd wasn't the first Welshman to be slain by Norman hands, through treachery or in battle. And, for her, Wales only stretched as far as the borders of her village.

'So, will you help me, Cristin? Will you open the castle gates tomorrow night? It is asking much of you, I know. It is dangerous and will take courage and if there was any other way…' His breath was urgent on her face as he bent his head lower. 'But there isn't. This may be our one chance and we *mustn't* fail!'

Cristin felt fear dry her mouth. He'd asked much of her once before and she'd given it willingly and without hesitation. But this was different. *He* was different. Before, she'd *loved* him, but now…

And yet, even if her country was smaller than the one he meant, it was hers all the same.

'What would I have to do?'

'Tomorrow remain in the castle instead of returning here, conceal yourself somewhere where you will not be discovered. When the Compline bell at the abbey church ceases, try and entice the guard at the postern gate away.'

Cristin's head began to swim at the enormity of what she'd agreed to do, what it might entail, how it might end. 'How?'

'Are there any Welsh at the castle who are still loyal?'

'Gronw Gof, your father's blacksmith. He was forced to work for the Normans when their own smith died of the pestilence. He is loyal but he is old now.'

'He was always a good man.' He nodded. 'We must trust he is still. Get him to help you and invent some urgency, tell the guard that he's wanted by his superior, anything you can think of. With luck, he may have fallen asleep anyway.'

'And if he's not asleep and won't leave his post?'

'Then Gronw must use that knife of yours, or one of his

own. The guard needn't be killed, just disabled enough to give you a chance to open the gate. We will do the rest.'

Cristin forced herself to think calmly. She might carry a knife, but she'd never had to use it, though once she'd had to draw it when the lewd teasing of one of the soldiers at the castle went too far. If the guard at the gate wouldn't comply…could she and Gronw Gof do the deed? Dare they?

But the answer was a simple and inevitable one. She'd always been there when he'd asked, when he needed her, and she could not refuse him now. 'Yes, I will help you, and I know Gronw will too.'

His eyes closed for a moment and his hands came to rest over hers where she clutched her bundle to her midriff. His forehead dipped and touched hers. 'Thank you, Cristin.'

They stood like that, in silence for a long moment, the sounds of the night all around them. And all at once, yet so slowly that it hardly seemed to happen, there was a change, a shift.

As if Llywelyn felt it too, his head lifted and he stared down at her with gleaming eyes, their expression unfathomable, yet intense. The twilight took on an eerie nature, as if the whole of the landscape had stilled too, and was watching them, wondering what would happen next.

His hands curled tighter over hers and his mouth came down close to hers, his breath warm on her face. And, on a murmur, the sound of her name, soft and low, erased seven long years as if they'd never been.

'Cristin…'

But those years *had* been. Things had happened that he didn't yet know about, might never know about if the battle went ill. Things she needed to tell him…show him…tonight.

Cristin wrenched herself away. 'There is something you must know…'

His brow lifted, his eyes gleaming differently now. 'What is it?'

She shook her head. 'Come with me, to the village.'

Turning swiftly, she began to walk, her footsteps brisk despite the dark. Llywelyn falling into step beside her as his long strides caught her up easily.

'Where are we going?'

'To my house.'

His tone became wary 'Why?'

Cristin evaded his question. It was better to let him see than to try to tell him in words, or at least she hoped it would be. Even so, she began to doubt. Should she have kept her secret hidden? But it was too late to go backwards now and, if the battle was won tomorrow, he would find out anyway.

'You will see for yourself very soon.'

He asked nothing more but she felt him glance frequently at her face, in between furtive glances ahead, to the side and to the rear. It was as they entered the silent village that he put his hand on her arm, slowing her progress.

'This is too dangerous for my plans. If the castle is to fall, I cannot be discovered here, Cristin.'

'We are nearly there. No one will see you.'

The sound of a door opening took up where her voice left off. A beam of light snaked across the ground, and a moment later her name came. But this time it was said, not in the tone of a childhood friend, nor that of an erstwhile lover, but in the way a mistress speaks to her servant.

'Cristin!'

Llywelyn jerked to a halt as a woman's voice shattered the silence and the light from the open door ahead illuminated the darkness. Too bright a light—a light that could upset everything. With a curse, he started to drag Cristin into the safety of the shadows, and then the figure of a woman stepped over the threshold of the doorway. She was just a silhouette, but something familiar about her stopped his heart as well as his feet.

'Who is there with you?'

The voice was not just familiar but unmistakable. Unheeding now of the need for secrecy or disguise, Llywelyn dropped Cristin's wrist and strode across the road to the house. And there, on the threshold, he met Tangwystl *ferch* Tewdwr, his mother.

'Llywelyn…is that you?'

His name on her tongue came strangely to his ears, since it had been a long time since he'd heard it. The ravages of her face, now he saw it clearer, were terrible to behold. And her hair—once lustrous and raven-black—hung in silver straggles over her shoulders. She didn't look at all like he remembered her and yet…

'Llywelyn…it *is* you…isn't it?'

Tangwystl stared at him at if seeing a ghost, or perhaps his peasant garb was too effective a disguise. But before he could speak, Cristin suddenly appeared at his side.

'Quickly, we must go back inside. The shepherd is returning from the pens.'

Llywelyn felt himself being pushed from behind, his mother retreating before him. The dark of the night became the light of candles and then the door slammed. He spun round, his hand going to his sword hilt, to see Cristin shoot the bar across.

'Keep still, make no noise!' She leaned back against the ill-fitting wood, one palm raised in warning, the other clenched to her midriff, her thin body no barrier at all should that door be forced.

Llywelyn cast his gaze quickly about the tiny room, made smaller by the curtain drawn across its length down the centre, but could see no other way in—or out. A poor fire crackled in the hearth to one side, an ancient grey cat curled there, its amber eyes regarding him with no curiosity whatsoever. A memory stirred and vanished as the shuffling footsteps of the shepherd slowed and stopped right outside the house.

There was no sound from without, but the presence of the figure beyond the door was palpable. He could almost see the man leaning close, his ear to the wood perhaps, a cunning expression on his face. Even the cat got up, its bony back arched and its fur in spikes as it sensed the tension.

At last, the footsteps moved on and faded away. Still, nobody moved nor spoke. A rodent scratched in the rafters. The shutter over the window creaked. Then silence again. Llywelyn exhaled and dropped his hand away from his sword hilt.

Cristin was still at the door, not looking at him, but at the woman who stood behind him. Slowly, his feet feeling as if they'd sunk into the earthen floor, he turned around to face his mother, and the sense of horror returned.

Even though she was not yet fifty, she was shrivelled, smaller in stature than he remembered her. In the glow of the rush lights, the skin of her aged face stretched tight over bone, and her gown, once of fine jaune wool, was threadbare.

'Mother,' he said, all other words out of his reach for the moment as he bit back the utterances of outrage that surged into his mouth. 'What are you doing here?'

The cat came to wrap itself around his boots and began to purr, but Tangwystl seemed to have no words at all now, her shock appearing even greater than his. Taking her hand,

Llywelyn sat her down on the stool before the hearth and dropped to his haunches before her.

'I thought you were safe in the north…with Rhianon?'

Tangwystl was composed now, her face set into the dispassionate mask he'd known so well. But the bones of her fingers in his were so fragile they might have broken had he held too tightly.

'No, as you see, I am not in the north.'

Llywelyn frowned. 'But a message was sent south, telling me so.'

'I was there, yes, for a while and then I returned.'

He shook his head, nothing making any sense, though her words were clear enough. 'You journeyed from Gwynedd…a dozen leagues or more…all alone?'

'No, Iago ap Dafydd, the priest, rode with me.'

'Iago ap Dafydd?'

'A layman of Llanbadarn, who trained with your uncle Edwin for the priesthood. He has been ministering to us here since the Norman priest fled the pestilence.'

He glanced up as Cristin answered and came to stand quietly beside his mother, putting a hand on one thin shoulder. A gesture of a trust, a familiarity, affection even, between them that he hadn't noticed until then.

'What is going on here?' he asked of both of them. 'Why, in God's name, would you leave safety to return here, into the midst of our enemies?'

There was a pause as the two women exchanged glances. And, as brief as the exchange was, it held a multitude of secrets. Llywelyn waited, still on his haunches, rubbing his mother's cold hands to warm them. But after a moment, she withdrew them and folded them in her lap. He forced himself to ignore a little sense of rejection, and all the rejections of his childhood that came in its wake.

'Mother…did you not consider the danger you would be in?'

'I knew the danger well enough, my son.' Tangwystl nodded. 'When Roger de Clare came and took Ceredigion, not long after you left, we had to surrender Ystrad Meurig to the Normans. I fled to Meirionnydd, with Rhianon and her children, and also Edwin and Iago, to the family of Eilyr ap Bleddyn. Your father remained here and fought on as best he could.'

'Yes, all that I know.'

Llywelyn curbed his impatience as a dreadful thought struck him. She had suffered much these past seven years, and more the long years before, married to Cadwgan. Her husband—having castrated and blinded his brother Edwin to steal Tangwystl from him—had then shown her, and their children, not love but unrelenting violence. *Dduw annwyl!* Had all that suffering finally robbed her of wits?

It wouldn't surprise him. His earliest childhood memory was of her running along a corridor, her black hair streaming behind her, her blue eyes awash with tears and her face a mask of terror. She'd scooped him up in her arms and kept on running. And, from somewhere beyond, Cadwgan's roar shook the walls, followed by a scream from his sister Rhianon.

'I know also that Cadwgan was killed in battle three years ago,' Llywelyn said, cursing his sire for all the harm he'd caused on that vaguely remembered day, when he'd been too young to understand, and on so many other days down throughout the years, when he'd come to understand only too well.

'But I believed you safely away,' he went on. 'Otherwise I would have returned before this. I could have asked that you be given shelter in the household of the Lord Rhys, further south in Cantref Mawr.'

'I would not have gone.'

He shook his head, truly baffled now. 'Wouldn't have gone? Why not?'

The thin shoulders lifted and then drooped again. 'Because your father wasn't killed in battle, Llywelyn. He was attacked, yes, but he wasn't killed.'

Llywelyn felt himself totter on his haunches, and his skin turned to ice beneath his clothes. 'Go on.'

'He was set upon, while hunting in the forest of Cwm Berwyn. A band of Flemish knights beat him nearly to the death.'

His mother paused, drew a laboured breath, and Cristin supplied the rest of the story. 'My father found him two days later, still alive.'

Llywelyn looked from one to the other, saw a bond of trust that neither he, nor his siblings, had ever shared with *either* parent. His father had cared nothing for familial bonds and his mother had been too distracted by fear to form *any* sort of bond with her children. For a moment he knew a pang of envy at what he'd missed. It shocked him.

'Cadwgan *would* have died if Ifor hadn't saved him, brought him to this house. Word was sent to me and so I came back.' His mother took up the tale again. 'If it hadn't been for Cristin, we would have died in the pestilence that came soon after. But it took her poor parents, God keep them.'

Tangwystl reached for Cristin's hand and squeezed it. 'Through her care, we've survived these last two years. It is because of *her*, and the food she brings from the castle, and the silent tongues of the villagers—thus far—that we are still alive at all.'

'We?' Slowly, Llywelyn rose to his feet and looked from his mother to Cristin and back again, the conclusion of the story, yet unuttered, dawning all the same. Horror closed in about him and suddenly he was in that corridor again, staring at his mother running towards him, Rhianon's scream echoing in his ears. 'Are you saying that Cadwgan...*lives*?'

His answer came, not from the mouths of either of the women, but from behind the rough woollen curtain that divided the room. It wasn't a coherent answer, only the unintelligible muttering of a man's voice, as if in sleep or delirium.

Lifting a hand, Llywelyn pointed, aware his finger trembled, as if the pestilence had remained and now possessed *him*. 'Who lies beyond that curtain?'

The two women exchanged glances once more and then his mother rose to her feet and met his eyes. 'Cadwgan, your father, lies there.'

'No...' He shook his head, though the effort at denial was futile. He *felt* the evil in the room without having to see it. The wonder was he'd not known it at once, so ingrained in his soul was the stench of it. 'No! That cannot be... I don't believe it.'

Tangwystl reached out a thin arm. 'It *is* your father, Llywelyn. Come and look.'

'No, never!'

From beyond the curtain, more muttering came, and the material moved as if a hand had clutched at its folds. Llywelyn didn't wait for that curtain to part, revealing the monster that lay beyond. Turning on his heel, he made for the door, tripping over the cat that had come to swarm around his legs once more.

The house was suddenly suffocating, the walls closing in on him, choking him like a fist around his throat. The rush lights flickered so brightly that they dazzled him as he fumbled for the bar, his hands clumsy and missing their hold.

'Llywelyn! Don't leave. Come…see you father, speak with him!'

Llywelyn paused at his mother's command, cold fury drenching him like a shower of hail. Speak with the devil? Look upon the man who'd beaten his mother and sister into a state of constant terror? Who'd brutalised his brother Rhodri until, in order to defend himself, he'd turned into a brute himself? Who'd tried to do the same to *him* and, when it had failed, had not desisted but tried harder still—with words and threats, fists and leather—until he *had* almost broken him?

'No!' He shook his head and grasped the bar of the door firmly. 'I will not see that man, not now, not ever. Cadwgan may live but he is dead to me and always will be.'

The hatred in the words filled the house, right up to the rafters, shaking dust from the beams. Cristin ran to the door and clutched Llywelyn's arm as he lifted the bar and threw it to one side. 'Stop! Heed your mother. Don't go… not like this.'

He turned his head, his eyes blazing with a fury she'd never seen there, not like this, because, for the first time ever, it was directed at *her*. 'Why didn't you tell me at once, Cristin?'

She flinched as if he'd raised his hand and struck her. 'I… I couldn't. I didn't know how, or if it was even my place to tell you.'

'Was it your place to keep silent?' He hissed a profanity under his breath, something else that she'd rarely heard from him. 'No wonder you were so reluctant to bring me here when I asked!'

'It wasn't like that!'

'Then how was it?'

'You coming so unexpectedly tonight... I needed time to think about *how* to tell you.' Cristin was still clutching his arm but she couldn't let go. 'I know how things were between you and Lord Cadwgan, and I knew you thought your father dead...'

'Stop calling him that!' The anger in his eyes was so terrible now that she recoiled, snatching her hand away from his sleeve. 'You of *all* people, Cristin, should know he was *never* a father to me!'

'My lord—please! Don't leave, stay and—'

But it was too late. Llywelyn was already wrenching the door open. Then, without a backward glance, he lurched out into the night, as heedless of the need for caution as he'd been heedful of it when they'd stood in secret behind the church.

'Wait!'

He disappeared into the darkness, as shockingly as he'd appeared, hours before it seemed now. Surely he wouldn't go like this? Surely he couldn't be so callous as to shut his ears and his heart to his mother, even to his father? Time had passed, things had changed, more than he knew. If he would only return, listen and learn, perhaps even relent...

But he didn't. The night closed in again. Tangwystl sighed and Cadwgan called from the bed. Slowly, Cristin turned and went back inside, shutting the door behind her.

Dawn had hardly broken the next morning when a banging on the door woke Cristin from a troubled sleep. She jumped up from her pallet next to the hearth and the cat, which was curled up beside it, spat and shot into a corner.

The banging went on, loud enough not only to rouse the

house, but also the whole village. She reached for her kirtle, dragging it over her head, her hands shaking and her heart pounding. The hem of it had barely fallen below her knees when the door burst open with a splintering of wood, and she whirled around, a scream dying on her lips.

Maelgwn ab Eilyr was standing on the threshold, a sneer on his face and a body of soldiers at his back. With the purple dawn light behind him, he looked more like a demon than a man, and Cristin's hand almost lifted to cross herself. Instead, it went to her throat in horror. A malicious smile pulled his mouth wide and her knees almost buckled beneath her.

There was an instant of absolute stillness and then they both moved at once. Cristin cried a warning at last, one that she already knew was futile, and ran towards the sleeping area where Tangwystl and her husband were surely awake by now and lying in terror.

As she clutched at the curtain around the bed, Maelgwn grabbed her hair and yanked her backwards so violently that the bones of her neck made a snapping sound. She screamed again, twisted and raked her fingernails down his cheek. Then her feet went from under her. The walls and the ceiling flashed across her vision, and she hit the floor.

Chapter Three

On the slopes of Pen y Graig, Llywelyn sat his horse and stared at the castle of Ystrad Meurig. Barely visible through the darkness, it crouched like a brooding demon on its mound, with its new tower of stone and mortar high and forbidding in the east wall. The erstwhile seat of his family, it had been built by the Normans, then captured by the Welsh, and now was back in enemy hands. But not for much longer if everything went to plan.

At Ystrad Fflur, the Compline bell began to ring. Tonight, however, he didn't picture the monks filing into the chapel and he didn't pray. His prayer of last night had had too many repercussions already, consequences that now drew his eyes towards the distant village.

It was dark, too, the shadowed dwellings shrouded in slumber, but even from this distance, he knew which one was Cristin's house. Even though he couldn't see it clearly, he could feel it, imagine the people inside, what they were doing, saying, thinking...

His hands tightened on the reins and his stallion tossed its head. He relaxed his fingers but his heart continued to rage. To meet Cristin again had been ordeal enough. To meet her, touch her, breathe her into his senses, almost taste her…and then to discover her deceit.

Why hadn't she told him at once about his parents? Did she think he wouldn't discover for himself that his mother had become an old woman, that his father wasn't dead, after all?

Llywelyn shook his head, the mutterings he'd heard from beyond that curtain filling his ears once more. Cadwgan might live, but so did the hatred he had for the man who'd sired him. How could such a man—who knew nothing of compassion, of kindness, of love but only of brutality and violence—ever deserve anything *but* hate, from him, from *all* those he'd hurt, irrevocably and unforgivingly?

He glanced up at the night sky, pushing that impossible quandary from him. It was time. Thank God there was no moon tonight and the sky was too cloudy for starlight. He turned to Gwion ab Adda, his *penteulu*, and spoke in hushed tones.

'I will take half a dozen men with me, on foot. Wait here and as soon as I have the gates open, you will see a torch flame. When you do, ride like the hounds of hell.'

'And if there is no flame?'

Llywelyn smiled grimly. 'Then you will know that we have failed and are doubtless dead. In which case, it will have to be a siege. Take command, surround the castle and send word at once to the Lord Rhys.'

The man nodded. 'Fortune be with you, my lord.'

Slipping from his saddle, Llywelyn handed him his reins. 'We will need more than fortune, Gwion.' Beckoning to his chosen men, he led them along paths he'd known all his life, to the place that had been his home.

The night was kind to them, the ground firm beneath their feet, no squelching mud or treacherous loose stones to betray their footsteps. Despite the moonless night, he knew every blade of grass, every rise and fall of ground, and they scurried, invisible and as soundless as mice beneath the castle ramparts.

They were at the postern gate in moments. Flattening himself on the ground, his men doing likewise, Llywelyn listened. All was quiet apart from the noises he expected to hear. The nearby stream was merely a trickle since there'd been no rain for days. A footfall came on occasion from the men on watch. Closer, the stamp of a restless horse in the stables that ran along the south wall.

The Compline bell had stopped long since but the postern gate remained shut. He frowned, chewed his lip in consideration, then motioning to his men to remain where they were, he inched forward on his belly. He pressed a palm to the wood, but it didn't budge. From the other side, a man grunted, another answered, followed by silence.

Llywelyn cursed silently. Something had gone wrong. Cristin and Gronw Gof weren't there. Either they hadn't found an opportunity to open the gate, or had decided it was too risky even to try…or they *had* tried and had been caught in the attempt.

Or perhaps, given what had taken place in her house last night, she'd decided not to help him, after all.

Fisting his hands in the warm grass, he battled a moment with each of those awful possibilities in turn. But there was no time to waste on futile speculation, and making assumptions was pointless. Whatever had happened, whatever the reason, it would doubtless become clear, one way or another, once they got inside—*if* they got inside.

Returning to his men, Llywelyn gestured to them to follow. Stooping low, moving slowly so that their weapons made little sound, he led them around to the west wall. With any luck, there might yet be a way in.

He found the place he was looking for and, for the first time that night, he prayed, for it was perilously close to the keep. Shoving his hands into the undergrowth, as noiselessly as he could, he dug down and found the ditch at the base of the wall. It had been filled in, of course, but the ground held a fault here and was too unstable to put down deep foundations. And the earth was dry, soft, workable. It would take time, but it was the only way.

Taking out his dagger, Llywelyn began to loosen the soil, scooping it away, handful by painstaking handful. It took an hour, perhaps more, but at last a gap was made under the wall, big enough for a man to ease himself through and into the bailey. That was all he needed.

The work of an hour became mere minutes now. Dispatching three men to deal with those guarding the postern gateway, he led the rest to the main gate, keeping in the shadows of the walls. The watch there were taken completely by surprise, not expecting attack from behind. Judging from the lack of commotion from the other gate, Llywelyn surmised that the surprise had been as complete there too.

And it took less than another minute to slide the bars across, take down one of the torches on the wall, and wave it frantically over his head, the signal his *penteulu* was watching for.

Gwion ab Adda's response was instant. The ground began to rumble beneath Llywelyn's feet as his army appeared out of the night. Thirty mounted men and fifty foot soldiers, they came sweeping across the plain like an avenging host risen from the underworld.

In the strong room on the ground floor of the tower, where she, Tangwystl and Cadwgan had been imprisoned, Cristin listened to the sounds of fighting without. There was only a small window set high, and they hadn't been left a light, so in the blackness that surrounded her, awful things took shape.

Every ring of steel on steel, every scream from man and horse, the yells of anger, hate, vengeance and fear left little doubt that terrible slaughter was being wrought outside. And knowing that death accompanied every sound shrouded her in horror.

Tangwystl and Cadwgan were huddled on the floor at the back wall, so still that they might have been ghosts. She suspected they were only still alive because Maelgwn had had no time to interrogate them yet, torture them before killing them, as he surely intended to do. They might *still* suffer that fate depending on the outcome of the battle because, instead of the bloodless victory Llywelyn had said he favoured, it had turned into anything but.

It raged for what felt like hours, fierce and fearful, and Cristin wrung her hands and bit her lip until it bled. And then, when it seemed the fighting would go on forever, it ceased with startling abruptness. She waited, her eyes fixed on the doorway, merely a dim arch in the wall. A long time elapsed before anyone came, but finally, there was the sound of the bolt being drawn.

Cristin blinked as the light of a flame dazzled her and, when her eyes had adjusted themselves, she saw a man standing there with another behind him holding a torch high. Quickly, she put herself between them and the two crouching figures behind her, her heart pounding. Were the soldiers Welsh…or were they Norman?

The first drew his helmet off. His hair lay flat against his skull and his face was in shadow. He wore a leather hauberk, but no chainmail, and carried a sword in one hand. In the other, he held a shield, on which was painted the heads of two hounds, both white with red eyes and ears.

The Cwn Annwn—the hounds that harried the souls of the damned into the depths of hell! Cristin shrank back in awe, although she knew that those were not the colours of Maelgwn ab Eilyr.

'Cristin?'

Sheathing his sword, the warrior stepped forward, sweeping back the hair from his brow with a gauntleted hand. She knew then who it was, but it was Tangwystl behind who spoke his name.

'Llywelyn!'

The word filled the small cell and there was a moment of stillness, when even the sounds from without faded. Behind her, Tangwystl started to get to her feet and, instinctively, Cristin turned and went to help her.

However, Llywelyn was quicker. Dropping his shield, he rushed forward, but even as he reached to aid his mother, he froze, his hands still outstretched. An instant later he lurched backwards, as if he'd been dealt a mortal blow.

Cristin froze, too, but as Tangwystl put out a hand, she bent and aided her to her feet. The proud old woman leaned heavily on her, for all that she weighed nothing, and it was with difficulty that she managed to support her.

'Assist me,' she urged of Llywelyn. He stood as if turned to stone, his eyes fixed, not on her or on his mother, but at the man on the ground. His father. Even with the torchlight behind him and his face in shadow, Cristin saw his expression. And fear closed over her, worse even than when the killing had been raging outside.

Because he looked at Cadwgan as if he would kill him too.

For an eternity it seemed, no one spoke. Then Llywelyn spun on his heel, turning his back on his father, and beckoned to a man behind him. And his tone was as hard as the stone walls that surrounded them.

'Take my mother and her husband to the main chamber in the keep. Get the physician to tend them and see that they have food and drink, whatever they require.'

The man called others forward and they lifted the frail old man and carried him out. Cristin watched Llywelyn's expression. It was grim, his features streaked with dirt. He didn't look at his father again, even though Cadwgan's eyes sought his, and one broken hand lifted in a gesture of supplication that was pitiful to behold.

In answer, his son turned his head away.

Tangwystl followed her husband, pausing a moment before going through the door. 'As you see, Llywelyn, your father is not the man he once was.'

He looked down at her and his reply came hard and hurtful. 'If you believe that, you are *still* as you always were, Mother. In his power, no matter how cruelly he has used you, and your children too!'

His mother bowed her head, her face sadder than Cristin had ever seen it. 'If you refuse to see him, or speak with him, then you will not see or speak to me either, since I will not leave his side.'

'But…why?' Llywelyn shook his head, his eyes bewildered. 'After all he's done to you, to us all, to me, to Rhianon, to Rhodri?'

'Because it is my duty as his wife…a duty that you, as his son, have as well.'

'Duty!' He gave a bitter laugh. 'It would take a saint to perform such a duty, madam, and I am only a mortal man.'

'Then I will pray that, given time, you will change your mind.'

With a lifting of her chin, Tangwystl moved on past him and out into the dawn. Cristin went to follow but Llywelyn stepped into her path.

'Not you.'

She stared up at him. And suddenly, whether it was due to the fear of before, the relief now the battle was won, or simply the wound on her head, she didn't know. But her knees buckled, her vision became a haze and she swayed.

'I… Oh!'

His hands caught her and she leaned into him, her fingers clutching at his tunic. Above her head, his voice came as if from far away.

'Are you faint?'

Cristin tried to gather her wits. 'I feel…strange…sick.'

The next moment she was swept up into his arms. The stench of blood and death about him made her feel sicker still, and she squeezed her eyes shut as he carried her out of the fetid cell and into the fresh air.

When she opened them again, she saw the dawn was breaking, the sky a light grey edged with rose, the castle walls looming up darkly. Below those walls, all around them was carnage. The bailey littered with bodies, Norman and Welsh, most dead, some wounded, one or two groaning and writhing pitifully.

There was a spattering of blood on Llywelyn's cheek, too, and Cristin's stomach heaved all the more, even though she saw it wasn't his.

'Can you stand?'

She nodded, not at all sure that she could, and Llywelyn put her gently down upon her feet. Then he called a man to him.

'Gwion will take you to the keep and find you a chamber.'

His eyes sharpened as they lit on her hair. Cristin put a

hand up, felt where the blood had dried from her wound, after her head had hit the ground that morning. No, that was yesterday…this was a new day.

'What happened to you?' His mouth tightened. 'What caused this wound?'

She told him. 'Yesterday at daybreak, Maelgwn ab Eilyr came to the house. I don't know how—by way of Owain Dafad perhaps—but he'd discovered your parents were hiding there. He came for them…'

Drawing off his gauntlets, he touched his fingertips to the place with infinite lightness. 'Maelgwn did this?'

'Yes, when I scratched his face. But I couldn't fend him off, he was too strong.' Cristin looked not at him, but at the scenes around her, where far more blood had been let. 'It isn't as bad as it looks, though my head aches.'

His hand dropped away and a muscle clenched in his jaw. 'Still, it needs treating. I have things I must do now, but go with Gwion. He will get the physician to tend to you.'

Abruptly, he turned on his heel and marched across to where two Norman knights stood in the middle of the bailey, hemmed in by Welshmen with swords levelled.

Cristin saw no more as the man called Gwion led her away, picking a path through the bodies and up the blood-spattered steps to the keep. In the hall, too, there were bodies, and vomit rose up into her mouth. Somehow, she kept it at bay until Gwion had installed her in a large chamber aloft and there left her with a promise to send the physician as soon as he could.

Then she crumpled and retched, but since her stomach was empty, it was only a thin and bitter liquid that came up. Later, she cleaned it from the floor with a cloth she found lying over a chair and sank onto the bed, still fully dressed, shoes and all.

Shutting her eyes, Cristin fell instantly into a deep sleep, the ache in her head splitting her skull in half, not knowing or caring if she'd ever wake up again.

Later that day, as the sun began to slide towards the horizon, Llywelyn stared down at Cristin, asleep on the bed, looking as if she'd been sleeping for a hundred years.

Her kirtle of pale green was old and faded, and the shoes on her feet nearly worn through at the soles. She was dirty and unkempt, her face so wan it seemed the blood had stopped flowing through her veins. And she was so thin that he could count every rib as she breathed.

But her hair was as it had ever been—thick and lustrous and like dark fire against the pillow. And, close to her left temple, a different hue of red, the dried blood of the wound she'd sustained when Maelgwn had misused her, though thank God nothing worse had happened to her.

Llywelyn's fingers clenched into a fist and he swallowed a curse, at Maelgwn and, even more vehemently, at himself. Even as he'd crouched in the dirt outside the gate last night, she must have been lying in that strong room, hours since, blood seeping into her hair, expecting death.

As if she sensed the turmoil of his thoughts, she stirred, a hand lifting and then falling limply down upon the coverlet. Her lashes fluttered and her lips parted in an incoherent murmur, as if she dreamed.

Llywelyn signalled to the physician—*his* man, not the one who'd served the Normans—to inspect the wound, softly, so as not to wake her. The man did as he was bid and, after a few moments, came quietly back to his side.

'The wound is not too severe, my lord, and the skull is intact. It is only the skin that is broken, though the bruise is deep. When she awakes, I will clean it and make up a balm to speed the healing.'

'Good.' But the simple word didn't come near to expressing the relief he felt. 'And my parents—how do *they* fare?'

'Undernourished, both, but otherwise Lady Tangwystl is well.' The man paused. 'Lord Cadwgan, I am sorry to say, will not mend. His injuries are too—'

Llywelyn cut the man's apologies short and dismissed him. 'Thank you. I will send you word when the maiden is awake.'

He waited until the door had closed and, pulling a chair to the side of the bed, dropped down into it. Drawing a deep breath, he scented the blood that still lined his nostrils even though he'd washed his body clean and changed his clothing.

It had been one of the longest days he'd ever known but, in reality, it had been *two* days. A day of planning to kill and a day of doing the killing. Of watching men die, quickly or agonisingly slowly, and then ordering the digging of graves to hide all that death away.

The battle hadn't gone well at all. The bloodless victory he'd hoped for had been instead a bloodbath, and now he could sleep for a sennight under the shame of it.

Llywelyn willed his heart to stop dwelling on what was done and looked around the room. At the walls, the floor, the ceiling, the furniture, some of it familiar, some of it new. It was a strange experience being home after seven years of exile.

And it was even stranger that Gwion had brought Cristin *here*, to the chamber that had formerly been his, and before him, his sister, Rhianon's. And that she slept now in the bed that had also been his.

Closing his eyes, he sent his thoughts backwards to that

more peaceful time. Before Rhianon had been wed and had left for her new home to the north. Before Rhodri had thrown his life away so recklessly, only two days after that wedding, pursuing the fleeing Normans who had failed to take this castle—though they took it a year later.

Before Cristin, only a week after they'd parted, had left his sister's service and returned so unexpectantly from Abereinion. He hadn't gone to the village to see her, as he was about to depart and join the forces of the Lord Rhys in the south, preferring to fight alongside his prince, rather than alongside his father.

He *could* have made the time to go to her, even then, but he hadn't. Not only was he ashamed of leaving Cristin as he had, and hurting her by doing so, there was also still no future for them. Monk or warrior or lord, it made no difference, and so there was no purpose in torturing her, and himself, all over again. That painful but necessary parting at Llanbadarn had been final—or so he'd thought...

Llywelyn dragged his mind back, forcing himself out of the past and into the present, to listen to the sounds from the bailey as his men cleaned up, the noise from below as the great hall was stripped of its Norman trappings and made into a Welsh hall again.

But through all that noise, Cristin's soft breathing came like a soothing lullaby to his ears. It seeped into him, easing his muscles and entwining him in silk, and those other sounds from without faded away.

Would it be so wrong to lie down beside her as she slept? Not touch her, nor kiss her, nor hold her—just lie beside her and rest. Let himself feel her warmth, her softness, the beat of her heart next to his. Let himself sleep and dream, not of killing and wounding, of war and of Wales, only of her.

His eyelids grew so heavy it was impossible to lift them.

His body felt like lead, his blood sluggish in its flow, and like a man dragging his soul out of a swamp, Llywelyn tried to harness his consciousness, but it was impossible.

He must actually have dozed for, when at last he forced his eyes to open, the sun outside the window had set and twilight shadows reached out from every corner of the room. Cristin's eyes were open, too, and she was staring at him so keenly that he could feel it, feel *her* so intimately, so thoroughly, that he might well have been lying right next to her, after all.

And then her gaze altered and she bolted upright into a sitting position, staring at him aghast now, as if she'd been dreaming and, waking, found it had been a nightmare instead. Or, as if he was the last person she'd expected, or wanted, to see!

'Llywelyn…my lord…'

Llywelyn sprang to his feet, his cheeks flaming and an excuse for his presence leaping to his tongue. 'The physician said your wound is not serious,' he said, turning away and taking up the trencher of meat and bread he'd brought with him. 'I will send for him to treat it but first, eat.'

He put the trencher on the bed, thought about retaking his chair, but went to lean against the table instead. She frowned down at the food and looked up at him, her eyes dark and puzzled.

'This is all for me?'

'It is little enough,' he said, folding his arms, feeling the pounding of his heart below, the rushing of his blood, not sluggish now, but hot and swift. 'The physician advised that you take food little and slowly at first, since…'

Llywelyn bit back the rest. He didn't have to emphasise the fact that she was half-starved. Even if he hadn't seen it for himself, she'd told him as much in plain words. 'So, eat,' he said, cursing his desire when he should be feeling only concern and care for her. 'There is ale too.'

If he'd thought she'd fall upon the food like a ravenous animal, he was wrong. Tentatively, she reached for a piece of roast fowl and took it into her mouth as reluctantly as if she thought it might be poisoned!

She chewed and swallowed and then her eyes filled. Her lashes lowered immediately as if to hide it, and she reached out, more eagerly this time, for another chunk of meat.

Llywelyn's gut twisted, and he had to plant his feet firmly on the floor to stop himself from rushing down to the strong room, where the two Norman knights were incarcerated, and beating them to dust for their master's neglect and ill treatment of her, of all the villagers.

After a few more mouthfuls, she met his eyes again. 'May I have a drink now? My throat is dry.'

He took up the cup of ale from the table and crossed back to the bed. His fingers brushed hers as she took it and a wash of colour entered her pale cheeks as she took a sip.

'Is the battle over?'

He nodded. 'The castle is back in our hands. The two survivors will go as hostage to the Lord Rhys, since they are noble.'

Her eyes flared. 'Only two survivors?'

'Most of the common soldiers were slain in the battle, and those few that were not have been dispatched cleanly by my men.'

Her face went from pale to ashen. 'You mean they've all been...killed?'

'It was what would have happened to my men, had we lost, and with far more pain than they suffered.'

Cristin was staring at him in horror now, her mouth open in a silent gasp. She lifted the cup to her lips and then lowered it without drinking. 'There is no end to cruelty, is there, even in victory?'

The remark was so simple and so true, that it needed no response. But he gave her one anyway. 'We are a long way from victory yet, Cristin.'

'But to slaughter those who had been vanquished anyway! Why?'

Llywelyn sighed. It had sickened him, too, to learn his *penteulu* had acted without his orders, killing those men he would have spared, but there was no undoing the act now. He should have made his orders clearer, *before* the battle, not afterwards.

'To spare an enemy only means having to fight him another day,' he said, the remark all victors used as an excuse, as he'd long discovered. It didn't make it excusable, however.

Her eyes dropped to the hands she wrapped around her goblet. His gaze followed and, as he saw the reddened skin, the roughened nails, his gut twisted again. Retribution was always bloodthirsty, as justice was often cruel. Those men who'd been killed by his soldiers had inflicted far worse on his people in the past seven years.

So why didn't it feel just? Why did it make him ashamed instead? He should be used to it by now!

'And Maelgwn ab Eilyr?' she asked after a moment. 'Is he hostage or dead?'

'Neither. He has escaped, God only knows how.'

As he spoke, his eyes went to the wound at Cristin's temple and, once more, he cursed his vile kinsman. The mercy was she hadn't suffered worse, been tortured or killed, his parents along with her.

She seemed to read his thoughts. 'When he came... I thought he meant to kill us. Why didn't he?'

'I suspect he hoped to get information from them in due course, and from you too.'

'I… We would never have betrayed you.'

'No, I know that.' Llywelyn's flesh shuddered at what she might have suffered for her loyalty. Under duress, and the sort of persuasive methods Maelgwn was known to employ, she may have had no choice *but* to betray him in the end. 'I will send for the physician now, to treat the cut on your head.'

'You haven't told me yet how your parents fare.'

He'd turned for the door when her statement halted him, stopped him from leaving, because what he really wanted was to *stay*. To sit and go on talking, to share memories and forget about war altogether, none of which was possible.

'Well enough, so I am told,' he said, turning back.

'You haven't seen them since…?'

He shook his head. 'No.'

Cristin laid the platter and the cup aside and got off the bed, a little unsteadily, but she wasn't as weak now as she'd been when he'd brought her out of the strong room. Smoothing down her skirts, she twisted her hair and tucked it back over her shoulder. Then, coming to stand before him, she drew herself up straight.

'What is to happen now?'

Llywelyn looked down at her. 'Happen?'

'To me?'

It was astounding but he hadn't considered that far ahead. He hadn't known the outcome of this battle, so hadn't looked beyond it. 'For now, I think it best you continue to serve my mother, since she seems to value you.'

'Yes, my lord.'

Llywelyn bit back the urge to tell her not to call him *lord*. If she were to remain as his mother's maid, until other arrangements could be made, they must both forget those days when they'd been equals, in soul if not in status. Forget, too, the later years when they'd grown closer still, yet in a different way, a growing up that had led inevitably to that night at Llanbadarn.

The night that had changed everything and yet had changed nothing. She was still a servant, and he was what he was. Although he may have abandoned his religious vocation to take up the sword, this war would not last forever. And one day, when it was ended…

Llywelyn drew a deep breath. That day was far away yet. 'But it is not fitting you sleep in the same chamber as my parents, for obvious reasons. You will occupy this one instead.'

Her eyes flew wide. 'You mean…*your* chamber?'

'I will take the one next door, which was my brother's.'

She inclined her head and, as if unsure what to do or say next, linked her fingers in front of her. 'I'm sorry I could not open the postern gate for you.' A little frown settled on her brow. 'And sorry, too, that your battle was not the easy victory you hoped for.'

Llywelyn shrugged but it was like moving a mountain with his shoulders. 'In war, not everything goes to plan. The garrison was more alert than I'd anticipated.'

Her frown deepened. 'But how did you gain entry?'

'The ditch under the west wall.'

'Oh…of course!'

He saw the memory flash across her eyes even as it flashed through his mind. They had made good use of that tunnel as children, sneaking in and out of the castle, under the noses of his parents and the guards. It was their secret…one of many.

'It had been filled in since the old days,' he said, 'so it took some digging.'

She nodded but, in her eyes, he saw the memory remained. 'Perhaps it is as well to refill it again, lest some other enemy use it as you did.'

Llywelyn nodded, too, but sealing up that tunnel couldn't seal up the past as well. No amount of earth would cover those memories, any more than her tossing her hair over her shoulder hid its colour, or the lowering of her lashes covered the beauty of her eyes.

'That work is already in hand.' He turned on his heel, lest she see the desire in *his* eyes. Desire that had grown out of childhood affection into mature love and finally into a carnal joining of body, soul and heart.

'My parents are in the chamber next door to this one. Perhaps, when you feel better, you would go and see to their needs before nightfall?'

And with that, he left her. Cristin Gwalltcoch. His past love, his only love. Changed, yet still the same, just as *he* was changed but unchanged. But too many years had passed since Llanbadarn, too much had happened to them both, and nothing now could be as it once was between them.

Chapter Four

Cristin sat at the servants' table in the great hall, far down its length, near the door. At one side of her sat Dyddgu, the laundress, a crafty, gossipy woman of the village. At her other side was Gronw Gof, the blacksmith, whose aid she'd intended to seek to open the gates to Llywelyn, two nights ago.

The hall was much changed. The language all around her was Welsh, not Norman-French, or English or Flemish. The castle's ancient *bardd*, Rhirid Hen, had regained his corner once more, frail and white-haired now as he tuned the strings of a *crwth*. Peat, not wood, smoked on the central hearth, and at the high table presided not Maelgwn ab Eilyr now but Llywelyn ap Cadwgan.

However, tonight he seemed anything but the reinstated lord of Ystrad Meurig. Even from where she sat, Cristin could see that he ate and drank sparingly and engaged little in conversation with the men who sat with him. He looked like he was at a wake, not a feast to celebrate a victory!

At her elbow, Dyddgu was speaking with her mouth full of mutton. 'Fancy you getting away with hiding the old lord all these years, not that we of the village would have betrayed them, of course…' Her eyes gleamed. 'You're a cunning one, Cristin, and no mistake. Paid you well, did they?'

Cristin bit her lip before the words *pot and kettle* slipped out. It was a wonder that Dyddgu, or one of the other villagers, hadn't betrayed her long before Owain the shepherd had. 'They had no money, so how could they pay me?' she said. 'Anyway, I didn't want payment.'

'More fool you then to go hungry while they ate! At least the new lord has seen fit to clothe you decent.' The woman took another bite of meat. 'They say the *old* lord will never walk again, and his wits have deserted him. Is that so?'

'I don't know.' Cristin picked up her goblet of ale. After so long without, when they'd drunk nothing but water, the brew tasted sweet and heady enough to addle *her* wits with only a sip or two. 'Perhaps, with sustenance and care, Lord Cadwgan will recover.'

But she couldn't help but delight in her new kirtle, an old one of Lady Rhianon's that had been discarded and hurriedly left behind with other belongings when the family had been forced to yield the castle to the Normans. Of rich blue, woven in fine wool, the kirtle had been brought to her the morning after she'd opened her eyes and seen Llywelyn sitting at her bedside.

Even now, her cheeks reddened at how she must have appeared to him, with her hair matted with blood, her face dirty and her old gown faded and patched. And her mortification deepened as she remembered how she'd longed for none of that to matter to him, that Llywelyn would rise from his chair and come to lie at her side, as he once had.

Gronw Gof butted into the conversation, the ale he'd drunk with abandon loosening his tongue. 'Is it true that Lord Llywelyn has locked his parents in their chamber because he can't bear the sight of his father?'

Cristin stamped out that untruth at once. 'Of course not! The door isn't locked at all and they are free to come and go as they please.'

'Then why aren't they at table?' Dyddgu leaned across her to reach for some bread. 'It's no secret that Lord Llywelyn hates his father enough to finish the job those Flemish knights started.'

'Aye, that he does…and no wonder, some might say.'

As the blacksmith nodded sagely and refilled his cup, Cristin put hers down, the ale tasting not sweet now but bitter. This time she had no denial to offer. That moment when Llywelyn had opened the door of the strong room, the words that had passed between him and his mother, the mangled, pleading hand Cadwgan had stretched out to his son that had been cruelly ignored, was proof enough that the blacksmith spoke true.

Llywelyn's hate for his father had grown, not diminished, over the years.

But hate was one thing…killing was another. She knew Cadwgan had killed his two brothers in battle, more than twenty years since, and maimed another through his lust for power. Surely Llywelyn could *never* become a man capable of the same?

Or had he already become that man? Cristin looked up at the top table to where he sat. On the wall behind him, in place of the hooded crow of Maelgwn ab Eilyr, the Cwn Annwn had been painted—the hounds of vengeance and retribution in vivid white against black, right against wrong, good against evil.

The legend of the hounds that harried the wicked to the gates of hell suddenly seemed ominous as she studied the man who'd chosen them as his insignia. Is that why he was so changed, so hardened, capable of having the Norman soldiers who'd survived the battle put to the sword? Was he, like their prince, the Lord Rhys, also bent on bloody vengeance, but towards his father as well as his enemies?

Llywelyn's gaze lifted suddenly and locked on to hers. She sat too far down the hall to see clearly but she didn't need to. The intensity in his eyes seemed to penetrate right through her and pin her to her stool.

Gronw and Dyddgu were talking across her now, but she didn't hear a word they said. She didn't hear the hissing of the fire, nor the plucking of the *crwth*, nor even the thumping of fists on tabletops and the boisterous voices of soldiers still harking on their glorious victory.

Everything around her seemed to recede into the distance as the power of that stare held her as fast, as surely as if he'd stretched out his hand and closed it around her heart, as he'd done in that other hall, seven years ago.

Just like then, nothing else existed, only she and Llywelyn—servant and lord—childhood friends and one-time lovers, and now…what?

The door was suddenly flung wide and the messenger who had been sent to the Lord Rhys with news that Castell Ystrad Meurig had fallen, strode up the hall towards the top table. Llywelyn's eyes released her at last and he leaned forward, head bent, to listen to the missive.

Cristin couldn't hear, of course, but the entire company had fallen silent, everyone waiting expectantly for the word from the Prince. And, after a moment, Llywelyn got to his feet and gave it.

'The castle of Llanbadarn has been taken by the Lord Rhys and Abereinion, too, is back in the hands of its lord, Peredur ab Eilyr, husband to my sister Rhianon.'

The news was received with a cheer that reached the rafters. Cups were raised, backs were slapped, faces beamed and even the old *bardd* got to his feet and began to sing and jig.

As Llywelyn retook his chair, however, his features were solemn. He shook his head as the servitor leaned in to refill his cup and, as his gaze found hers once more, the words of Gronw Gof at her side sent a thrill of horror down her spine.

'Well, there's no going back now. King Henry of England will soon bring his army into Wales and, when he does, it will be a long and terrible war between him and the Lord Rhys.'

Llywelyn stared down the hall at Cristin. The message hadn't been a surprise knowing the Prince's determination, though to learn that Peredur had taken Abereinion without a blow being exchanged, thanks to the loyalty of his people in that district, was good to hear.

Rhys, on the other hand, had been merciless in his capture of Castell Llanbadarn, his wrath focused on the men who had brought about the murder of Einion, his nephew— Gwallter ap Llywarch, who had driven a dagger into the youth as he slept, and Roger de Clare, who'd commanded the deed and then given the murderer shelter under his roof.

They were now both prisoners of the Lord Rhys and a banner had been hoisted, high and proud, a challenge that King Henry of England could not ignore. They had triumphed in Ceredigion, yes, but repercussions were bound to come, and sooner rather than later. War, one way or the other, was inevitable now and when it came...what of the common people, who'd already suffered so much? What of *his* people here in Uwch Aeron? What of Cristin?

She sat where his steward had placed her, far down the hall according to her status. He'd almost given the man a tongue lashing for that but where else could he have put her? Here, at his side and thereby given rise to gossip and speculation? Embarrass her and torture himself by flouting the rules and putting temptation within his reach?

Llywelyn pushed his trencher away. He didn't have to place Cristin at his side at the high table at all. She was temptation enough just where she was.

Gwion ab Adda, sitting on his right, spoke, bringing a welcome distraction.

'How many men will you take with you on the morrow, my lord?'

'Ten will be sufficient,' Llywelyn replied. That had been the second part of the message from the Lord Rhys, a summons to Llanbadarn for a war conference. 'It's unlikely we'll encounter any Normans along the way, since doubtless they are either fled or dead.

Disgust rose up into his throat. The Prince's orders had been clear—none of the garrisons of the three castles was to be allowed to escape—and his *penteulu* had taken that command too far. Hopefully, the reprimand he'd issued earlier—in private and less harsh than it should have been because Gwion had lost his wife, and also the babe in her womb—would ensure the man would await *his* orders before slitting enemy throats.

Llywelyn took a mouthful of ale but the disgust remained. *He* was the one at fault, no one else, and he must be more vigilant in the future. Not just of his *penteulu*, but of all his men who'd suffered and resented Norman rule for so long, and were more than ready to wreak vengeance even on the vanquished.

'Take charge here in my absence, Gwion,' he said. His head was aching from the noise in the hall, as much as from the strong ale, and he got to his feet. 'With luck, I'll not be gone more than three days.'

Everyone else had risen, too, in reverence to see him out. It still surprised him how quickly, and how readily, they had accepted him in place of his father. Even though they all knew that Cadwgan lived, none wanted him back as their lord. His harsh rule over kin, soldiers and servants alike had reaped a fitting reward. Everyone had walked in terror of him during his life, but now nobody cared if he were alive or dead, himself the least caring of all.

Llywelyn started to walk down between the two flanking tables, his mind calculating strategy, his eyes fixed on the oaken door ahead, but all his senses were arrowing against his will to the end of the table to his left, where Cristin was.

She stood as everyone else did, with head bowed, her hands clasped in front of her, a coif covering her hair. In the edges of her vision, as insignificant as she was among that whole multitude, only she existed.

He halted, spoke a moment with Rhirid Hen, thanked the old *bardd* for his songs, poor though they were compared to those of days gone by when he'd been young and vigorous. Then, delay turning to awkwardness, he passed on.

Just a few strides more and he would reach the doorway, only yards away but seeming leagues distant. But Cristin was there, in front of him, at the end of the table nearest that door. He could pass on, of course, since there was no reason for him to stop, least of all to talk to a servant, but stop he did.

'Cristin,' he said as she dipped him a curtsey, her lashes lowering. 'How is your head wound? Healing, I hope?'

Llywelyn heard his voice come without inflection. No shake or strange pitch to betray the fact his breath had become lodged in his throat. And the burn of his cheeks might well be attributed to too many cups of ale, or to the fire that was banked high despite the clement evening.

She nodded, touching the spot, covered now with a coif. 'I... It is healing very well, thank you, my lord.'

'Good,' he said, his voice still that of a considerate lord not a man of flesh and blood. 'The physician's balm proved soothing, I trust?'

'It did... Thank you.'

That should have ended the conversation, but it didn't. Why couldn't he stride on by, now that he was reassured of her well-being, as a good lord should? Why had he even stopped at all? Everyone was still on their feet, unable to resume their seats until he'd left the hall. Yet still, he couldn't move.

'And, in all other respects, you are well too?'

'I am very well in *all* respects, my lord, thank you.'

She might not thank him if she could read his thoughts. If she knew how much he wished he were not a lord at all, that time could go backwards to how they'd been before. To the day he'd first seen her, when they'd both been children, and he'd gone to the village with the castle steward on some business he couldn't remember now.

Cristin had caught his eye at once, her long red hair—brighter then than now and so different to the dark heads of all the other bond tenants—flying around her thin shoulders in the wind. She'd stood at the well and stared straight into his eyes, as if she knew, as he did at that moment, that they were two souls destined to find each other. He'd sought her out again the next day, spoken with her for the first time and felt as if he'd known her forever, as if she were one side of a coin and he the other, and together they were one. And he'd kept on seeking her out, on days when his father's violence knew no bounds, and he'd been afraid to go home, so he'd gone to the village instead, to *her* home.

And later, as they'd grown up, they'd become inseparable, necessary to each other, and he'd sought more than just her friendship. He'd sought her counsel, her comfort and her love, and she'd given all, innocently and generously, without question or hesitation.

'I am glad to hear it,' he murmured. It would be a small step from lord to lover again, at least for him. All he had to do was step closer, no more than a half pace, to be able to breathe her in, to touch her, to sweep that coif from her head and feast his gaze on that glorious red hair once more. A mere dip of his head to capture her lips with his…

But it was a step he could never take, and would never take. He'd forfeited the right to do so when he'd lain with Cristin in a stable and left her two days later, forever or so he'd thought, cleaving that coin and himself irreparably in two. And he had no right to ask now, either with words or with his heart, not even if he needed her, tonight, as much as ever.

'If you require anything, be sure to ask it,' he added instead, as any good lord would.

She inclined her head—like a lady not a servant. Rhianon's old blue gown suited her well, flowing down over her slender body, still too thin, but with the hint of curve at breast, waist and hip. He lifted his eyes from her body to her face, to find her gaze speculative, as it had been that very first day at the well.

As if she still saw right through his skin to his needs, as if she still knew him better than he knew himself, even after all these years. But then, how could she not, since he'd bared his whole soul to her once, as she had to him.

Llywelyn nodded a farewell, tore himself away and

strode towards the door, which was being held patiently open for him. He walked through it, his gaze fixed in front of him, those years that were gone forever following in his wake.

Even after he'd passed from the hall altogether and placed his foot on the first step that led upwards, an invisible rope seemed to drag him backwards, to the days of their youth. A thread spun so thin by the passing of time but one that nevertheless wound around him and tied him in knots.

The following day, Cristin stood behind Lady Tangwystl and, the combing done, began to plait her mistress's hair. It had once been a mass of long black curls, just like her daughter Rhianon's, but was now thin and coarse, its abundance turned to a straggling fall of silver.

'And what news did the messenger bring last evening, *forwyn*?'

Cristin told her the bones of the message but omitted the rumours of war that had begun to spread after Llywelyn had left the hall. Alarming rumours that even now made her blood run cold.

'And how did my son take the news?'

'Without excitement. In fact, he seemed…preoccupied, *meistres*.'

Tangwystl gave a nod. 'Llywelyn was always preoccupied, even as a boy, spending too much time in his thoughts…so deep, and so different to Rhodri…'

The words were wistful, as they so often were when she talked of her three children—Rhodri, killed in battle before his time, and Rhianon, married to Peredur ab Eilyr, and a mother herself now. But of them all, she spoke most of Llywelyn, and her reminiscences had been torture to Cristin over the years.

Like spikes driven into her flesh, they had pricked and drawn a constant trickle of blood from her heart. But even so, her ears had sharpened, each and every time. Painful or not, she'd clung on to every word, every memory, because it was the only connection between her and Llywelyn too.

'If he hadn't had to abandon his religious calling and take his place as his father's heir,' her mistress was saying now, her gaze going through the open window and far away, 'perhaps his resentment wouldn't have become so deeply rooted, so irreversible.'

Cristin had begun to ask herself the same since Llywelyn's return, though not out loud, of course. It wasn't her place to voice her thoughts, for all the trust that had built between Lady Tangwystl and herself over the past two years.

'He was always secretive but now he seems so enslaved by his hate that he is unreachable, so hostile, even to me, his mother!'

'Perhaps he doesn't mean to be so, *meistres*. Mayhap he has too much responsibility now on his shoulders.'

'Mayhap…' Tangwystl shook her head and the plait slipped through Cristin's fingers, so that she had to start over. 'But that is no cause, nor excuse, for such hate.'

The bittersweet reminiscing was interrupted by the calling of her husband. Cadwgan was bad this morning, his muttering words incoherent, his mood fretful. So tying the end of the plait quickly, Cristin helped her mistress up off her stool and put away the comb and braiding.

She didn't go to Cadwgan because Tangwystl always went, swift and without fail, day or night, whenever he needed her. It was Tangwystl, too, who bathed and fed him, soothed and comforted him, bore his rages when his mind cleared and succinct and terrible anger rained from his lips.

Now her mistress hurried to his bedside and took up one

of the gnarled hands between her own. 'Go and fetch something to break my husband's fast, Cristin. *Cawl*, if there is any, with a little meat in it.'

Cristin curtseyed and went to do as she was bid. She'd long stopped wondering why Tangwystl had left her safe haven and come back to nurse him after everything she'd suffered. Perhaps it was duty, just as she'd told Llywelyn. But incapacitated and dependent, Lord Cadwgan had turned to his wife, his need of her growing into a kind of love, on his part at least, that Cristin had seen blossom before her eyes.

Was he truly penitent for all the violence of his past? Tangwystl seemed in no doubt and had dedicated herself to caring for him, despite all the cruelty he'd dealt her and their children, despite even the cruel blinding and castrating of Edwin, her former betrothed.

If Cadwgan, of all men, could feel love, could Llywelyn not set aside his hate and feel love again too? Could he, like his mother, accept this change in his father, to care a little at least, if not forgive nor forget? And, if he could do that, could he change in other ways, too, back to how he'd once been?

The question was still nagging at her when she came up from the kitchen with a trencher of food. There had been no *cawl* so she'd brought some cheese and oatcakes and a jug of ale. Balancing them carefully on one hand and lifting her skirts with the other, she went to mount the stairway that led upwards to the chambers, but seeing the door of the hall ajar, she paused and then went in.

The hall itself was empty though not dark, since daylight came in through the windows, even if it didn't reach into the corners. At the far end, flanked by torches either side, the Cwn Annwn presided and, mesmerised, she walked towards them, as if they'd beckoned her.

Cristin put the trencher down and looked at them. Was it imagination or were those eyes redder than before, the ears pricked sharper, the jaws gaping wider? They were fleeter of foot than living hounds, with long noses that never lost the scent, and their howling, once heard, was never forgotten. And, even if they did represent justice, the relentless and merciless way they exacted it sent a shiver down her spine, just as they had when she'd been a child.

She could almost hear that howling now, almost see the desperate flight of their quarry as they sought a futile escape from their fate. But it wasn't the snarling of hounds but a footfall that sounded behind her.

Spinning around, Cristin saw Llywelyn, coming into the hall. He wore a russet-coloured riding cloak, below which a coat of chain mail glinted in the light that shone in through the windows. Calfskin boots reached to his knees, and he carried leather gauntlets in one hand, though his head was bare.

As he saw her, he hesitated and then strode purposely forward to greet her with a smile that was as brilliant as it was unexpected. '*Bore da*, Cristin Gwalltcoch.'

If he hadn't called her by that name, Cristin might have smiled too. Now the familiarity only brought hurt. '*Bore da*, my lord.'

At her use of his title—a title he'd asked her not to use—his smile faded and his mouth twitched, as if he was going to ask her a second time. But instead, his gaze lit on the trencher behind her.

'Who is that for?'

'It is breakfast for your father,' she answered. 'And I am late in taking it, so, if you will let me pass…'

His lashes flickered. 'I gave orders that meals be taken up to my parents when the rest of the household eats. How is it you are taking this food up now, at this time of day?'

The question came as a surprise, for he'd never yet asked her anything at all about his parents. 'Your father sleeps much of the time,' Cristin replied, 'and is not always awake at the set mealtimes, so Lady Tangwystl sends for food as and when it is needed.'

He frowned and a muscle moved in his jaw. His face was the same as it had always been, lean, sharp of bone, clean-shaven, with not a scar upon his skin, despite the battles he must have fought. Perhaps there were scars upon his body, hidden by his clothing, since few warriors escaped unscathed. But below the skin, deeper still, did inner scars lurk unseen and known only to himself…and to her?

'I see.' The response was given without inflection. 'In that case, you may continue to do as my mother commands.'

At her back, Cristin could feel the eyes of the Cwn Annwn burning through her clothes but that was nothing compared with the intensity of the blue gaze in front of her. She turned, reached for the trencher, paused.

'Why did you choose these hounds as your emblem?' she asked, suddenly needing to know. 'Because they are similar to the wolf's head insignia of your father—or because they are different?'

Llywelyn didn't answer her, but a shutter seemed to descend over his eyes as they locked on hers. He was standing so close that she could feel the warmth from his body, and yet he seemed so far away that, even if she reached out, she couldn't touch him, not really.

'People are asking why your parents keep to their room,' Cristin went on. 'There is a rumour you have become so cruel that you have locked them in.'

The blue stare sharpened. 'The next time you hear anyone say so, tell them to go up and try the door for themselves. They will see it is not locked and never shall be.'

'Why don't *you* go up and open that door?' she challenged, seeking some remnant of the man she knew. The man who had never glared at her with such hostility, nor shut himself off from her, as he now did. 'Go inside and see your mother…and your father?'

'So, as well as my parents' protector, you have become their advocate too?' He gave a twisted smile. 'Why do you care so much, Cristin? Why did you shelter them as you did? My mother, yes, I can understand why—but *him*?'

Cristin held her ground before the unexpected assault. 'How *could* we turn him away when your mother begged us to help him?'

'Yet some would have handed him, and her, too, over to the Normans, not lived in fear of discovery and possible retaliation.'

'But not me and not my father either! We would *never* have betrayed them.'

She lifted her chin, unwilling, unable, to tell Llywelyn—to whom once she would have told everything—that harbouring his parents wasn't just duty or pity. It brought *him* closer, kept the thread intact, even if only a little, no matter how far away he'd been in reality.

'Once, you would have understood that,' she said, 'but now…now you won't even *see* your parents! Do you think that if you ignore them they will go away?'

His head tilted, his gaze glittered, and, for a fleeting instant, he looked more terrifying than his father ever had. 'You talk as if it were *I* who inflicted those injuries on Cadwgan.'

Cristin knew she shouldn't go on, that she should fetter her tongue, bow her head, curtsey and escape. But she went on all the same, attacking him because she didn't understand him and yet understood him only too well.

'You may not have wielded the weapon but in your heart you've wished those wounds, and worse, upon him a thousand times over.'

'Even if that were true, I was saved the trouble.' A ghost of a smile touched his mouth, chilling and terrifying. 'An apt fate for a man who used his fists so readily, not only on his enemies, but on those nearest him.'

'*Dduw annwyl*, that may be, but…what has happened to you?' Cristin heard her voice rise with feelings she couldn't suppress any longer. 'Have you become so cruel yourself, Llywelyn, that you have forgotten what pity is?'

'How can *you* have forgotten it all so quickly! His violence, his cruelty, the delight he took in hurting us all, kinfolk and bondspeople alike!' His face flushed and she saw his hands clench at his sides. 'Dear God, Cristin, you knew better than anyone how he tried to break, not only our bones, but our spirits, too, to beat all traces of kindness out of us, humiliate us to make us weak, stain our souls to make us like *him*!'

Cristin shook her head, the heat of his anger striking her like a storm of fire. 'No, I've forgotten nothing. But he is *changed* now, he is old and it is *his* bones, *his* spirit, that are broken. And, whether his fate is just or not, if a man repents for his past sins and asks for forgiveness, shouldn't he at least be *heard*? You—of all people—would have said so…once.'

'He robbed my uncle Edwin of his manhood and his sight, killed two other brothers in battle.' Llywelyn's voice was shaking now, as he told her things she was already well aware of. 'He terrorised my mother and my sister, brutalised my brother and…'

'And hurt you too! Beating you until your bones broke and your blood flowed and you wept! Yes, I remember it all, better than anyone, Llywelyn, since you came running to me often enough to stem your wounds. But now… I don't even know you.'

'Don't know me!' The blue eyes flared wide. 'For *you*, of all people, to say that, after all we've…'

At that moment the squire appeared at the door, his lord's shield and helmet in his hands. Llywelyn turned his head and sent the man a savage glare.

'Wait outside!'

And then the glare was aimed back at her, not just savage now, but burning with feelings so potent that she flinched. She waited for him to finish whatever it was he was going to say, but instead he gave a shake of his head.

'Perhaps it is understandable that you don't know me, Cristin. How can you, when my father did such a good job that even *I* don't know who I am anymore?'

And with that, he whirled away and strode down the hall and out through the door. Cristin sagged against the edge of the table, her body feeling bruised, her thoughts in turmoil. Silence fell and the hall felt even emptier than it had been before.

Had Cadwgan succeeded, after all, as he had with Rhodri? Had those pitiless, punishing lessons made Llywelyn, too, become like his father? No! The boy she'd once known could not have vanished so completely, surely, no matter how much he'd suffered. Not the gentle boy who'd shed his blood and his tears in her arms.

There *must* be something left, even if only a little piece, of the man she'd loved, and still loved under that hard and unremitting exterior. And, if there was not, why did her foolish heart—the heart that man, and that boy, too, had broken, over and again—still seek to find him?

Chapter Five

Llywelyn stood in the burned-out bailey of Castell Llanbadarn and watched the Lord Rhys hang the murderer of his nephew. It was a slow and agonising justice and by the time Gwallter ap Llywarch had gasped his final breath, his stomach was churning with nausea and his heart was wrung with pity.

He'd seen terrible things over the past seven years, done terrible things himself, but had never become used to the brutality of war. Sometimes, like now, he almost wished he *could* be as hard and as indifferent as the men he commanded and fought alongside. But he couldn't and so he would always be sickened by the violence he had to wield, the battles he had to wage, the endless killing.

Next to him, his brother-in-law, Peredur ab Eilyr, spoke quietly, reminding him he wasn't alone in his abhorrence of war. Peredur, too, did what he had to do out of duty, taking no pleasure in it, although there was nothing meek about his half-Welsh, half-Flemish kinsman. He'd been the hero of many a siege even before he'd reached the age of two and twenty—the bloody battles for the castles of Llanrhystud and Aberllwchwr, and the ravaging of the lands of Gŵyr and Cyfeiliog, in the cause of the Lord Rhys.

'Murderer or not, it's a terrible way to die, Llywelyn.'

'Yet Roger de Clare goes unpunished,' he replied, 'apart from the inconvenience and indignity of being held hostage.'

Peredur nodded. 'At least his ransom price will help refill Rhys's coffers—if the King agrees to pay it.'

'And if he doesn't pay,' Llywelyn added, 'it wouldn't surprise me if *he* didn't hang too. Rhys was very close to Einion.'

'And to his other nephew also, the son of his dead brother, Maredudd. The lad was murdered by Walter de Clifford himself, they say.' Peredur ran his fingers through his wheat-gold hair. 'It is a miracle that Rhys has stayed his hand this long. But now he *has* struck back, the King has to act, and doubtless he will uphold his Marcher lords' vile crimes and we will be in the wrong, even though right is on our side.'

Llywelyn looked again at the gallows. If this war was lost, they may *all* be swinging at the end of a rope soon, condemned as rebels for the crime of fighting for their own lands, their rights, their freedom.

'It might prove a repeat of the swift campaign of six years ago,' he said, knowing that prospect was a doubtful one even as he voiced it. 'When Rhys was forced to submit to the King with hardly a blow struck.'

'It might, though things are very different now. Rhys is stronger, more powerful, and he has support.' His brother-in-law suddenly looked much older. 'This war won't be like the last one, Llywelyn. Henry of England blundered badly at Woodstock by demanding our princes do him homage for the kingdoms they hold by lineage and royal right.'

Llywelyn agreed. 'If the King had sought to unite all of Wales against him, he couldn't have done it any better.'

There was a long silence, as if each of them reflected on what that unity might mean, before his kinsman opened a different topic, a sigh in his voice.

'I hear my brother, Maelgwn, escaped during the battle for Ystrad Meurig?'

'Yes, he did. There has been no sign of him since, though we searched the lands about the castle.' Llywelyn knew, as did everyone, that there wasn't and never had been any affection between the two brothers—Maelgwn the true son of Eilyr ap Bleddyn, and Peredur the adopted son. 'Doubtless he has made his way into the March, or to England.'

Peredur's mouth tightened. 'I hope to God he has and that he never comes back into Wales. If he does, there is only one fate awaiting him, and I fear he'll not escape his sins the next time.'

His gaze flickered towards the gallows where Gwallter ap Llywarch's body still swung. 'Perhaps I should not have spared him that day he tried to abduct Rhianon, when he confessed to the killing of the garrison at Abereinion.'

'You did what you thought best, Peredur, the only thing you *could* do, and you cannot hold yourself responsible for your brother's acts since.' Llywelyn turned the talk to more pleasant topics. 'How is my sister? I have not seen her since the baptism of your firstborn.'

'Marared, yes.' The other man's face softened. 'She is grown so tall and only six summers old! Rhianon and our children are all well and safe, *diolch i Dduw*, though it's nigh on two years since I last saw them, with only sporadic news of them during all that time.'

'Then you will be glad to have them home.'

Peredur shook his head. 'I dare not bring them out of

Meirionnydd yet, not until our hold in Ceredigion is certain. But I ride north today, at last, to visit them.'

'Take my greetings with you and tell her I, too, hope to visit her soon—when this war is over.'

'I will, and I know she will be glad to see you when that moment comes—if it ever comes.' With that, his brother-in-law clasped his forearm in farewell. 'Doubtless we two will meet again rather sooner, Llywelyn, in battle. Until that day, God keep you.'

Before departing Llanbadarn, too, Llywelyn paused and looked around him at what was left of the castle. He'd been here seven years ago, for his sister's marriage feast, before it had fallen to the Normans, but it was hardly recognisable now. Inevitably, his gaze was drawn to the far side of the bailey where the stables had been. Only charred remains were left, still smoking in parts, the wood blackened and turned to ashes.

Why couldn't the memories that this place held be charred remains too? Why couldn't they be cold, dead ashes instead of smouldering like a fire that refused to be doused? Perhaps if he hadn't seen Cristin again they might have burned themselves out eventually, leaving his heart withered but still intact. But he *had* seen her and now…

He banished that thought before it took root. The private talk he'd requested yesterday with the Lord Rhys had settled his future. Once the war was over—whether the Prince or the King emerged victorious—he would put down his sword for good and take up instead the monk's habit.

But as he rode out, Llywelyn knew himself to be as torn as he'd been the last time he'd ridden from Castell Llanbadarn. His future might be settled, should he survive the war, but in the weeks, months, perhaps years ahead, there was still Cristin.

Living under the same roof as her, seeing her day in and day out would be like purgatory on earth. He couldn't touch her, hold her, kiss her, because there was no going back in time, and no place for her in his future.

But the knowledge that she would follow him into the cloister all the same was a penance that he would have to bear until the day he died.

As she'd done the previous two days, Cristin walked to the village to search for her missing cat. It looked as desolate as ever and a pall of nervous apprehension hung in the air. The invaders might have gone from Uwch Aeron, but they hadn't gone for good and everyone knew it. The Normans weren't likely to relinquish these lands they'd coveted and conquered as meekly as all that. Sooner or later, they would return.

At least Lent was over and, for once, the villagers had food to eat, plenty of it, too, and ale and medication, whatever was lacking, all provided by Llywelyn from the castle stores. And people were out of doors now instead of huddled fearfully inside, tending to their livestock and their crops, mending their homes and their lives, even if they did look over their shoulders frequently, just in case...

Owain Dafad, the shepherd, had disappeared the night of the battle, doubtless to avoid paying the price for his treachery. Maelgwn ab Eilyr, too, had vanished without trace, although his presence still lingered, like an evil force awaiting reincarnation.

Cristin nodded to some of her former neighbours, stopped to pass the time of day with one or two, helped another to draw water from the well. Then she went into her house and stood for a moment looking at the bare interior, the cold hearth, with not even the scratching of mice breaking the lonely silence.

This house had never really been a home. It was smaller than the one the Normans had burned, for her father had been headman of the village, a man of importance despite not being a freeman. There'd been a loft there, where Llywelyn had slept, but only once, when he was eleven. It had been the day Cadwgan had broken his nose and she'd known, although he was too proud to say it, that he was afraid to go home.

So she'd asked Idris to persuade him to help gather the harvest, before the threatened rain came. And, when darkness had fallen, fed and exhausted, Llywelyn had fallen asleep in the loft, alongside her brother. The next day *his* brother Rhodri had found out, however, and Cadwgan had punished Llywelyn worse than before, and so he'd never slept under her roof again.

It all seemed so long ago now. Even the death of her parents two years ago seemed to belong to another lifetime altogether, even though she missed them every day. The loss brought a well of tears to her eyes, the flood thickened by the loss of Llywelyn, too, even though he was alive and well. It was their love that had died.

Closing the door behind her, Cristin left her tears inside and resumed her search. But still, Mwg was nowhere to be seen. The cat had fled for its life when the Normans had come for them that dawn a week ago and hadn't been seen since.

To the south of the village, just beyond its boundary, was the pestilence pit where too many villagers were interred, along with her parents, although her brother's body had never been brought back for burial after his death at the siege of Llanymyddyfri. Cristin paused there a moment, said a prayer for them all and then continued on her way, searching every possible hiding place.

Finally, at the corn mill at the very end of the village, when she was on the verge of accepting that she'd never find the cat, a flash of grey caught her eye. There, slipping out through the open door and darting under a low cart that had lost a wheel and lay askance at the side of the road, was Mwg.

Relief quickened her steps and, kneeling, she ducked her head under the cart. Two round amber eyes peeped back at her. 'Mwg…' She put out her hand. *'Dere 'ma, pws.'*

But Mwg didn't budge no matter how much she called and coaxed him. His thin tail began to swish back and forth and his mouth opened and shut in silent miaows, showing teeth faded with age, the gaps where one or two had fallen out.

Cristin sat back on her heels for a moment and bit her lip. There was only one option. If he wouldn't come out, she'd have to go in and get him. She was just about to flatten herself on the ground when the sound of horses approaching came to her ears.

Backing out quickly from under the cart, a cry of warning leaping to her tongue lest it be the enemy come back, she sprang to her feet. But her cry withered and died. It wasn't the Normans at all. It was Llywelyn returning from Llanbadarn.

His chestnut stallion's great hooves sent the dirt of the road spiralling upwards and the heads of the Cwn Annwn danced upon his shield. He was mailed, spurred and gauntleted, as were all his men, and like them, travel stained. But even so, his armour seemed to glint far brighter than theirs, even under this grey and sunless sky.

Brushing the earth from her gown, Cristin stood respectfully to the side of the road, like any good peasant on the approach of her warrior lord, and dropped a curtsey, glad of the need for reverence that hid the flushing of her cheeks.

He hadn't looked at her yet, his eyes set on the road ahead, and she prayed he would pass by. But just as it seemed he would, he halted. Drawing rein, he removed his helmet and looked from her to the cart and back again. Then motioning to his men to continue onward to the castle, he dismounted.

'Has something happened here?'

Cristin's heart began to beat hard. 'No, my lord.'

His mouth tightened and she remembered he'd told her not to call him that. Or perhaps it was because of the way they'd parted three days earlier that displeasure rather than greeting marked his fine features. 'So, why have you left the castle?'

She drew herself tall, though still far short of his height, which seemed greater than ever in his light armour. 'I came to find my cat.'

'Your cat?'

Cristin gestured behind her. 'He's under the cart but I can't reach him.'

Llywelyn's eyes scoured hers, a frown furrowing his brow. Was he, like she, reliving that bitter moment when they'd stood before the Cwn Annwn? If he was, he chose not to speak of it. Handing her his reins, he placed his shield and his helmet to the side of the road and unclasped his cloak, throwing it over the saddle.

'I'll see if I can get at him.'

But he didn't need to even try. To Cristin's astonishment, Mwg came out at once and began to rub himself around Llywelyn's boots, purring loudly, tail up like a staff. To her greater astonishment, he grinned and stooped to pick the cat up, cradling it in his arms. And, as he began to stroke the matted grey fur, the years came full circle.

'I gave you this cat.' He lifted his head. 'This is Mwg, isn't it?'

It was such a little thing, such a simple statement, but along with it came a past filled to the brim with feelings. 'Yes, this is Mwg.'

An awkwardness fell between them, and the horse began to paw impatiently, its hooves raking the dust again, choking her until she struggled to catch her breath.

'But this cat must be fourteen, surely? He was naught but a kitten when I gave you him, one of a litter that had been born at the castle.'

This cat? Had he so completely forgotten the past, their past? Did it mean nothing at all to him now? Did he not feel it with the same intensity, mourn it with the same agonising sense of loss?

'Yes, but he is nearer fifteen,' she said. 'You gave him to me for my saint's day.'

The breeze picked up, blew through Llywelyn's black hair, and one gauntleted hand lifted to sweep it back. 'Your ninth birthday…yes, I remember.'

The anniversary had been and gone a week since. No one had remembered it, in the aftermath of the battle for Ystrad Meurig. She herself had almost forgotten it, except that it had been the day he'd given her the blue kirtle. Not as a gift for her saint's day, which was also the day of her birth, but from expediency, since her old one had been falling to rags.

Was the same thought crossing his mind too? Cristin searched his face but it was impossible to tell. Even though his eyes bore down into hers, she couldn't read what was in his mind. Once, she didn't have to, because he always spoke his mind, and if he didn't, she'd always known what was in his heart without the need for words.

Now his mind, and his heart, too, were closed to her. Something that was made painfully clear as he shoved Mwg into her arms and took hold of his horse again.

'Well, if you mean to bring it to the castle, one more cat will make little difference to the gaggle that roam the stables already.'

Cristin stared aghast as he bent to retrieve his helmet and shield. The dismissive remark hurt far more than Mwg's claws as they dug into her sleeve, so hurtful that, lord or not, her response came tartly to her tongue.

'But he's not a stable cat! He's…mine.'

Cursing under his breath, Llywelyn wished he could take those words back. Callous and thoughtless words that had come too quick and without caution. Straightening up, he hitched his shield over his shoulder and turned back to face her.

'I'm sorry…that is not what I meant. Of course, you may keep him in your chamber.'

A flush mounted her cheeks and her lashes lowered. But he'd seen the hurt in her eyes all the same, hurt that *he'd* put there. He'd seen the same hurt three days earlier, as they'd stood before the Cwn Annwn and she'd called him hard, cruel, and he'd not been able to deny it.

Llywelyn gripped his helmet firmer lest he tell Cristin how holding the cat in his arms had made him want to hold *her* too. To hold her so tight that he might even, by some miracle of love, take them both back to the day he'd given her Mwg, here in this village, on her saint's day.

The day he'd known, for the first time, that he loved her. Until then, he'd thought only grown men loved, but he'd discovered that a boy of ten could also love. Not ardently, with his body, but deeper with a heart he hadn't been able to understand, not until years later.

Turning away from the bewildered look in her eyes, that shock stopping his breath all over again, he twitched his stallion's reins. 'I'll escort you back now, if you are ready to return?'

She hesitated and then dipped her head in acquiescence, although he had the impression she would have preferred to refuse. But since he was her lord, she could not, even though his words had been an invitation, not a command.

They began to walk back to the castle, through the village, drawing curious looks from the villagers, not just those out of doors but out of open windows too. A scrawny dog ran out and barked and a man called it to heel. A flock of geese scuttled out of their path, their necks craned high as they honked loudly.

Cristin walked a few paces behind him, as befitted a servant, though once, that wouldn't have mattered, and they would have walked, boldly, side by side. Llywelyn slowed his pace, but she slowed, too, maintaining a respectful distance between them, until at last he *did* have to resort to a command.

'Walk at my side, Cristin.'

Immediately, she quickened her strides and fell into step beside him, but the promptness of her compliance irked rather than pleased him. She might be his mother's maid, but she'd never been his servant and she never would.

The blue kirtle—a lady's gown—flowed down over her supple form and caressed her long legs. He'd given her new shoes and stockings, too, on her saint's day, though without marking it. Neither did he mark it now, as her attire provided a safe topic of conversation and they left the village behind.

'I saw Peredur ab Eilyr at Llanbadarn,' he said. 'He sends news that Rhianon is still safe and well in the north, her family too.'

'I am glad to hear that.'

Llywelyn waited but she said nothing else. In the awkward silence—an awkwardness that once would never have existed between them—other sounds seemed too loud. The creak of his boots, the jingle of his horse's bit, its hooves like a drum beat in his head. His armour chafed and the day's growth of beard on his jaw itched. But the gulf between them was the most uncomfortable of all.

'She has three children now,' he went on, attempting to close that gulf. 'Two girls and a boy...but doubtless you know that from my mother.'

This time she made no response at all. The castle seemed farther away than ever, though in reality there was hardly any distance at all between it and the village. Not even a quarter league to walk yet the way seemed endless, the going as arduous as wading through mud.

'Why did you leave my sister's service so unexpectedly?' Llywelyn turned his head to look at her. 'Your father told me himself that he deemed it an honour that you should be maid to a lady, that you should rise so high, even if it meant leaving here. And Rhianon would never have dismissed you, since she was fond of you, so the wish to leave her and return must have been yours.'

Her chin, level with his shoulder, lifted a little higher. 'I was...unsettled at Castell Abereinion.'

'Unsettled by what?'

'It's a lonely place, hemmed in by mountains and sea.

The people are unfriendly and strange creatures called *mor-loi* inhabit the shore.'

Llywelyn had often seen the *morloi* she spoke of, not at Abereinion, but on the beaches of the western shores, during his years of exile. 'Sea calves, you mean?'

She nodded, glancing askance at him and then away. 'They frightened me and so Lady Rhianon engaged a new maid and gave me permission to return.'

'You were never one to be afraid of anything, Cristin,' he said, lightly, since the admission was a startling one. 'Least of all God's natural and harmless creatures.'

Suddenly, as if his words had lit a torch inside her, Cristin stopped in her tracks and turned to him. Her eyes blazed like flames through a dark wood, green fire amid soft hazel.

'You are wrong. I have been afraid, all the time—of the Normans, of the sickness returning, of betrayal by someone from the village, of every knock at the door.'

She looked back towards the houses behind them and Llywelyn could read her thoughts as clearly as if she'd voiced them.

'It was a miracle Cadwgan and my mother were not discovered earlier,' he said. 'The enemy are not usually so lax.'

'The soldiers avoided the village for fear of the pestilence lingering there, which it did, for a whole winter afterwards.' Her eyes met his again. 'Once, on a bitterly cold night, wolves came to scavenge on the corpses of those who had perished. The pit had been dug too shallow because there were too many dead. It was the pit that held my parents' bodies.'

'*Dduw annwyl*, Cristin.' Llywelyn reached for her but she moved away and his hand dropped into the empty space between them. 'I'm sorry.'

But even though he wasn't touching her, he could feel

her distress as if it seeped out of every pore of her skin and into his. Distress he wanted to soothe away, make her forget all she'd endured and never let her suffer such things ever again.

'You should never have had to endure those things. You never will in future, I swear it.'

Her eyes held his, full of pain and grief, of shared memories and precious moments that neither of them could speak of, or recapture. 'And you should not have harboured Cadwgan,' he said, harsher than he'd intended. 'You put yourself in grave danger, the villagers too. He's not—'

'Not worthy of it? You don't have to say it again, though once you would not have said it at all, not even about your father.' She looked suddenly weary and at the same time infuriated. 'You have changed, Llywelyn.'

'So you have told me.' Llywelyn didn't try to deny it. 'Yet you have changed, too, Cristin.'

She gave a bitter little smile. 'Did you expect me to remain the same, after all these years?'

'No.' And all at once, there it was, hanging between them like a sword suspended by an invisible hand. One of them had to say it and it might as well be he. 'That night in the stable at Llanbadarn changed us both, did it not?'

Colour swept into her cheeks. 'Yes.'

Llywelyn drew a breath. The simple word held a multitude of others, accusing, damning, and all the worse because they were justified. 'It spoiled… I spoiled everything that we had before.'

'No.' She shook her head. 'It wasn't what we did that spoiled things. It was what happened afterwards…'

'Afterwards?'

'When you didn't even bid me farewell the morning I left for Abereinion.' Cristin's eyes raked his, filled with accusation. 'Why? Were you ashamed to speak to me, in front of your sister, or your mother, or all those fine people?'

'I'd said my goodbyes already.'

'It still hurt me and you must have known it. Or did I mean so little that even courtesy was beyond you?' She held the cat up to his face, the creature's amber eyes full of accusation, too, it seemed. 'And now Mwg...*this cat*, as you called him, means nothing to you anymore, does he, when once...'

She bit her lip, leaving her words unfinished, but Llywelyn didn't need to hear it. He knew what she was going to say. That once, the cat had symbolised everything that had been between them, a gift that had brought them as close as it was possible for two innocents to be.

'I never meant to hurt you, Cristin, that morning—'

But she cut him off. 'You did more than that. You... insulted me, and belittled me, after all we'd been to each other...'

'I've *never* belittled you, Cristin!' That she should even think he *could* hurt him as much as he was hurting her. 'Rhodri's death changed the course of my life, and my vocation, overnight. It altered everything, and I was still struggling to accept that, to come to terms with what it would mean.'

Her eyes blazed. 'But even when I returned to the village, barely a week later, you never came to see me...'

Llywelyn shook his head. 'I couldn't.'

'Why?' Her lips quivered and she looked away. 'Because I was a bondswoman and not worthy of your time?'

'You know that is not true, Cristin!' But even he knew he was trying to excuse the inexcusable. 'I rode south the next day, to join the Lord Rhys. I'm sorry.'

He reached for her but she moved away with a dismissive jerk of her chin. 'It's too late for sorry. And I don't know anything any longer, only that you are a stranger when once you were not.'

Silence reigned between them for a moment and then she settled the cat more firmly in her arms. 'I don't need you to escort me to the castle, my lord. I've been walking there by myself for years now. I know the way well enough.'

With that she strode ahead, her spine rigid, her head high, the cat's tail swishing a furious farewell, too, or so it seemed.

Stranger? The word echoed in his ears and lay heavy over his heart, while every sinew urged him to run after her. Tell her she was wrong, that he *wasn't* a stranger, that she still meant everything to him and always would. Show her he loved her as much as he had, more even, if that were possible.

But his feet stayed where they were, in the place where the old village had stood, almost where her former house had stood, burned to the ground by the Normans. His eyes found the exact spot, right in the centre, or where the centre had been. Nothing remained now, only scorched earth and brambles, and memories. And suddenly those thorny briers entangled him, so thickly and so painfully, that he winced and struggled for breath.

He'd chosen a different path through life since the last time he'd stood here, in this vanished village, with Cristin. A path he still adhered to, in his heart at least, because it was the only path that could lead a man to peace instead of war, to life instead of death—and the dealing of death. A spiritual and not an earthly path, and one that she could not tread with him.

So would it not be better, then, to *remain* the stranger he'd become to her? Forget that he'd ever crossed from his world into hers, from the castle to the village, from the *crug* where they'd sat as children to the stable where they'd become man and woman?

It had seemed, at the time, a culmination of a love that had grown strong, true, unassailable and irresistible. Their two hearts had sped towards an inevitable expression of that love through the joining of their bodies. But nothing had been fulfilled in the end. Instead, everything they'd had before had been destroyed, as completely as if it had never even existed.

Chapter Six

Sewing at the window, Mwg curled at her feet, Cristin glanced for the twentieth time down to where the men were erecting the May Pole in the bailey. Her fingers worked deftly, hemming the narrow swathe of green material she'd cut out of the bottom of her old kirtle, but her attention kept wandering to the excitement building outside.

Calan Mai hadn't been celebrated under the years of Norman rule, but now the Welsh victories of Easter week were cause for rejoicing. So this first day of May, Llywelyn had thrown the castle open and the villagers would soon be arriving to feast and drink and dance and enjoy a day free from toil and trouble.

Five days had passed since she'd last spoken to Llywelyn, words of anger and regret and accusation…and lies too. Yes, the *morloi* of Abereinion *had* frightened her but the greatest fear during the short time she'd spent there had been that she might be with child. That Llywelyn's child had already begun to grow in her womb and, having sinned as they had by lying together outside wedlock, their child would be born cursed.

In the event, there had been no child and the strangest and most fearful thing of all was that she'd been sorry. If there *had* been a babe, she would have had *something* of him. And now, even though Llywelyn was back in her world, she had *nothing* of him.

She looked around the chamber that had been his. There was no trace of him in it, of course, no belongings or clothes. The Normans had occupied it for the past six years so how could there be? Yet, he was here, in every beam of the roof, in every knot of wood in the walls, in every plank on the floor.

The sound of the gates opening below brought her to her feet. Craning her neck to look through the window, she saw the Lord Rhys riding in at the head of a small entourage. As a mark of favour towards Llywelyn, he was passing the celebrations at Ystrad Meurig before returning to his royal seat at Dinefwr.

The next moment, Llywelyn appeared and walked quickly forward to hold the Prince's horse as he dismounted. A man among the entourage, whom she'd not noticed before, was hauled down from his mount. There was a brief interchange and then he was led, his hands shackled, to the strong room.

From his attire, as well as his arrogant manner, it could be none other than Roger de Clare. Still haughty as he went to join the two vanquished knights, all of them prisoners of the Lord Rhys until the King deemed to pay their ransom—or not to pay.

There would be no May Day celebration for them.

As Llywelyn and the Prince passed indoors and out of sight, Cristin went over to her coffer and put her needles and thread away. Smoothing out the creases in her blue kirtle, she placed the green sash she'd made over one shoulder, so it sat about her body crossways. The faded material looked drab against the rich blue, but it would suffice.

Calan Mai was the turning of the calendar, a celebration of life, procreation and renewal. She'd risen early, before dawn, washed her face in the dew outside the walls, threaded spring flowers through her hair and gone to the village to bring in the May with everyone else. The beasts had been driven to the high pastures the day before, and the bonfires of the night were still smoking as the villagers decorated the outside of the windows and doors with hawthorn blossom.

And today would also be *her* renewal. The past was gone and the Llywelyn she'd known was gone too. So today she would dance and sing and make merry with everyone else. She might even forget, for this one day at least, that those years had ever existed at all. Pretend that they didn't lie hidden, shrouded in sadness, beneath that green sash over her heart.

The afternoon sun beat mercilessly down into the bailey of Castell Ystrad Meurig and turned the grass underfoot to parched gold. Llywelyn walked with the Lord Rhys as the Prince mingled with his people. High and low, soldier and serf, good and bad, they were all gathered to celebrate Calan Mai.

Not only the village had turned out but folk had come from settlements farther afield, too, and from the outlying farms, eager to see the Prince and seek his favour or voice a complaint and, above all, toast his military successes of Easter week.

Sounds and smells and sights bubbled together like oil in a vat. Bunting and banners of primrose and bindweed decked the walls and stalls and, in the centre of all, the May Pole itself reared a dozen feet into the air. In the cooler shadow of the walls, meat roasted on spits and barrels spilled ale and wine into eager cups. The dancing had begun long since and music filled the air, *crwth*, pipe and harp competing with the twittering and swooping of swallows.

Sweat pooled between Llywelyn's shoulder blades and bathed the palms of his hands, and it was a relief when the Prince—who seemed hardly to feel the heat at all—paused beneath the east wall to take a mutton patty from a passing tray.

'It grieves me to find your father confined to his bed, Llywelyn.' Rhys licked meat juice from his fingers. 'A pitiful state for such a vigorous and brave man to have to endure.'

Vigorous and brave, yes, but so many other, less commendable descriptions could be applied to Cadwgan ab Ieuaf. Llywelyn didn't voice them, however, as he glanced towards the keep, where his mother sat at her open window, watching the festivities, her white head just visible. His father would be listening from his bed perhaps, or asleep, as he often was now, despite the noise. Cadwgan couldn't come down, not that he'd been invited, and Tangwystl *wouldn't*, even though she had been.

'My father will have been glad you took the time to visit him, *f'arglwydd*.'

As he spoke, a flash of blue and green caught his eye. Cristin, dancing gracefully and with abandon, like everyone else did, except him. Her figure, though still slender, was fuller at breast and hip now and her feet nimble and light as they followed the tune faultlessly. Her face was alight with excitement and her hair tumbled in abundance about her shoulders, glinting like autumn leaves under sun.

'Your mother, too, I find much changed, braver than I remember her. An extraordinary lady indeed, to leave her sanctuary and come to her husband's side, as she did.' Rhys finished his patty and dusted crumbs from his hands. 'She made a request of me, as it happens, concerning you.'

Llywelyn tore his eyes from the dancing figure. He could well imagine what his mother's request was and he wasn't wrong.

'Lady Tangwystl asked me to persuade you to reconcile yourself with your father before it is too late.'

'Is that a command, *f'arglwydd*?'

'No—but it is my advice. I was fortunate to be born into a family blessed with love and loyalty.' Rhys's face sobered as they moved on a few yards to the huge barrel of Gascony wine. 'Both my parents died when I was a child and now I am the only one left of four brothers, apart from Cadell, who has retreated from the world.'

Prince Cadell had suffered the same fate as Cadwgan, many years before. Attacked and left for dead, he was now a monk at Ystrad Fflur, an irony that wasn't lost on Llywelyn as he refilled the Prince's cup. He didn't fill one for himself. His head already swam with wine and heat and noise, and his eyes were dazzled with colours of every hue.

'I have two nephews dead by treachery,' Rhys was saying now, 'and two sons held hostage by the King of England at this very moment, not knowing if I will ever see them alive again.'

Llywelyn murmured words of sympathy but, as Cristin came into sight, lifting her skirt high as she laughed and sang gay May songs, his mind followed the dancing feet, ensnared as securely as if in a trap.

'So, no, I will not *command* you to heal the rift in your family, Llywelyn, but I will tell you that, in your place, I would not hesitate to do so. I have learned to my sorrow how precious family is. And when gone, it is too late to say the things that should have been said long before.'

The Prince turned and began to walk again, the topic thankfully closed. Llywelyn followed in his wake, like a good host should, attentive to his royal guest's every whim, away from where Cristin danced.

But all the time, her feet beckoned him, her brightness dazzled him, making his head spin even as the ribbons were spun round and round the May Pole. She was dancing now with old Iorwerth Foel, who shouldn't have the energy to twirl a woman about like he was, nor leer and paw at her like a lusty youth.

Llywelyn had never known jealousy before but now the taste of it soured his tongue. He'd lost count of how many had jostled for a dance with her, not just the young and ardent among his soldiers, but men of more advanced years whose bedding days should have been far behind them but who butted and gawped like rams at covering time!

And when the moment arrived to crown y Frenhines Fai—the May Queen—his stomach hollowed and heaved as if it was poison not wine that churned there. The choice was unanimous, as he'd known it would be. Cristin, however, looked stunned as her name rang out and she was led forward for the crowning.

She shook her head and tried to hang back but nevertheless she was ushered into the presence of the Prince of Deheubarth. Rhys placed the wreath of spring flowers on Cristin's head and then he gathered her in his arms, slapped one hand to her bottom and gave her a hearty kiss on the mouth.

Cheers and lewd calls filled the air and, if he'd thought himself jealous before, Llywelyn found himself seething now. The Prince, barely past thirty, wedded, and a father several times over, was almost as famous for his amorous exploits as he was for his military ones!

The kiss went on, the Prince plundering Cristin's mouth with relish, though in good sport. Llywelyn's fists clenched at his sides and outrage, as well as jealousy, boiled in his blood. Whether he'd have gone so far as to yank his over-lord off her, he never had to discover, for the next moment Cristin pushed Rhys away and, with a mock frown, wagged her finger at him.

'Even a *prince* may not kiss a queen, nor fondle her without permission!'

There was a moment of stunned silence and then Rhys roared with laughter. All those around followed suit as Cristin wagged her finger again and tapped it on the tip of his nose.

'But come back next year, my handsome young Prince, and I might find it most pleasing to *grant* you permission.'

Llywelyn couldn't believe his ears nor his eyes. Not just because Cristin was flirting with a prince but because she knew, or had learned, *how* to play the flirt! Her cheeks were pink with pleasure, almost exhilaration, and her eyes twinkled with a dark and sensual promise.

Rhys's laughter died away and his eyes grew darker too. With a bow, he lifted her hand to his mouth, turned it and placed a lingering kiss on her palm. 'I shall not forget the date, Frenhines Fai, you may be sure of that.'

Freeing her hand with difficulty, and an inclination of her head that she hoped was worthy of *any* queen, Cristin turned and walked away through the crowd, as steadily as she could. People parted to let her pass, then closed in around her, like a welcoming and disguising cloak.

Behind her, she heard Rhirid Hen's harp start up and, as the crowd fell silent to listen to the ancient verses that announced the season of growth and fertility, she quietly made her way to the shadow of the stable block.

Leaning back against the wall, Cristin wiped her mouth, the taint of wine on the Prince's breath still turning her stomach. Her limbs were trembling from the onslaught of that kiss, the sheer strength of those arms, and she'd bet there was a bruise on her bottom from where he'd grabbed it.

It wasn't that Rhys was repulsive, quite the opposite, but it had been the final indignity of a day that had gone horribly awry. From setting out to enjoy the freedom of the feast, after so many years of fear and deprivation, she'd felt herself engulfed in frenzy. Everyone had drunk too much, eaten to excess, sang and laughed as if demented and danced as if it was the day before the final judgement.

She'd tried to be like them, but in truth, it had shocked her to see such abandon, and alarmed her to be swept up in it and carried helplessly along, like a twig in a flooded river. And worse, the countless men she'd danced with seemed to think it all part of the celebration to grope at her breasts and bottom with their rough hands or kiss her neck with their greedy mouths.

Llywelyn alone had stood apart, watching it all with a hooded gaze and a face like thunder. She'd almost seen that storm break when the Lord Rhys had kissed her. Then, for a dangerous moment, she'd thought he'd take hold of the Prince and haul him clean over the castle wall!

Cristin pressed a hand over her heart. It was still racing, not because the Prince had kissed her and squeezed her bottom, nor because she'd been so bold as to push him away and—with the May Queen's licence—chastise him, though that had been momentous enough.

No, it had been Llywelyn's reaction that had set her heart a-pounding. His agony of restraint had *pleased* her, there was no denying it. Not since they were children had she seen him so…put out! And to know that he still felt *something*, if not *for* her, then at least on her behalf, made her feel…satisfied.

Suddenly, the sound of a footfall came, and a shadow blocked out the afternoon sun. The next moment Llywelyn was standing in front of her, the thundercloud still on his face.

'A performance worthy of a courtesan, Cristin.'

Cristin suppressed an urge to giggle, for he was rattled, like Mwg was when his fur was brushed up the wrong way, and was apt to swipe with his claws. Lifting her chin, she gave a shrug. 'I'm glad you appreciated it.'

'I didn't say I appreciated it.'

There was a strange accusation in his eyes and his mouth was set even angrier than before. Doubt flittered across her mind. Had he drunk too much? He never used to, but then he never used to do a lot of things he now did.

'Well, everyone else appreciated it,' she retorted, glibly, 'even the Prince!'

'Especially the Prince. And doubtless he's already looking forward to next year.'

Cristin smiled sweetly up at him. 'As am I.'

'Because he kissed you?' He moved closer, planting his hand on the wooden wall behind her, close to her ear. 'Or because he desires you?'

The sleeve of Llywelyn's tunic brushed her cheek, the warmth of his arm penetrating right down to the marrow of her bones. 'He does *not* desire me!' she retorted. 'The

Prince was merely entering into the spirit of the day, and mayhap had taken too much wine, judging by his breath.'

His mouth set. 'Yet his hand was steady enough as it grabbed your rump.'

'My *rump*!'

'That is what I said.' He scowled. 'Had he got hold of you somewhere less public, he would have grabbed you in other places too.'

Cristin's mouth dropped open. And, as he glowered down at her, his jaw set so sternly it was a wonder his teeth didn't shatter, she finally gave vent to laughter. Whether it was the word *rump*—that made her sound like a filly at the market—or the fact that she, too, had drunk far more than she'd ever drunk, or the sheer absurdity of the moment, she didn't know. But the tension broke like a thread of silk before a blade.

'I thought he was going to swoon with shock when I tapped his nose!'

Llywelyn's gaze flared and then his lips twitched. Was that a smile, too, or even a chuckle? Was the sunlight dazzling her and making her see things that weren't there? Or was the nearness of him making her even more dizzy than the wine had?

'I'd wager no woman has ever admonished him so sweetly, nor so cleverly,' he said, his lips twitching once more, 'not even on May Day.'

Cristin steadied herself against the wood at her back as those blue eyes blazed down at her. 'Of course, it *is* tradition for the lord to kiss the May Queen,' she said, 'and I won't have been the first to get groped as well into the bargain.'

'Nor the last, either.' Llywelyn's tone was dry, but humour, albeit restrained, hovered about his mouth. 'Such is the privilege of a prince...' He plucked a daisy from her hair and twirled it between his fingers. 'Your garland is beginning to wilt already…'

The scent of him filled her nose far headier that that dying daisy, making her breath hard to draw 'Even the hardiest of flowers wilts eventually.'

The poetry reciting ended, and the music began again. 'If the Prince hadn't been here today, it would have been *I* who had crowned you.' His eyes burned into hers. 'I who would have had that honour, as lord.'

'Next year, if I am chosen, and the Prince is not here, it *will* be you who crowns me…' Cristin moistened her lips as the sun crept slowly around and shone full upon them. 'Will you kiss me, too, Llywelyn, as tradition demands?'

'Come next May Day, there may be a different lord at Ystrad Meurig to crown and kiss the May Queen.'

'A different lord?'

He nodded. 'This war has only just begun. And even when this is over, there will be another war, and another, until either we are victorious and free…or vanquished and enslaved once and for all.'

Cristin felt a shiver slip down her spine. His words were so solemn that the cloud that passed just then over the sun might have been an omen.

'If that is so,' she said, 'perhaps we should live for the moment, enjoy every day as it comes, in case it should be the last.'

'Should we, Cristin?'

'Yes. And we should dance, and laugh and kiss, too, without the need to be drunk to be so bold.'

Abruptly, tossing the wilting daisy to the ground, he flung himself away, twisting his body so that his back was against the wall too. 'I don't have to be drunk to want to kiss you, Cristin. I only have to be near you!'

Cristin's pulse began to pound in her ears as the music from the bailey was whisked away on the breeze. The singing and the laughter around the May Pole faded to faraway echoes. 'You can be nearer still,' she breathed, 'if you want to.'

'Even though I am a *stranger* to you now?'

The word was not so much bitter as angry, and below it, an edge of sorrow sounded. Cristin moved a little closer until their shoulders touched, and tentatively, she sought his hand.

'I should not have said that, for we don't *have* to be strangers, Llywelyn…' Carefully, she let her fingers brush his, felt his curl and entwine with hers. 'Not if you kiss me now, in case there *is* no May Day next year, and this is the last there will ever be for us.'

His head turned slowly, and his eyes met hers. They were dark, turbulent, as they lingered for a moment before dropping to her mouth. 'But, if we are not strangers…what *are* we, Cristin?'

Cristin's breath quickened and her heart started to bang against her ribs. 'I don't know…'

'Do you *want* to know?'

She nodded. 'Yes…do you?'

There was a long moment before he nodded, too, his eyes darker and more turbulent than ever, as his head lowered slowly towards hers. 'Yes.'

It was then that Gronw Gof and Dyddgu rounded the corner of the stables and, as one, halted in their tracks, their mouths agape. Llywelyn's body jerked and his head snapped back.

'M-my lord…?'

The blacksmith bowed and, a little tardier in her reactions, the laundress dipped a curtsey. But as she straightened up again, Cristin saw her eyes gleam with malice and with mischief.

Llywelyn moved first. Pushing himself away from the wall, he let go of her hand and took her elbow instead. With a nod of acknowledgement, but not a word of either excuse or explanation, he led her briskly away from the avid stares and into to the midst of the crowd.

'Wait…' Cristin ran to keep up with him. 'They will think…'

But he neither responded nor slowed his pace, until they were back in the bailey. Like a huge and engulfing wave, the noise and the heat, the stench of roasting meat, swamped her, and, even before she'd regained her breath, Llywelyn was gone from her side.

Cristin stood rooted to the spot, as bodies surged and sang, intoxicated with ale and misrule, pressing all around her. Someone barged into her, almost knocking her off her feet, and the crown of flowers slipped from her head to the ground.

No one was looking at her now, nor asking her to dance, and she might not have existed in this world, or in any other, but only in a place between reality and fantasy.

The reality was there, under the royal awning, as Llywelyn, back at the Prince's side once more, served him with a fresh goblet of wine and a plate of sweetmeats, all thoughts of kissing doubtless forgotten, or *wishing* to be forgotten, a stranger once more.

The fantasy was that May crown that was now being trampled into the earth, unnoticed, by careless dancing feet. Perhaps it was just as well, since it had beguiled her into thinking that the world really *could* be turned upside down. But not even a kiss could turn a stranger into a lover, nor a servant into a queen, not even on Calan Mai.

* * *

Early the next morning, Llywelyn escorted the Prince and his party, bound homeward, as far as the old Roman road at Sarn Helen. In their midst rode the hostages, Roger de Clare and the two captured knights, bound not for home, but for the strong room of Castell Dinefwr. The day was already warm, the sky cloudless, the grass glistening with dew beneath their horses' hooves as the sun rose slowly.

'All the enemy castles in Ceredigion are taken except two, Blaenporth and Aberteifi. They must fall within the year, Llywelyn, without fail.'

Llywelyn's heart sank at the prospect, but he offered an opinion all the same. 'The news of our victories will surely have reached their ears by now, *f'arglwydd*, and they will be preparing for us.'

'Of that I have no doubt.' The Prince chuckled as he guided his stallion around a small boulder in the path. 'And I imagine Robert Fitz Stephen at Aberteifi is praying his kinship to me through marriage will save him. He is wrong.'

As Rhys proceeded to outline strategy, Llywelyn continued to listen with one ear, nodded in agreement or shook his head in dissent and commented where required. But only half his mind was in the present conversation—the other half kept returning to the previous day's celebrations, and to the consequences of them.

How the madness of May Day had made him forget himself, even though he'd drunk moderately, kept aloof and alert, as his duty demanded since he had a royal guest under his roof.

But his vigilance had failed him. Worse, it had led him into Cristin's wake after the Prince had kissed her, his jealousy overriding his common sense, and desire eclipsing decorum. And, most compelling of all, the need to be with her, away from everyone, as if May Day were for them alone.

'Doubtless you know that Blaenporth is garrisoned by Flemings, not Normans,' the voice of the Lord Rhys hardly penetrated his thoughts. 'So it will be a vicious fight.'

Llywelyn had no doubt either of the Prince's prediction, and his hold tightened on his reins at the thought of yet another brutal battle, so soon on the heels of the taking of Ystrad Meurig. But as he'd said to Cristin yesterday, the war had only just begun.

Was that why he'd curled his fingers around hers when she reached out her hand? Leaned his shoulder against hers when she'd moved nearer? Dipped his head to hers? Listened when she'd said that they should live for every moment in case it should be the last?

'I will recall Peredur from Abereinion and put him in charge of the siege, with you as his second,' Rhys went on. 'With, say, thirty of your men to complement his forces.'

Perhaps the coming siege was just as well. For, if those servants hadn't come around the corner when they had, he might have accepted that invitation, agreed that they must embrace every moment, and, far from being strangers, had kissed her!

'Peredur knows the Flemings better than anyone.' His murmured response came tardy, but the Prince was too preoccupied to notice. 'It will be my honour to serve under him.'

What of *Cristin's* honour if he had kissed her, gone further still, and drawn her into his arms, as he'd longed to do? Pressed her back against the warm, welcoming wood and let his body, his heart, his soul, rediscover hers? Make them anything but strangers once more?

There would have been no slander aimed at him if he

had, for it was almost expected that a lord take a mistress, more than one, even. His own father was an example of that! But Cristin, a servant and his bondswoman, would have no such respect, and no blind eyes would be turned. The malice he'd seen yesterday, on the face of the laundress, the leering look of the blacksmith, was certain proof of that.

'And after Blaenporth falls, we will turn our sights to Aberteifi.'

Llywelyn was about to respond, though not with the same eagerness with which the Prince had spoken, when his gaze caught something glinting in the grass to the side of the path. Drawing rein, he swung himself down from the saddle to pick it up. It was a copper belt buckle with the personal insignia of a man of rank carved upon it. And, as he brushed the dirt off its surface, he knew at once what—and whose—it was.

'What have you found?'

Llywelyn rose from his knee and held out the badge. 'An insignia, *f'arglwydd*. The hooded crow of Maelgwn ab Eilyr, brother to Peredur.'

Rhys leaned from his saddle and spat on the ground. '*Y 'sglyfaeth diawledig!* That man is vicious, a traitor and a murderer, and much else besides!'

The condemnation was an understatement, but Llywelyn said nothing as he put the badge into his pouch and remounted. They were several leagues south of Ystrad Meurig, so it was unlikely Maelgwn was anywhere near the castle. Yet, his nerves tightened and his scalp began to prickle as he cast his gaze in all directions, squinting against the sunlight.

That day he'd freed Cristin and his parents from the strong room, when he'd seen the blood in her hair, heard how Maelgwn had handled her, *his* blood had run cold at what might have befallen them had he been defeated. Now it ran cold all over again.

'He has not been seen since he escaped the battle for the castle a fortnight ago,' he informed the Prince. 'We thought him dead, of wounds, or else of thirst and starvation, yet no body has been discovered.'

'A pity he escaped, be he dead *or* alive. He is one that I would enjoy hanging very much.' Rhys's tone was ominous. 'But if he still lives, and is found in my realm fighting for the enemy, I may yet have that pleasure.'

They continued on their way, reaching the Roman road just after noon. There Llywelyn left the Prince's party and headed homeward, at double the pace. As he neared Rhydfendigaid, the bell of Ystrad Fflur rang the hour of Sext, and, drawing rein before crossing the ford, he paused, removed his helmet and listened.

The notes were clear in the distance, deep and pure, and so beautiful that a tingle of awe slid down his spine. They called to him, as they always had, and always would, until he eventually answered that call. Yet, to the north, something…someone…else called, as strong and as irresistible.

The bells stopped, and all was silent, leaving only the trickle of the river and the song of the birds. War and treachery seemed far away, not looming on the horizon, as the sun warmed his face and, the reins loose in his hands, his stallion dropped his head and began to crop the grass.

Llywelyn sat for a long time, with the sense of being at a crossing place that led in many different directions. South to the monastery, west to Blaenporth, north to Ystrad Meurig. And, for the first time in his life, he had no idea of which road he was supposed to take.

But staying in one spot forever wasn't possible either, so gathering the reins again and touching his heels to his

horse's flanks, he continued on the route he had to follow—
for now. Northward, but not direct to the castle. There was
another place to the north, too, one he'd not visited for many
years, but a place that suddenly called to him as well, just
as strong, just as loud, just as irresistible.

Chapter Seven

When Cristin left her chamber and went outside, the cleaning up after the celebrations of the day before was going on everywhere. The May Pole had already come down, the grass around it yellowed from the sun and flat from the dancing. Flowers and greenery lay scattered on the ground, her May Queen crown among them, sad and forgotten.

The Prince's party had departed at break of day, Llywelyn accompanying them so far, as his duty as host demanded. She hadn't seen him nor spoken to him since they'd parted yesterday. After taking the evening meal up to Cadwgan and Tangwystl, she'd retired early to her chamber, her stomach revolting at the thought of food and her heart still bruised at the way Llywelyn had left her.

As she made her way across the bailey, Dyddgu was coming towards her, and she paused to bid the woman good day. But the laundress sailed past without a word or a glance, the same malicious smirk on her face that had been there when she and Gronw Gof had discovered her with Llywelyn.

Her own face reddening but her head held high, Cristin

walked on and out through the gates into the solace and solitude of the countryside. The landscape opened up before her in all directions, the peaceful expanse an escape from the turmoil of her thoughts.

Taking a deep breath, she went eastward, her feet leading her way without her having to think about it. At the bend in the path, she turned north toward the *crug*, the high place where kings had held assemblies in centuries gone past. The place that had been her sanctuary in her childhood, hers and Llywelyn's.

It had always existed, the *crug*, but the day they first went there, it had seemed like *they* had discovered it, that only *they* knew about it. And, without either of them saying a word, they both knew, too, that it would be the place where she would wait and he would come. As he did, more and more often as his father's brutality got worse and worse.

At the little river of the Meurig, she took off her shoes and waded through, the water low from lack of rain. Barefoot just for the blissful feel of the earth between her toes, she lifted her skirts and threaded her way through the cowslip and long grasses.

The sun was warm and, her spirits lifting, too, Cristin began to hum a tune under her breath, startling a hare from cover. She watched it bound away, the unexpected encounter so delightful that she smiled. Then the jingle of a bit broke the moment and, looking up, she saw Llywelyn, sitting atop the *crug*, not fifty yards ahead.

The summer day suddenly turned cold. Could she go back the way she'd come? Turn in a different direction completely? But he'd already seen her so there was no purpose in that, or in pretending she wasn't heading to their special place at all.

Her skirts clutched in one hand and her shoes in the

other, Cristin approached, climbed the mound and sat down next to him. 'I didn't expect to find you here,' she said, not knowing what else to say. 'Nor for you to return so soon from escorting the Prince homeward.'

'I felt it prudent to return as soon as I could.'

She glanced at him, but he didn't elaborate. Instead, he stared outwards to where the hills shimmered like a magic kingdom. They'd often sat here as children, looking out over those vast lands, imagining that they were king and queen and ruled all they beheld.

Today, too, as in those long-ago months of May, the blue speedwell—*llysiau Llywelyn* in the Welsh tongue and the same colour as his eyes—bloomed on the summit of the *crug*, bright among the buttercups and daisies.

Cristin put out a hand to pluck one, feeling suddenly shy. He seemed awkward, too, as he shifted and lay back on his elbows, knees bent.

'It's been a long time since we sat here together, Cristin.'

'I don't know why I came here, really,' she replied in like tone, while the sea of speedwell dragged her down with their colour and their fragrance and their painful memories. 'I wanted to walk a while and somehow my feet found their way to our…the *crug*.'

'I'm not sure why I came either today, except that I felt the need.' There was a pause as his eyes narrowed against the sun. 'I'd forgotten how far you can see from up here.'

'I hadn't.' Cristin followed his gaze outwards, over those brilliant emerald-green hills. 'Although I haven't been here either…much.'

Though she *had*, on occasion, on long summer evenings when her work was done and the past called too strongly to resist, and even the sorrowful memories were not enough to keep her away. When, even though Llywelyn wasn't here and had no need of her as he once had, her need of him had grown not lessened in his absence.

'I'd almost forgotten, too, how much I love these lands.'

Llywelyn's voice was soft. He sprawled as he'd done so often in the old days, his limbs relaxed, his lean body flattening the grass and the flowers. *These* lands were *his* lands, lost and now regained. Was that why he'd come here today, to survey his restored territory? Or, like her, had he really felt compelled to come?

'Do you remember how we flew my falcon from here, Cristin?'

His tone was wistful now, not just soft, and, for a moment, he seemed almost as young as he'd been when they'd sat here together—at first, in companionship, and then amid the blossoming of something deeper.

'He never caught very much, though, did he?' she said, her voice wistful too. 'At least not that I remember.'

But that wasn't true. *Everything* was remembered with bittersweet clarity, since it was all around them—the heady scent of the *clychau gog* that the Saxons called bluebells, and the dazzling dandelions—but now in a choking sea of blue and yellow and green as those memories drowned her in sadness.

'No, he didn't.' He glanced across at her briefly. 'Doubtless, I trained him badly.'

To their right, barely a quarter league, the castle looked peaceful, smoke rising from the kitchen and spiralling up into the cloudless sky. It hadn't always been peaceful, though, in the days when Cadwgan had ruled. Then it had been his father's violence, the rages and the beatings, and not just the flying of falcons that had driven Llywelyn to seek her out here.

'Mayhap he was just a poor bird of prey, no matter how

much training you gave him?' Cristin suggested, every bone in her body longing to lie down, too, feel the warm grass at her back, *his* warmth at her side. Simply look up at the sky, as they used to do, counting clouds and wondering what lay beyond.

'Perhaps he was.' Llywelyn's wistful tone turned bitter. 'But my father never allowed me to keep another falcon after that one died.'

Before them, due south though hidden by the hills, lay the abbey, its bell sounding the hour of Nonce. They both fell silent to listen, as if it would be sacrilege now to speak. And when it had faded, Llywelyn turned towards her, his hair lifting from his brow in the breeze.

'Yesterday…'

Cristin's heart missed a beat…but one of them had to refer to it sooner or later. 'What about yesterday?'

'Yesterday, when we stood by the stables, I spoke of war.' There was a hesitation before he went on, looking away and a muscle clenching in his cheek as he frowned into the sun. 'Today that war has come a step closer.'

Cristin snatched a breath. 'What do you mean?'

'The Lord Rhys has given me, and Peredur, the task of taking Castell Blaenporth.'

The statement sent a thrill of fear down her spine. She looked back at him just as he turned to look at her. His expression was stern now, his mouth set into a grim line, and, suddenly, he wasn't like the boy who'd sat here so long ago at all.

'When will you go?' she asked, as the breeze cooled suddenly, making it seem as if summer was over already instead of just beginning.

He shrugged, but there was nothing careless about the

movement of his shoulders. 'I don't know, before the week is out, certainly.'

A stone rolled somewhere nearby where the black cattle grazed on the *ffridd*, and a pair of small white butterflies flittered by in a mating dance. They both watched the sparring wings until they'd disappeared.

'But that isn't all I need to tell you. I wanted to tell you also…' His cheek clenched again. 'That you made a beautiful May Queen, Cristin. You dazzled everyone who watched you.'

Burying the fingers of one hand in the grass, Cristin anchored herself to the earth. 'It is the role of the May Queen to dazzle. She would be a poor choice if she did not.'

High in the sky, a lark swooped and sang and in the forest of Llwyn y Gog to the east, a cuckoo called, its voice merry in comparison to the sombre note that marked Llywelyn's voice when he continued.

'The problem was that I was dazzled too.'

Cristin dug her fingers deeper, clutching a handful of clover, as a fist seemed to close around her heart. 'We never used to talk in riddles when we sat here as children,' she said. 'What is it you are trying to say, Llywelyn?'

A stone rolled again and the chestnut stallion, grazing below, raised its head and pricked its ears. Its nostrils flared as it scented the air before it returned to cropping the grass.

'The same thing you told me when we parted at Llanbadarn, seven years ago?' she pursued, when he remained silent. 'That there was no room in your life for earthly love, or for me, even though you had just enjoyed both?'

His eyes lifted to hers and his face flushed red. 'You are angry with me. You were then too.'

'Yes, I was!' Cristin felt her breath tremble as a wave

of anger swept her. 'I *believed* you, Llywelyn! When you said you loved me, I thought…'

'I didn't lie in that, Cristin.' Llywelyn twisted towards her and the intensity of his gaze seemed to peel her flesh from her bones as he'd once peeled her clothes from her body. 'When I told you that you were the only woman I would ever love, it was true. It still is true. I wish to God it wasn't!'

Cristin plucked a sprig of the blue speedwell from the grass and began tearing the petals apart. 'In that case, perhaps you should *pray* to Him! Ask Him that it *not* be true!'

'Don't you think I have!'

She looked away, her eyes following a bumblebee as it buzzed from flower to flower. 'And has He answered your prayers?'

'No.'

'Evidently, you are not praying hard enough,' she retorted, with a lightness that belied the heaviness that had settled over her heart. 'Or else you have forgotten to pray at all and know only how to wield a sword!'

'*Ar fy llw*, Cristin!' He turned away from her, back onto his elbows. 'These last two weeks, I've done nothing but pray!'

'For what?'

'For the strength of will to not take you in my arms and kiss you…even though I want to, more than I've ever wanted anything.'

'Then it's just as well you go on praying, if kissing me is such a sin on your soul!' Tossing the remnants of the speedwell away, Cristin leapt to her feet, her heart not just heavy now, but starting to crack. 'If you are too holy, or too afraid, or too proud, there are plenty of *others* who will kiss me!'

As Cristin dusted grass off her skirts, Llywelyn rose to his feet too. 'I know there are others, Cristin!' he said through gritted teeth. 'I watched them all yesterday, so many of them that it made my head spin.'

She glared at him, two spots of indignant colour high on her cheekbones. 'Mayhap you shouldn't have watched!'

'I couldn't do otherwise.' Llywelyn felt his cheeks heat, too, not with indignation, but with shame. 'You are always in my sight, in my mind, Cristin, even when you are not near.'

'Well…' Straightening up again, she planted her hands on her hips. 'Since it appears that prayer has failed you, what do you intend to do about that dilemma?'

'*Dduw annwyl*, if only I knew!' Although he *did* know, and that was the problem. 'But yesterday, as I watched you dance, I hated all those men who watched you too. I could have killed them for daring to touch you, to kiss you… when I could not.'

'Surely you were not jealous?' Cristin's eyes grew wide and he saw himself reflected in their hazel-green depths. 'Hardly a *pious* virtue, Llywelyn!'

He reached out and touched her cheek, letting his fingertips trail downward to the pulse that beat fast at the base of her throat. 'No, it is not pious at all, Cristin.'

Beneath his fingertips, her flesh was warm and soft, and he felt his own pulse quicken too. 'Even if it was in my heart, not with my sword, the thought was there. And thought is sinful if it is the wrong thought…'

And it would be so wrong now to draw her down upon the ground again, lie beside her in that long grass, among the buttercups. Wrong to leave off praying altogether and let himself love her, just once more…so why did it feel so right?

It was then, just as Llywelyn tottered between right and wrong, that his stallion suddenly started at a noise and threw its head up again. In an instant all his senses were sharpened in a different way completely and he wheeled around in the direction of the sound.

Cristin turned with him, one of her hands brushing his. 'I heard that sound earlier, and so did your horse,' she said. 'Like feet slithering on stone. Perhaps it is the men cutting rocks at Tancnwch?'

Llywelyn shook his head and resisted the temptation to link his fingers with hers. 'The quarry is too far away for any sound to carry. This was much nearer.' He frowned and cast his eyes all around, but there was nothing untoward to be seen nor heard now.

And yet…the danger was there, real. He could feel it with every nerve, every pore of his skin. He glanced around a second time, but there was still nothing—and yet…

'Shouldn't we go and find out what it is?' Cristin chewed her lip, drawing his gaze to her mouth. 'Someone, or something, might be in distress.'

The noise came again, this time accompanied by the splash of water from the nearby stream. On the *ffridd*, the black cattle had all stopped grazing and were staring right back at him. Llywelyn considered a brief moment. No Norman soldiers had been seen since the fall of the castle. But finding Maelgwn's badge was an ominous sign, one that had unnerved him more than he cared to admit.

'No,' he said. Just because none of the enemy were visible, it didn't mean they weren't there, deep in the forest, biding their time. 'I'll return with some men and search this area thoroughly later.'

'But why don't we search now?' She turned to look at him, her brows lifting. 'There could be a simple explanation.'

There could be…but if war had taught him anything, it

was that a wounded man, like a wounded wolf, was dangerous. It lurked in cover, licked its wounds until, driven mad by pain, it was apt to turn and bite. If Maelgwn were in the vicinity, perhaps with reinforcements, he wouldn't be able to defend Cristin on his own.

And, worse, if she'd happened to be sitting here alone, or walking to the village as she often did, unaware of danger, that kitchen knife of hers—if she still carried it—would be no defence either. He had to warn her, at least, but not alarm her.

Drawing the hooded crow emblem from his pouch, Llywelyn held it out on his palm. 'Do you recognise this?'

She looked down at it and her face paled. 'It's the insignia of Maelgwn ab Eilyr. Where did you find it?'

'Not near here, but not very far away either. Maelgwn hurt you once and the fact you hid my father right under his nose for nigh on two years will not have endeared you to him, Cristin, nor to *any* Norman.'

Llywelyn shoved the badge back into his pouch. When he looked up, she'd moved closer, so close that he could count the light cluster of freckles on her nose.

'So, you think he is still here, somewhere?'

He shrugged, felt her soft breath tickle the base of his throat. 'It's possible.'

At that moment a small bullock clambered up over the bank of a deep crevice through which a stream ran. They both turned their heads at the sound, and when their eyes came back to meet again, at the same time, hers were dancing with mirth.

'So your lurking danger was naught but a beast after a cooling drink of water.'

'It is not a topic for jest, Cristin. It is a matter of safety,'

Llywelyn replied, knowing he should be taking her away from here, homeward and out of harm's reach. But his feet seemed to have taken root in the earth, held fast by the grasses and the flowers, and by the past they'd shared here, on this spot. 'It might have been anything. An enemy advance scout, survivors from one of Rhys's battle, brigands…'

'Then it is not just jealousy? You *do* still care?'

The cattle moved away, their hooves brushing through the grass as they sought shade from the sun under the trees, higher up on the pasture.

'I've always cared for you, Cristin,' he said, feeling his heart begin to thump. 'You know that without me having to say it.'

Fewer swallows swooped now, their morning feeding frenzy giving way to midafternoon rest. Time ceased to exist, only Cristin existed just as she always had, as she lifted a hand and removed a blade of grass that had stuck to the sleeve of his tunic.

'So we are not *strangers* any longer?'

Llywelyn shook his head. 'We were never *really* strangers, and never *could* be, no matter how long apart.'

'And now that we are together again…?' She tilted her face up to his. 'And if we are *not* strangers…then what *are* we? Friends? *More* than friends?'

The impulse to show her what they *could* be was almost overpowering. All he had to do was dip his head, let his lips touch hers and kiss her as he wanted to, as she clearly wanted him to also.

'I don't *know* what we are now, Cristin,' he said instead, his voice shaking as his breath evaded him and his heart thundered in his chest. 'But here is not the place, and now is not the time, to try and find out. Best we return to the castle. The day is fading fast.'

The day wasn't fading at all, but if they remained here, Cristin so warm and close, with the sunlight in her hair and promise in her eyes, he would never want it to end. Danger may be lurking but the greatest peril was the longing inside himself to disregard everything else. The yearning to accept that call of her eyes, the lure of her lips, a beguilement so strong he could almost taste it.

Wrenching himself away, Llywelyn stooped and brushed the grass from his leggings, denying himself all those things. Her shoes were still lying where she'd put them so, dropping to his knees, he took them up, replaced first one then the other. He tried with all his might not to notice the soft skin, the earth between her toes, the delicate ankle, but when she put a hand on his shoulder to balance herself, it was *he* who nearly toppled back down into the grass.

'Thank you,' she murmured when he'd regained his feet, her eyes thoughtful as they rested on his, and a host of other words seemed to hover unsaid behind the simple one of gratitude. Words of feelings.

Taking her hand, lest she say them, or he say them, and bring the years full circle again, he led her down the slope of the *crug* towards where his horse stood. The animal was unperturbed now at least, indicating that no hidden peril existed—at least not outwardly.

'We'll ride,' Llywelyn said, unlacing his fingers from hers before they could lace too tightly. 'My stallion can carry us both with ease.'

Swinging himself up into the saddle, he put out a hand to help her up behind him, leaving his foot free of the stirrup so she could place her foot in it and mount. This was how they used to ride in the old days, Cristin behind him, her arms around his waist, her cheek against his back.

And this is how they rode now, except instead of a child's slight body pressing into him, it was a woman's, still slight but now with curves where before there were none. Her arms felt different, too, the palms of her hands flattened against his stomach in a way they hadn't before. Her kirtle had ridden up, just like her skirts had then, but now the slender leg was longer, shapely. And the cheek that rested against his shoulder blade was no longer that of a girl.

There was no preventing it. He hardened at once and, short of moving forward and sitting on his mount's neck, there was nothing he could do about it. All he could do was grit his teeth as the short distance to the castle became countless leagues of utter torture.

If Cristin noticed his state of arousal, as she surely must, given the way his heart hammered and words evaded him, she said nothing. As they entered in through the castle gates, he'd begun to believe she hadn't noticed anything at all. Or he might have believed, had it not been for the flush on her cheek as he helped her dismount.

'Thank you,' she said again, as she'd done when he'd helped her on with her shoes. Her gaze met his, fleetingly, but as thoughtful as before, and then she turned and walked towards the keep, without looking back.

Llywelyn led his horse to the stable, his cheeks burning, too, his loins on fire. He felt stares following him, albeit hidden under brows, beneath hats and over shoulders. And no wonder! After yesterday, in the lee of the stable wall, tongues must be well and truly wagging by now.

A stable lad came to take his reins, but he waved him away, leading his stallion into its stall to see to the beast himself. As he scraped the sweat of its coat, he cursed under his breath. As lord, it was his duty to keep Cristin safe, and that safety included her good name, not just her life.

Calan Mai really did turn the world in somersaults, it seemed, upset the norms of life, made sense become non-sense and allowed passions to run free. And, on the *crug, his* passions had almost done the same. Run riot and made him forget common sense—and almost his vocation—altogether.

His vocation! He'd meant to tell her, there, that he still intended to take up the monk's habit, as he'd told her seven years ago. But just like then, his heart, his desire, had ruled his head.

Mwg crept into the stable and began to rub around his horse's legs. The stallion was inclined to kick and, just as he went to tie its rope more securely, it stamped a forefoot, almost catching the cat's tail.

'*Uffern dân!*'

Going down on haunches, he reached for Mwg, to put him outside, out of harm. But for his pains, he got a scratch on the back of his hand and a glare from two furious amber eyes, before the old cat shot from the stable far quicker than he'd come in.

Llywelyn rested his forearms on his thighs and hung his head. Taking up a handful of straw, he inhaled the sweet dusty smell, feeling sweeter memories stir, then let it sift between his fingers and fall back to the floor. It would be so easy to exist only for the present, not look to the fu-ture. Yield to desire and embrace the love that bound them, tighter than ever, in case that future never came. But that future might yet come—and when it did…

He'd hurt Cristin so much when he'd left her, without a farewell and with no promises, that winter's morning at Llanbadarn. More than he'd realised or intended. He stared down at the spots of blood on his hand. A scratch from the claws of a cat was nothing compared to the rupturing of a person's heart. And he couldn't—he wouldn't—hurt her like that ever again.

Chapter Eight

The hour was late! Hurrying out through the door of her chamber to wait upon her mistress, Cristin almost fell headlong as Mwg darted out in front of her between her flying feet. As he vanished down the stairs, she swore quietly but there was no time to go and try to catch him now.

Considering the cat's age, he could move fast enough when he chose to, and when a certain she-cat of the stables was in heat and ripe for mating—as if fathering half the kittens in the village wasn't enough, *y cwrcath*!

Her curse vanished before a smile. This morning, for some reason, her heart felt as light as her feet as she made haste for the adjacent chamber. Although, in truth, the reason was as plain and as bright as the sunshine outside. Yesterday, on the *crug*, she'd glimpsed the old Llywelyn, dimly, but he'd been there.

She'd sensed it—in his gaze, his touch, his voice, his care for her, when the strange noise had puzzled them, when he'd placed her shoes back on her feet, his fingers soft on her skin. Beneath the warrior's armour, that boy she knew, the man she loved, had always loved, still existed. She just needed to find him.

Knocking, Cristin entered her mistress's chamber and found Lady Tangwystl already up and dressed. The curtains around the bed were drawn back and Lord Cadwgan was propped up against the pillow. His face looked clammy and the sheen of fever glazed his eyes.

Her smile fading, she crossed quickly over to where Tangwystl was plaiting her hair. 'I am sorry for my tardiness, *meistres*,' she said. 'I slept badly.'

Although this fell badly short of the truth. For she'd tossed and turned, reliving that moment when Llywelyn's lips hovered close to hers in the promise of a kiss that hadn't come.

'Never mind that now. Lord Cadwgan is unwell.'

With that, there came the sound of choking and both women turned at the same time to see Cadwgan had vomited into his pillow. Tangwystl ran to him, her half-tied plait streaming out behind her.

'Hush, husband, hush. Be calm.'

As his wife stroked his brow, murmuring reassuring words, Cristin mopped up the vomit and replaced the pillow with a clean one. No sooner was it done, than Cadwgan vomited again, though thankfully not as violently as before, and this time she had the basin ready.

Tangwystl turned to her with dread in her eyes. 'Is it the pestilence come back, Cristin?'

Cristin resisted the temptation to cross herself just in case. 'No, *meistres*, I don't think so. With that sickness, the skin becomes yellow, and Lord Cadwgan is pale.' Too pale, she added, silently to herself.

'Yes, you are right, of course, but there is something gravely wrong.' Tangwystl touched her husband's hollow cheek. 'Can you tell me what it is, my lord?'

Cadwgan made no response, but a mangled hand lifted

and clutched that of his wife, moving it to lie entwined with his over his heart. It was the last thing Cristin expected to see him do, this man who had used his hands—before they were cruelly broken by the men who'd attacked him—only in the performing of equally cruel acts.

And then, as she wondered yet again at the change in him, Tangwystl turned to her, her eyes wide and her voice urgent. 'I can hardly feel his heartbeat. Quick, Cristin, fetch the physician!'

When the physician entered, Lord Cadwgan was no worse, but no better either. The man could do little but confirm it wasn't the pestilence and advocate clean bedding and clothing at once to destroy any risk should he be wrong.

Then he bled Cadwgan, but only a little, to stem any fever and left, muttering under his breath about the need to send for a priest, just in case. Lady Tangwystl, quiet and composed, remained at her husband's side, and bade Cristin to take the soiled bedding to be cleaned.

Cristin was glad to go. It was hard watching a man die, slowly, without dignity, instead of in battle, the way a warrior would choose to die. That at least was quick and, so they said, if done quickly enough and with skill, almost without pain.

When she entered through the open doorway of the washing room, Dyddgu was there, bending over the water vat from which steam billowed up in clouds.

'Good morning, Dyddgu. I have some bedding that needs washing.'

The woman turned, her face flushed from the heat. 'Do you, indeed!' She dried her hands on her apron. 'As if I've not got enough work to do this morning—unlike *some*, who think they have risen so high as to be above such menial duties now!'

Cristin stopped short on the threshold, the unexpected attack heating *her* cheeks too. For the curt retort was one she couldn't deny, even if her change in fortune had come unlooked for and unexpected.

Before, when the castle was in enemy hands, *she* would have been doing the daily washing, too, alongside Dyddgu. And she'd sensed from the start that the other woman resented her elevation to lady's maid. But until now, the depth of that resentment hadn't been voiced so openly nor so spitefully.

'I have *other* duties now, Dyddgu. Like you, I carry out whatever tasks I am told to do.'

The woman smirked, her round face a mask of malice. 'Perhaps so, but I'll warrant your tasks aren't quite so disagreeable these days!'

Cristin flung her chin up. 'What is *that* supposed to mean?'

Dyddgu eyed the bundle of dirty bedding. 'Some folk know how to feather their own beds, don't they? And have no shame in taking their pleasure therein neither. But if they think their shame can be washed clean and no one will be any the wiser, they are greatly mistaken.'

The pungent stench of Cadwgan's vomit became even more distasteful, and Cristin had an urge to fling the bundle away from her. Instead, although her stomach turned, she gripped it hard, as if it were a shield.

'This is the bedding from my lord and lady's chamber, *not* from mine!'

'So *you* say…' Dyddgu's red mouth curled. 'But who is to know for certain, since you sleep in a bed just as fine?

And you don't sleep alone either, I'll wager, for all your meek looks and innocent manner!'

'How dare you say such things!'

'I'll say what I like. Your pretence at playing the virgin fools nobody, *y butain*!'

Cristin felt her face go redder still, her mind reeling at the unprovoked attack. Dropping the bedding down next to the other soiled garments waiting to go into the vat, she drew a calming breath.

'I will try and forget what you have said to me today, Dyddgu, but if you ever call me a whore again, I will repeat your slander to Lord Llywelyn.'

'Tell him!' Dyddgu folded her arms smugly over her ample bosom. 'It is not only *I* who call you that. Everyone knows what you are, and I'm not saying anything that others haven't said.'

Cristin's stomach churned worse than it had from the stench of the bedding. That stench was at least clean, in a way, whereas the words that filled her ears now were filthy and wicked.

'No, but I'll wager it was *you* who said it first. *You* who began these rumours that have no truth to them at all.' She held out a hand, palm upwards, and struggled to keep her temper as well as her dignity. 'Why, Dyddgu? What have I ever done to offend you?'

'Placed yourself above me, above us *all*, that's what!' The laundress spat. 'Licking the boots of the lords of the castle, be they Welsh *or* Norman, ay, and bedding with them too!'

Cristin's temper finally boiled over. 'Fine words from you! Have you not bedded with half the men in the village in your time?'

Digging her nails into her palms lest she actually slap

the woman, she spun away and, steam blurring her eyes, stumbled towards the door. But the laundress's spite followed on her heels.

'That's right, the guilty always run! How fine you look in your new blue kirtle, Cristin, but you'll never be a lady for all that, *yr ordderch!*'

Lurching out into the daylight, Cristin steadied herself a moment against the wall. Tears of outrage stung her eyes even as the vicious slander stung her ears.

*Putain...gordderch...*whore!

It *wasn't* true, none of it, even if it had been once. It was all lies, spread by folk who were ignorant, jealous and wicked beyond words. But thanks to Dyddgu, those lies would run in rumour all over the castle and the village before too long.

Crossing to the water trough from which the livestock drank, Cristin plunged her hands into the cold water. She scrubbed them over her face until the odour of the soiled bedding was washed away, though the rottenness of false rumour remained, deeper than the skin.

Drying her face with her skirt, she took a deep breath and made her way back towards the keep. She held her head high, as if nothing at all had been said, or heard, or felt. But she noticed now what she hadn't seen before, like a mist lifting before her eyes.

The knowing looks from the men going about their tasks, surreptitious leers and sniggering mouths, whispers behind hands into eager ears. It seemed not only the servants but the soldiers, too, had cast her in the role of the lord's *gordderch!*

Cristin ran up the steps of the keep, the bell at Ystrad Fflur starting up and speeding her way. Escaping into the welcome shadow of the doorway, she leaned back against the inner wall and pressed her palms to her midriff, then to her cheeks, to try and cool the burn, but to no avail.

Her kirtle was wet from the trough, the shift below wet, too, and clinging to her body. She realised that the shape of her breasts were prominent beneath her bodice, visible to all those men she'd just passed by, and her cheeks burned hotter still.

The gown Llywelyn had given her was too fine a garment for the likes of her. It was a gown a lord would give his lady—or his mistress. But she'd worn it all the same, with pleasure, and with pride too, and today in particular.

For he still loved her, she was certain of that now. Even if it was different now to before, their love still lived, as strong and as sure as ever. What did gossip matter?

But was Dyddgu right? Had she put herself above her station on the basis of that love? Yesterday, on the *crug*, she'd longed for his kiss, yearned for him to take her in his arms, lay her down in the long grass, and she'd known he'd wanted the same.

Did the wanting, as much as the doing, make her wanton, even so? Should Llywelyn ask, would she give everything, just as she'd always done? And if she did, was that right or wrong? And could love—true and lasting love that encompassed heart and soul as well as body—transcend everything else, even slander, even sin?

It was noon when, after some brief strategic discussion with Gwion ab Adda in the empty hall, Llywelyn dismissed his *penteulu*. Getting to his feet, he stretched his arms above his head to ease the tightness in his spine, and turned around to look at the Cwn Annwn.

The red eyes stared back at him, the eyes of pursuit, retribution and justice, albeit a terrible one for the transgressors they brought down with those sharp teeth—an eternity of torment in fires of hell. He flinched at the thought of the souls he'd sent there, albeit cleanly by the sword in battle, over the years.

Yet, who was he to judge whether their fate was deserved or not—he who was as damned as any of them? Could the Cwn Annwn condone everything—his weakness, his needs, his sins?

A footfall sounded behind him. Turning, he saw his mother walking up the hall towards him.

'*Dydd da, fy mab i.*'

Her greeting was firm, her voice strong. She was still thin, but her bones were not so brittle now. Her hair shone silver and was neatly bound into a coil below her veil. There was colour in her face, too, now, instead of the ashen hue she'd had the night he'd discovered her in the village. But as she came to stand beside him, it was the colour of displeasure that warmed her cheeks as she went to her point like an arrow to its target.

'You will have heard that your father is unwell?'

'Yes.'

She tutted. 'And yet you have not been to see him!'

He shook his head. 'No.'

'Not even now when he may even be dying?'

'Not even now.'

Llywelyn stared up at the hounds on the wall and his mother stared up at him, her eyes burning into his cheek far more fiercely than those red eyes ever could.

'Then I can only leave that between you and your conscience—if you still possess one.'

'*My* conscience? What about *his*?' He turned to look at her, bewildered that she of *all* people should be so blind. 'Does he feel remorse for the beatings, the curses, the cruelty? Does he seek atonement for what he did to you, to Rhianon, to all of us?'

'Yes, I believe he does.'

Llywelyn clenched his teeth. 'Cadwgan might fool you, Mother, but not me. Even if he *were* sorry, now when it is too late, it wouldn't undo any of it.'

'You have become hard, Llywelyn, as hard as he ever was. At least his rages, as terrible as they were, flared and died swiftly, and there were moments of calm in between. With you, there seems to be only rage, constant and unrelenting, and nothing else.'

Llywelyn folded his arms across his chest. All his young life, he'd seen her meek and afraid, silent and invisible lest she incur his father's wrath. So terrified of Cadwgan that she didn't even protect them, her children, from that wrath, but let them face it alone.

That day when she'd run down the corridor, sobbing and clutching him tightly in her arms, flashed back. Perhaps she *did* try, at least in the beginning, but Cadwgan broke her spirit as well as her body, and she didn't try anymore. And, as they'd got older, he and Rhianon had stood up for themselves.

Yet now Tangwystl had become a tower of strength and courage, as well as sharp of tongue. When had she changed? From where had she found her bravery at last? Or was it *easy* to have courage now that her husband could no longer hurt her or anyone else?

She spoke again, her tongue sharper still. 'I have heard rumours about you and Cristin!'

'Have you?'

'Yes. What do you intend to do about them?'

'What do you *expect* me to do?' he said, mentally asking

forgiveness for an untruth even before he voiced it. 'There is nothing to either confirm or deny.'

Tangwystl frowned, the furrowing of her brow adding to the lines on her face, but her wit was as keen as a knife edge. 'You and Cristin were always close as children, despite the differences in your standing. And, when you were older, I often wondered...'

'We are not children now.'

'No, and because of that, perhaps it is best if Cristin goes back to the village.'

Llywelyn held her gaze. 'And who will attend you if she goes?'

'She can continue in her duties, come to the castle daily, but she mustn't sleep under this roof, in your former chamber, for a night longer.'

'No.' He didn't even have to ponder it. 'Cristin will remain. It's not safe in the village, for one thing, and for another...'

That *other* was something he could never admit to but his mother had no such qualms, it appeared, about giving voice to his conscience. 'She is too good to be your bedfellow, Llywelyn, if that is what you mean to make her. And if you *do* mean that, shame on you!'

Llywelyn felt his face burn hot. 'Cristin is the last woman I would bring shame upon, and you mistake me in that, madam. I seek no bedfellow.'

'What *do* you seek, Llywelyn? Of my children, you are the one I have understood the least.'

He shrugged, though her remark struck him painfully, for he'd always thought she'd understood him only too well. 'I mean to take up my vocation at Ystrad Fflur. The Lord Rhys has already given me his blessing and his patronage.'

'Then you have not changed your mind over all these years?'

'No. If anything these years of war have only convinced me more.' Llywelyn looked back at the Cwn Annwn, the pricked red ears listening for an explanation, just as his mother did. 'For men born into a noble house, there is only the sword or the cloister, Mother. There is nothing in between.'

'And Cristin knows of your intention?' his mother asked.

Beyond the walls, through the unshuttered windows, the sun dipped lower, slanting into the hall and sending beams of golden light across the flagstone floor. 'Yes…but I will tell her again, in case she has forgotten it.'

'But what of your duties here, your responsibility to this place and to these people? Who will be lord of the castle when your father dies? Who will protect our tenants, Llywelyn?'

'Rhys will install a new lord,' he replied. 'One who will do those duties better and more willingly than I. And Gwion ab Adda will remain here as steward.'

A grey shape came out of the shadows. Mwg. The cat dropped a dead mouse at his feet as if expecting a reward! Llywelyn ignored it. For reasons he couldn't fathom, the creature constantly sought him out. It irritated him and yet he could never kick it away.

For Mwg was a thread that linked him to the past, to Cristin. A thread that, instead of weakening over the years, seemed to have only grown stronger until now it seemed unbreakable, despite all the conviction of his intended vocation.

'And will this new lord allow me, and your father should he live, to remain? To exist on his bounty and at his mercy?'

'The Prince will provide for you and Cadwgan too.' Llywelyn felt a niggle of discomfort all the same. He'd never wanted the responsibility of lordship in the first place, any more than he'd wanted to wield a sword. And yet, as his mother took him to task, he realised just how much he'd adapted to those duties already, how keenly he felt the responsibility for his tenants. 'He has assured me that neither of you, nor any of our people, will want for anything.'

'Doubtless he will…if he wins this war. If he *loses* it, there will be no provision for *any* of us.'

Llywelyn dropped his gaze to the dead mouse at his feet. Did the souls of animals go either to heaven or hell too? Because his mother was right. If this war was lost, things like duty and responsibility would matter little, since they'd *all* be dead. 'The outcome is in God's hands, Mother.'

'Spoken like a true son of the Church!' Tangwystl's tongue cut sharper still. 'In his prime, your father placed his faith in his sword, as well as in God.'

'Yet he lost this castle and all our lands.'

'And with God's help, you took them back! You had Cristin's help, too, in that, don't forget, or would have, had the Normans not come for us.'

Llywelyn nodded, a shudder passing through him at what might have happened. 'I'm well aware of the fate that would have fallen you, and Cadwgan, had I not retaken the castle. Cristin might have paid the highest price of all for giving you shelter all those years.'

'So you *do* still care for her.' The blue eyes, so like his own and Rhianon's, studied him shrewdly. 'I've always known about you two, you realise?'

Llywelyn took a breath, let it out again. 'What have you known?'

'That your closeness as children grew into something deeper. That she loves you and always has.' Her brows knit. 'And yet at Llanbadarn all those years ago, you didn't bid her farewell. Why, Llywelyn? What happened between you then? Did you argue?'

'No.' And he left it at that.

'Keep silent, then, but I know without having to hear. Women always do.' Tangwystl's shoulders lifted in a sigh. 'There is another thing also that I've always known about you, *fy mab annwyl*. You have chosen a difficult path through life.'

'Perhaps it has been chosen *for* me?'

'No, it is your choice alone, Llywelyn. I pray it is not the wrong one.'

Llywelyn said nothing in response. *He* prayed, too, night and day, for the certainty that his chosen path was the right one. It had seemed a simple choice once, since it was the only way to avoid the violence he abhorred. Even when he'd left Cristin at Llanbadarn, it had still been simple, though not easy. It had been anything *but* easy then.

And now…here he was, embroiled in violence anyway, and Cristin filled his vision, his senses, his heart, day and night, too, until not even his prayers showed him the way any longer.

'I will ask you one more time and one more time only.' His mother's thin mouth pursed. 'The priest has already been to see you father. Will you come now and make your peace with him, before it is too late?'

'If he has had absolution from a priest, he has no need of me, since I cannot give him the same. I am riding out shortly in any case.'

'For what purpose?'

'To search the area round about. There are signs that the enemy may still linger, or have returned. I must find out if that is so, and how many they number.' Stooping, Llywelyn picked up the dead mouse by the tail and, striding to the hearth, tossed it into the flames. 'And you are wrong when you say I have chosen my path, Mother. It was my *father* who chose it for me, not I myself.'

Tangwystl moved away then but, after a few steps, turned back. 'That isn't the path I am really talking about, Llywelyn.' She became suddenly kinder and more courageous than he'd ever seen her. 'You might be the deepest of my children, the least fathomable…and I have not been the mother you, that all my children, needed me to be. But I see very clearly that you love Cristin as much as she loves you. And for that, I pity you both.'

She left him with those startling words, her footsteps fading away and the door of the hall closing quietly behind her. Llywelyn remained, the hissing of the peat in the hearth loud in his ears, the smoke filling his nose, choking him, and the cat coming to rub itself around his boots.

He looked down at the creature and it looked back up at him, its amber eyes seeming suddenly to delve as deeply and as all-seeingly as his mother's had, and to accuse as keenly. In the fire, the carcass of the mouse had burnt up to nothing. Soon, if the physician—from whom he'd already sought word of his father—was right, Cadwgan might be facing the same fate in hell.

And Llywelyn, too, felt as if he was being consumed by flames, the cold hard flames of the impossible choices that faced him. War or peace. Hate or forgiveness. Love or denial. Cristin or the cloister…

Why, *why*, when he'd only chosen for himself the *one* path, the one that led to a spiritual and not a worldly life, where he could hurt neither Cristin nor anyone else, was there still so many others in front of him?

The moon was just cresting the hilltops when Llywelyn turned for home at last. He'd sent his men back hours since but he himself had stayed out, some inner sense convincing him that danger lurked. He just couldn't see it.

That afternoon they'd scoured the land around up to a distance of three leagues, and yet no sign of the enemy had been found anywhere. But he *knew* it was there with a certainty that went beyond the senses of sight and hearing and smell. It was something he could taste, as if evil hung in the air, thicker still now in the twilight.

But he was half-asleep in the saddle, his limbs were stiff, his head heavy. As he plodded through the village, hardly a light showed, the villagers already abed. Not even a dog barked and it seemed every living thing slept, oblivious to any threat of danger at all.

Perhaps it wasn't there, perhaps it was only *he* who sensed it—or imagined it. But yesterday, on the *crug* with Cristin, it was no bullock that had caused that noise.

Lost in thought, he nearly missed the creak of the church door but his horse heard it, starting and pricking its ears. Drawing rein, Llywelyn turned his head to look. The door was in shadow, but as his eyes peered into the descending dusk, he saw it was ajar.

His nerves tightening, he dismounted and, looping his reins over the wicker fence, approached, every sense alert. Doubtless, someone had been careless in closing the door behind them after Vespers…and yet the air inside the church as he entered seemed to crackle.

He was halfway up the nave, his hands outstretched as if to touch that which he could not see, when the door slammed shut. And then, in the fading echo, through the sudden hush, came the scrape of a sword being drawn from its scabbard.

Chapter Nine

That evening in hall, Llywelyn's chair was empty and, no matter how often Cristin looked up and towards the high table, it remained empty all through supper. Behind it, the Cwn Annwn looked lost, less terrifying, without his presence. To the right of the vacant place, even Gwion ab Adda, the *penteulu* and the head of the household guard, looked lost, his brow furrowed, his solitude conspicuous.

The party of soldiers that had ridden out that day, to scour the lands round about for any enemy presence, had come back well before dusk, but Llywelyn hadn't. On their return, they'd reported that he'd sent them home but he'd remained in the saddle, continuing to search.

Now an eerie sort of apprehension hovered over the room, like the cobwebs that hung from the beamed roof. Not just the expectation of inevitable war but the unsettling absence of their leader and their protector in that war when it came.

And Cristin was the most unsettled of all. After the incident in the laundry, Dyddgu had moved her place at table, taking old Gronw Gof with her. In their stead, some of the stable lads sat either side of her, speculating avidly on the reasons for the lord's lack of presence in hall.

'Not been seen for hours.'

'Can't have got lost, not he, knowing these lands since boyhood.'

'An accident, perhaps a fall from his horse?'

'More likely some marauders have waylaid him, just like they did his poor father.'

'Cut his throat, mayhap, or worse.'

'If that's so, then some will mourn him hard indeed, *one in particular*!'

At last, Cristin put her knife down with a deliberate clatter. She knew the speculation was partly for her benefit, malicious tongues revelling in teasing because they all believed she shared Llywelyn's bed.

'Stop your idle talk, will you! It helps no one and only causes more worry!' But she heard her voice quake all the same, since what they were speculating at might well be true. 'Or have you nothing better to do than gossip like women?'

Guffaws broke out all around, accompanied by winks and nudging of elbows. And as Dyddgu, farther down the table, glanced her way and bent her head to whisper into the avid ear next to her, Cristin couldn't bear it a moment longer.

Rising to her feet, she walked towards the door with a withering glance at the laundress. Iago the priest was also just leaving, since it was almost the hour of Compline, and he bowed and stood aside to let her pass out first.

Where *was* Llywelyn? Why hadn't he returned with the others? Could any of those terrible predictions be true? After all, his father had also been riding alone, that day he'd been set upon and callously left for dead...

No! Cristin pushed those unanswerable quandaries out of her head and mounted the stairs. The Normans had gone and the Flemings were far to the south. Llywelyn knew the terrain better than any, and his horse was too surefooted to stumble and throw him. There were no marauders lurking in dark forests, knives gleaming, waiting to strike him down either. There *mustn't* be!

She was passing his door when a noise from within stopped her. It was the mewing of a cat. Mwg! He must have been shut inside by accident when someone had closed the door earlier that day.

Putting her ear to the wood, she listened a moment in case Llywelyn *had* returned, after all and, beknown to no one, had gone aloft instead of coming into the hall to sup. But there was no other sound within, only the pitiful mewing that grew louder and more insistent as Mwg sensed her presence.

Lifting her hand to the latch, Cristin pushed the door open. The chamber was indeed empty, apart from Mwg, who darted out at once and vanished down the stairs, doubtless making for the kitchen where the cook always kept some scraps for him at mealtimes.

She stood on the threshold and looked in. The candles weren't lit, of course, but a faint light came in through the open window as the moon peeped over the sill. It was a room Cristin knew well, since she'd shared it with her former mistress, Rhianon, before her marriage. It had been rather less tidy then than it was now, more occupied somehow, even when no one was in it.

Now it was the room of a soldier, sparse and unadorned, a place to sleep and nothing else. The bed was neatly made but the pallet she'd spent her nights on then, as befitted a servant, was no longer there, so it seemed no minion kept guard at Llywelyn's feet of a night.

Leaving the door ajar, so that the torchlight from the corridor aided her way, Cristin went in. Sitting down upon the bed, she smoothed her hand over the woollen coverlet, imagined his form beneath it. Did he lie awake during the long dark hours, as she did, his black hair tousled on the pillow, his thoughts tousled, too, as they strayed beyond the wall to where she lay? Or did he fall asleep the moment his body touched the mattress, with no thoughts in his head at all?

Cristin shivered and clutched the coverlet tightly in her hand. She'd dismissed that idle speculation earlier as nonsense…yet, if it wasn't true, if nothing had happened to Llywelyn, then why was he not *here*, in this room, in this bed, either asleep *or* awake?

Llywelyn sprang to one side as the sword arced above his head, a bright flash through the gloom. The stroke hissed past his shoulder, so close that he felt the rush of wind. He drew his own weapon just in time to meet the second arc, the ring of metal loud in the silent church. And, as the echo faded, a voice came, low and menacing out of the shadows.

'So the monk *can* fight, after all!'

Maelgwn ab Eilyr! A cold sweat breaking out on his skin, Llywelyn backed carefully up the aisle, into the moonlight that slanted in through the window behind the altar. A strange laugh came, hollow and eerie, as his assailant followed, hunched low on soundless feet, like a wolf. The sword arced again and he parried a third time, the impact shuddering along his arm, making him gasp with the shock of it.

'Where have you been all this time, Maelgwn?' Llywelyn's mind raced after options and his nerves turned to steel, as a warrior's always did at the moment of battle. 'We searched high and low.'

Killing was the last option, but even in the moonlight, the glint in the other man's eye, the mask of evil on his face, didn't bode well for a peaceful solution. And he was right.

'I know, I watched you. I've been hiding…waiting… and now I have come for what is mine. This castle, these lands and your life!'

With that, Maelgwn lunged and Llywelyn had no time to think, let alone attempt to reason, as their weapons clashed and locked, just inches from his throat. All the skill he possessed was no match for the demonic strength of the man who pressed him backwards, inch by inch, until he was almost lying on the altar.

For an endless moment, they struggled, clasped together as if in an embrace not a contest of arms, the rasping of steel, of ragged breaths and grunts, echoing up to the domed roof. The candlesticks and silver cross on the altar clattered to the floor and Llywelyn knew that he was staring death right in the eye.

He heaved with all his might and pushed Maelgwn off him. There was a beat of silence, filled with the sound of his own heart as it thundered in his ears. Then a scream rent the air as Maelgwn came at him again, leaping like a devil out of hell. Llywelyn, still off balance, levelled his sword and the scream ceased abruptly to be replaced by a soft gasp of incredulity.

Maelgwn staggered, dropped his sword and fell forward. It was so swift and so unexpected that, in the moment of stillness that followed, it was impossible to believe it was over. And then his weapon was dragged from his hand by the weight of the body as it slid slowly to its knees and crumpled at the foot of the altar.

Llywelyn slid to the floor, too, his limbs trembling now with the shock of reaction that always came at the end. With his back to the stone altar, he stared at the grotesque form on the floor while, nearby, the two swords lay one over the other. But only one of them stained with blood—*his* sword.

He sat, struggling for breath and rigid with horror, for God knew how long, as the moon rose higher, bathing the dead man in a silver shroud. Then the door opened and Iago ap Dafydd came hurrying up the aisle, holding a torch high, his shadow lagging behind him.

'My son…what has happened here?'

Llywelyn looked up at the priest and tried to swallow down his guilt. 'Isn't it clear enough, Father?' As he spoke, the horror rose into his mouth, too, in a bitter surge of bile. 'I have killed a man, here, at the sacred altar.'

Iago frowned, glanced again at the dead man and then, placing his torch in a bracket, crouched down at the body. Turning it onto its back, he felt over its chest, the side of its neck, and then looked up, his face grim. 'This man still lives.'

Llywelyn's heart jolted and he almost reached for his sword again, despite the disgust at what it—*he*—had done. But there was no need. Maelgwn's breathing was laboured, barely reaching his ears, even though he sat right next to him. And when the priest went to the niche behind the altar to take out a vial, he knew Maelgwn would not live for much longer.

Iago replaced the cross and candles on the altar, kindling them from the torch and bringing some light into the darkening church. Then the last rites were administered, in haste, to salvage the dying man's soul, if not his mortal body.

Llywelyn listened, head bent, eyes closed, knowing he'd dealt Maelgwn far more than a quick end. For the wretch couldn't speak, to confess and ask forgiveness for his sins, nor could he swear to do penance to avoid purgatory…or hell.

The whispered prayers hissed around the church like ghosts, writhing among the empty benches, slithering up the walls to stare down from the black beams. Llywelyn opened his eyes, expecting to see those ghosts were slithering, not up the walls, but along the floor towards him, to wrap a shroud around *him*.

The priest was anointing Maelgwn's forehead with holy oil just as the final breath came at last, rattling and terrible before fading to an awful nothingness. Llywelyn stared at the lifeless face a moment longer and then he pushed himself to his feet. His body felt as if it had passed into nothingness as well, his soul departed, too, into a pit of utter blackness.

He cleared his throat, found his voice and then met Iago's troubled gaze. 'It is *I* who need to confess my sins and ask for absolution and penance now, Father, if you will hear me?'

Cristin didn't know how long she'd been sitting on Llywelyn's bed, thinking, remembering, worrying, lost in her thoughts. But the moon was high now and spilling across the table that stood before the window like a silver lake. In its light, she saw that items sat upon its surface—a pot of ink and some quills and a small oaken chest, its lid open.

Curiosity drawing her, she rose and crossed over to see what it contained. They were parchments, unbound and with writing and drawings upon them, and, taking one up, she studied it. The writing made no sense, since she couldn't read, but the lettering was beautiful, the first letter at the top larger than the rest and decorated with swirls in rich colours of red, blue and verdigris.

At the left-hand side, running almost the whole length of the vellum, was a staff such as that used by a bishop, intricately designed and coloured with green and gold. At the bottom right corner was a drawing of a white dove with a yellow beak, its soft round eye seeming to look right back up at her with wisdom and reproach, as if it knew she shouldn't be in this room.

'What are you doing here, Cristin?'

But it wasn't the heavenly dove that spoke. The parchment almost dropped to the floor as, her heart leaping, Cristin spun around. In the open doorway, silhouetted by the torchlight behind him in the corridor, stood Llywelyn. She gulped, her mouth full of shame and her face flushing hot. It was bad enough being discovered in his chamber, but being caught looking at his things, prying where she had no right, was beyond damning.

'Wh—where have you been?' she stuttered, her embarrassment staining her voice as well as her skin. I was… everyone was worried when you didn't return with your men.'

He stepped into the room, leaving the door open behind him, like an invitation for her to leave. And he repeated the question that, in her shock, she'd omitted to answer. 'Why are you in my room?'

Cristin clutched the parchment tighter between her fingers. 'I came to let Mwg out. He must have got shut in when you left.'

She stood still, unable to move, let alone leave, as he took up a taper and went out into the corridor again, to light it from the torch on the wall. Closing the door behind him this time, he lit some of the rush lights in the chamber, glancing around the room.

'Yet Mwg has gone and you are still here.'

He came to stand beside her. His short riding tunic, belted at his hips, smelled of heather, and his hair gleamed blue-black as he lit the candle. In its glow, she saw things she hadn't seen before—the blood on his clothes, the anguish in his eyes, the pale and tired face.

'I was about to leave when I saw these...' Cristin said, dread filling her throat. Was that *his* blood? 'What...what has happened, Llywelyn?'

He leaned forward, his hands flat on the table, and looked down at the parchments, his jaw clenching. For an age, it seemed, he didn't answer and, panic rising, she was about to ask again, to demand even, if she had to, when his lips parted.

'I killed Maelgwn ab Eilyr tonight...in the church... where the old village stood.'

The words, uttered so quietly, filled the whole room. Cristin stared at his bent head, the hair falling over his brow, hiding the awful expression in his eyes. His limbs were trembling and, as the sense of horror that seemed to grip him gripped her, she began to tremble too.

'Tell me...' she urged, one thought foremost in her mind. That blood on his tunic wasn't his.

His shoulders heaved. 'We searched far and found nothing...but I *knew*... I felt the presence of danger yesterday when we were on the *crug*.'

'So you went back there, after you sent your men home?'

He nodded. 'And found nothing. It was when I was returning that I saw the church door open.'

'And Maelgwn was inside?'

'Waiting for me. It seems he'd been nearby all along, biding his time, waiting to strike.' His shoulders heaved again. 'It was so quick…so unexpected. It was dark…or nearly so. He came at me and I struck back…and then he was dead.'

Cristin closed her eyes, relief making her limbs go weak. When she opened them again, Llywelyn was staring fully at her. And the agony in his eyes, the remorse, was so terrible she could almost touch it.

'And you…are not hurt?'

He shook his head. 'No…but I *killed* him, Cristin…in a church! I pierced his heart at the sacred altar!'

'In defence of your own life,' she said quickly, as the guilt on his face thrust a sword through *her* heart too. 'He would surely have killed you had you not defended yourself.'

'Yes, I know.' His mouth twisted. 'But that makes little difference to the sacrilege of the act…the shedding of blood there…'

Cristin reached out, touched his arm, felt the flesh beneath the sleeve recoil. 'Where is he now?' She didn't really want to know but she had to turn him from looking inwards and finding guilt to outwards and finding practicality.

'Still in the church. The priest is with him, keeping vigil. Iago heard my confession…he even granted me absolution, but…'

'Llywelyn…' As his words faltered, she spoke different ones, and with care. 'Maelgwn lived by the sword and he has died by the sword. If you hadn't killed him, someone else would have, one day. It is the way—'

'The way of the warrior?'

The bitter words cut through her own as cleanly and as cruelly as any blade. 'Yes,' she said, nodding, unable to deny nor condone it.

'That doesn't excuse it, Cristin.' He ran his hand through his hair and she saw the shaking of his fingers, the stringing of nerves stretched too tightly. 'Iago gave me a penance to atone…but that won't excuse it either.'

Cristin had seen him thus many times in the past, after one of his father's beatings, when he'd come to her and she'd comforted him, with words, distractions, or just silence. But silence wouldn't do now. Something more potent, more imperative, was needed to bring him out of that dark church where, for him, evil had been done, and back into this room, into the light again.

The parchment she'd picked up earlier was still clutched between her fingers. Putting it down on the table, she smoothed out the creases she'd made, unknowingly, and touched a forefinger to the script.

'What do these words mean?'

He turned to look at her, his face confused, stricken, all angles and shadows in the moonbeams. There was a long pause and then his eyes dropped to the table. 'They are the legend of a saint,' he said, touching a hand to the parchment, too, next to hers, its slight quiver making a scratching sound upon the paper.

'Which saint?' she asked, willing that tremble to stop, the remorse to fade, searching desperately for a way to reach him. 'A Welsh saint?'

He nodded. 'This is the *Vita Sancti Paterni*—the life of Saint Padarn, written half a century ago by Ieuan ap Sulien, high priest of the church of Llanbadarn.'

'I cannot read.' Llywelyn knew that, of course, but her ignorance, something that had pained her so often in the past, didn't matter now. 'So, I was looking at the—' Cristin searched for the word '—the illustrations. They are beautiful.'

His hand moved to the image of the staff. 'This is Cirguen, Padarn's holy staff and the symbol of arbitration, and this…' His fingers moved again. 'This is the dove of peace…'

Cristin's fingers followed. 'Why?' she asked.

'Because he was a wise and just man and a peacemaker.'

She looked up at him, seeing that the darkness still lingered, despite the illumination of moon and candle. 'I meant…why is it here?'

He met her eyes, his own dark, feverish almost, against the paleness of his face. 'I am transcribing the Latin into Welsh so that, on Padarn's feast day, it can be read out in our churches and understood by our people.'

That he was learned she'd always known, but she'd assumed he'd left that learning behind when he'd taken up the sword instead. '*You* are doing this work?'

'At the request of the Lord Rhys. I brought the book back with me from Llanbadarn. The *Vita* will reside at the abbey of Ystrad Fflur where it will be safer from theft or destruction, should…when…the Normans return.'

Drawing the oaken chest closer, he took two leaves of parchment out and placed them carefully down on the table. Slowly, his expression changed, anguish becoming awe, his breathing sounding easier, the quivering limbs growing stiller, calmer.

'You see,' he said, indicating the writing on the first piece of vellum, his hand steady now. 'Here is the page in Latin—' his hand went to the other '—and here it is in the Welsh.'

Cristin leaned closer, peered down, enthralled and enchanted. 'There is no bishop's staff or dove on the first one,' she said, encouraging him to talk on. 'Only on the Welsh.'

'No, there are no illustrations at all in the Latin. The ones in Welsh are mine.'

Taking more leaves from the chest, he spread them out, pointing to a drawing of a large pot. 'Here is the cauldron of bronze that Padarn used to prove his innocence when wrongly accused of theft by a fierce king of the north.'

'Tell me the story,' Cristin breathed, feeling herself drawn into the world he was talking of, even though she didn't really understand it. But it was enough he was telling her of miracles now, not of killing. 'How could a holy bishop be accused of theft?'

'The King was a wicked and suspicious man, and he believed the false tales his magistrates told him about Padarn stealing treasure. Having decreed that boiling water would reveal a liar, he tried to test Padarn's integrity. The saint put his hand into the boiling water but when he withdrew it, it came out as white and as cold as snow.'

'And these?' Cristin touched her fingertips to another leaf, where two black crows in flight were painted, their beaks gaping wide, as if in fright or despair. 'What do these signify?'

Llywelyn's fingers came to rest next to hers and the nearness of him made her heart beat faster, not in fear for him now, but with something else.

'The magistrates were forced to put their hands in the water, too, whereupon their lies were revealed. Their bodies burned up and they died on the spot.'

'Then the two birds are the magistrates?'

He nodded. 'Their evil souls, symbolised by crows, flew to the Graban River where they were swallowed up in eternal damnation.'

Cristin turned her head to look at him just as he turned

to look at her. 'Do you think Maelgwn's soul will fly there also, since it, too, is evil?' she asked carefully.

His gaze flared and for a moment she thought she'd gone too far, pushed him beyond the brink and into his own form of hell. 'Perhaps…and mine, too, someday.'

She took hold of his sleeve. 'Llywelyn, listen to me. Maelgwn would have killed me, and your parents, too, had you not come back when you did. He had already caused so much suffering in the village, and he would have gone on to do more.'

'I know that.' But there was no conviction in his words. 'And I know his end would always been a violent one but… I wish it hadn't come in a holy place…and by my hand.'

Cristin moved closer, the chill of his body despite the warmth of the night making her shiver. 'Tell me the end of the story,' she said, as the darkness threatened to engulf him once more. 'Did the King make peace with the saint?'

'Yes.' His gaze bore down into hers, grave still, but some of the anguish receding again. 'He gave Padarn the land between the rivers Rheidol and Clarach, where he built the church of Llanbadarn.'

'And that's where Ieuan ap Sulien wrote down the history…the one you are translating into our tongue now?'

'Yes.'

They had moved closer still until their clothing touched, until Cristin felt his breath on her face. The scent of heather, stronger even than the stench of dried blood, drifted into her senses like sweet marsh mist.

'I think Saint Padarn would be pleased at that…don't you?'

The light of the moon enfolded them in its bright beam, locking them into some celestial realm, while the outside world retreated far away. His hand lifted and his fingers touched her face. 'I hope so.'

An age passed. His palm caressed her cheek, warm now and steady, instead of cold and tremulous. His eyes remained locked on hers, searching, delving, right down into the heart that beat in her breast.

'Thank you, Cristin.' He nodded, at last, not to her, but as if to himself. 'You always know how to give...how to help without my even needing to ask.'

'Anyone would have helped tonight, when you needed it.'

'No, not anyone...only you, always you...'

And then, so slowly, his head lowered, or hers lifted, and their mouths touched at last. Yet, when the kiss came, it was so soft she might have only dreamed it, imagination made reality by a Maytime moon.

But it wasn't a dream and nor was it imagination. Llywelyn's quickly drawn breath, his hands closing around her waist, his body hard against hers as he drew her closer, were real. His kiss that went from soft to hungry, his mouth devouring hers, the taste of him that lit her senses, was real too.

The table rocked behind her as he pressed her backwards, the candle flickering and spitting in its dish. Cristin forgot about the saint, his church, the pot and the crows, even about Maelgwn's death, as Llywelyn's hand cupped her breast, smoothed down her body, over her hip. Her skirt moved and she felt the touch of his palm on the bare skin of her thigh, the long fingers beginning to caress and seek.

The table rocked again as he moved between her legs, making her shiver with anticipation. Her gown had risen up, almost to her waist, and she felt the ardent need of him against her womanhood, her own need matching his, the ache low in her belly making her moan his name out loud.

'Llywelyn…yes…'

She sensed him fumble with his clothing, and then he lifted her so that she was sitting on the table. His hands cradled her face, his lips finding her throat, her jaw, her mouth, and she clutched him close, wrapping her arms and her legs tightly around him. The candle flickered and went out in its oil, and with it, the absence of seven years ceased to exist, as if it were no more than a moment in time…the beat of a heart…a breath coming in and going out…

'Cristin…*fy nghariad i*…'

The groan of her name, the ragged endearment, was followed by the sound of the parchments slipping from the surface of the table and floating to the floor. It was nothing more than a whisper, from somewhere far away, another place entirely. A whisper so soft it was barely heard…but it was loud enough to shake the world.

At once, Llywelyn went still, as if the sound had turned him to stone. His lips froze on hers and his arms slackened about her. And then he pushed himself upwards, out of her embrace, and stared down at her like a man breaking free of a trance cast by an evil spell or waking from a terrible nightmare.

'*Er mwyn Duw!* What in God's name am I doing!'

Even before the shocked words had faded to an echo, he spun away, rearranging his clothing and cursing under his breath. Smoothing down her gown, Cristin slipped off the table and watched him pick up the fallen parchments, his hands groping, as if he couldn't see them clearly.

She waited, her heart racing faster than ever, until he'd retrieved all the leaves of vellum, placed them carefully in the chest and closed the lid. And then she forced the question out past the lump in her throat.

'Why did you stop?'

Chapter Ten

Llywelyn stared at Cristin from the other side of the table. Her cheeks were flushed, and her lips were parted, full and plump where he'd kissed them. Her coif was awry, although only a single lock of her hair had escaped its confines. It curled like a flame, its colour vivid against the pale column of her neck.

'Why did I stop?' He clenched his hands into fists to prevent himself from reaching across, taking her in his arms and starting all over again. 'I stopped because if I hadn't…'

'What, Llywelyn?' Her gaze grew accusing. 'Because, if you hadn't, we might have done what we did at Llanbadarn?'

'Yes.' He groaned inwardly as the taste of her lingered on his tongue. 'For God's sake, I had no right to even *touch* you.'

Llywelyn spun away, crossed to the opposite window and stared out. His heart still thundered, his lungs burned and his legs trembled so much it was a wonder he still stood upright.

'Why not?'

Beyond the walls, the abbey lay not a league distant,

but too far to reach. Not even the bells were tolling to help him find the answer. He dragged in a deep breath, let it out slowly, then took another, deeper still.

'Tonight I killed a man. His blood is still on my clothes, on my hands, on my sword. His body lies in the church but his soul surely is in hell. And tomorrow, or the next day, or the day after that, I will have to tell his brother what I have done. And you ask me why not?'

There was a pause and then she came to stand behind him, out of sight, not touching him but so near he could feel her.

'I may not have your learning, Llywelyn. I don't know the things you do. I can't read or write or understand Latin or French, or even Welsh. So, I need you to speak clearly, like you did when you told me about the saint and the pot and the crows.'

'I thought I *had* spoken clearly.' He turned and fought against the need to take Cristin in his arms once more, let her fill his need, as she always did. But now he could never desecrate her—so pure, without a stain on her soul or her heart—with his bloody touch. 'And even if I hadn't, you saw clear enough, surely.'

'Saw what?'

'The reality of what a warrior is. A man who has to kill even when he hates doing so. A man driven by only two things—lust and death.'

'That's not true, not of you!'

Llywelyn sighed. She hadn't seen clearly at all. 'Isn't it?'

'No, it isn't. We love each other, Llywelyn!'

'That wasn't *love*! That was carnal need, mindless desire.' He pointed across the room, accusing the moonlight, the table, even the *Vita* for what had nearly happened. 'God,

Cristin, I needed you so much that I was ready to take you there, across the table…like…'

Her chin tilted up. 'Like a common harlot?'

'Yes!'

Hurt flickered in her eyes. 'And at Llanbadarn, when you were *not* a warrior, was that just carnal lust too?'

No, it wasn't,' he said, shaking his head, ashamed of the words he'd used. 'There is more between us than that, Cristin, much more. How can there *not* be when we have known each other all our lives.'

'Then what is the matter?'

Llywelyn stepped forward and took her face in his hands, blood and all, willing her to listen, to understand. 'I cannot be two men, Cristin. I cannot be a warrior, and so I must be a monk.'

'I don't understand…'

'Yet I have told you, even when we were children, that I will enter the monastery one day.'

'I thought that you would change your mind…one day.'

'My intent has not changed. And what I did *today* has only convinced me that my course is the right one. When this war is over, I mean to take my vows at Ystrad Fflur.'

'Still…? Her quiet gasp filled the room. 'But…why?'

'Because the world is abhorrent to me.' How simple it sounded. So simple and yet so momentous. 'I cannot bear the violence, the cruelty, the killing, and I want no part of it.'

'Those things are abhorrent to many others, too, but we *must* bear them, since there is no other way.'

'There *is* another way, Cristin. To turn your back on it all.' He dropped his hands to his sides. 'I am a vassal of the Prince, Cristin, bound to answer his call to arms, whenever it comes. In the monastery, there will *be* no call.'

'And so you will pretend the world doesn't exist? Run away from it, as a coward would do?'

Llywelyn shook his head. How could she not understand, she who understood everything else about him? 'No, it will always exist. But in the cloister, it can be avoided, and if that makes me a coward, so be it.'

She was silent for a moment and then her hand touched his sleeve. 'No, you are not a coward, and never could be. But the world isn't always like that, Llywelyn. And the men and women in it are not always cruel or violent either. There is compassion and kindness, love…'

She was looking at him as if he'd suddenly started speaking in the Latin of the *Vita*, without comprehension, even though the words were clear enough.

'My choice is made, Cristin. It was a long time ago,' he said, making them clearer still. 'And, before it is too late for me to be anything *but* a warrior, I will not undo that choice, not even for you.'

There was a little pause, her gaze raking his, and he saw that it was belief, not understanding that she lacked, as she placed her palm on his chest, over his heart.

'Does the heart of a monk beat as yours is beating now?'

Llywelyn saw, too, where she was leading him, felt himself unwilling to follow, yet followed anyway. 'I don't know.'

Her palm pressed firmer. 'Does a monk feel what you are feeling at this moment?'

He shook his head. 'Perhaps they do even in the cloister, in the *dortur* at night…but they must deny such feelings and master them, not be mastered by them.'

'As you are doing?'

'Yes.'

Her hand lingered, searing like fire through his clothes,

into his flesh, deeper still. 'And when you are a monk, will you think back to this moment and what you have denied yourself…and me too?'

'That will be my penance.'

'And everything that we have shared?'

'Will not be forgotten.'

Her eyes burned into his, seeing far more than he was willing to reveal, as they always had. 'Choices do not always have to be final, Llywelyn. They can be made and then unmade. Or if not unmade, postponed…'

Llywelyn stared down at her. 'For how long? A week, a month, a year?'

'Longer…or at least for as long as we have together.'

'Would you be content to share my bed, receive my love, give me yours, knowing that it couldn't last?'

She nodded but he saw the swallow of her throat, the way her tongue moistened her lips. 'If that was all there could be, yes, I would.'

'Even knowing that, one day, I would leave you as I did at Llanbadarn?'

The words were deliberately cruel but he had to say them. Had to make her realise what she would suffer, as he would suffer, when that day came.

'Yes.'

He shook his head, even though every part of him longed to accept what she was offering him, here in this room where no eyes could spy on them, illuminated by moonlight and candles. A love too bright and too strong to deny.

But he had to deny before that longing conquered him. 'If we were to lie together, it would be even harder to leave you a second time.' He paused, drew a deep breath. 'And I can never let myself hurt you as I did before.'

She stared up at him. 'You are hurting me *now*, Llywelyn. Your leaving will hurt me, whether we lie together or not!' Suddenly, her eyes flashed with anger, and behind the anger, tears. 'I love you!'

'I know.' Llywelyn touched her cheek. 'And I love you.'

But Cristin jerked away and stepped back, her hands clenched at her sides. She stared at him for a long moment, her shoulders dropping in an acceptance that made him clench his hands, too, lest he reach for her, let himself be conquered and *unmake* his choice before it was too late.

But it was already too late.

'Then, *because* I love you, I will make it easy for you. *I* will leave *you*, here with your chastity and your beads and your precious parchments. Good night, my lord monk!'

The door closed behind her with a bang and, in the distance, over the hills, the abbey bell began to toll, drumming the midnight vigil into his head like hammers upon nails. He closed his eyes and counted the tolling notes until they faded away on the night air.

When only an echo remained, Llywelyn crossed the room to the corner that contained the small wooden *prie-dieu* he'd carved with his own hands, years before. And dropping to his knees, he took up his beads and began to pray.

He prayed for the soul of Maelgwn ab Eilyr, that he'd surely condemned to hell that night. Next, he prayed for the strength to resist his earthly love for a woman that would never die, whether he remained in the world or entered the cloister.

And last, he prayed for his own soul. Because this night's work, of killing and of loving, had shown him something not even Cristin could see. For when he'd slain Maelgwn, he'd felt—not just shock, or guilt, or shame, but greater than all that—a terrifying sense of relief.

Relief, and even gladness, that Maelgwn was dead and could do no more harm to Cristin, his parents, or anyone else. Even the desecration of a church, the spilling of blood upon sacred ground, had seemed irrelevant, an excusable deed, because it rid the world of a little bit of evil. Or so he'd told himself, and had believed it—for a moment, at least. Now alone, on his knees, he wondered... What did that say about his soul, his faith, his whole vocation?

Would a man who had dedicated his life to God really feel that relief? Would a man who abhorred killing in all its forms excuse it as a necessary and just act? Had he become more warrior than monk these past years without even knowing it? And if so, where did he go from here?

Stay on his path towards the cloister regardless...or turn aside and take another road? One that would mean more battles, more killing, more guilt. One that would make him loathe himself until he lost his soul completely.

And then...what of Cristin? How could he become that man and still deserve her love? A love that would surely die in disgust, just as any love his mother had ever felt for his father must have died. Llywelyn closed his eyes and prayed harder, but none of those questions were answered. Perhaps there *were* no answers, not even from heaven.

When day had broken, Llywelyn rose from his knees and went to do the penance Iago ap Dafydd had imposed on him. Dragging in a deep breath, he knocked on the door of his parents' room. There was no sound within and, as if a reprieve had unexpectedly been granted him, he turned to go. But Tangwystl's voice halted him in his tracks.

'Enter.'

Softly, he cursed and steeled himself to do what he'd sworn never to do again. To look upon his father's face. It was an ironic yet apt penance Iago had chosen to answer for the sin that he'd committed in the church the night before. For Cadwgan himself would never have shirked from such an abominable act.

His mother had urged him, Cristin had urged him, but it had taken the words of a priest, the atonement for an unspeakable act *he* himself had committed, to force his feet to the threshold.

Llywelyn pushed the door open. Inside, Tangwystl sat on a stool by the window. Cristin sat opposite her, head bent over some needlework, a coif as always covering her hair. Her eyes lifted, met his and then dropped away, a flush mounting her cheeks.

His cheeks burned, too, quick and hot, as the previous night's encounter brought all sorts of repercussions in its wake—the pull of desire, the struggle of the long sleepless hours afterwards on his knees before the *prie-dieu*, the prayers that had not been answered, no matter how fervently he'd uttered them.

At the other side of the room was the bed, the curtains still closed around it, but Llywelyn didn't look there. Not yet. Instead, he crossed over to the window and, not looking at Cristin either, bowed to his mother.

'I have come to see my father.'

Tangwystl's face lit up. 'Thanks be to God.'

Cristin put down her sewing, her face lighting up, too, drawing his gaze. She wore her old green kirtle, as she had last night, not the blue gown he'd given her. Why? Had she rejected it as he'd rejected her? He wouldn't blame her if she had.

'No,' he said, looking back at his mother. 'Thanks to Dafydd ap Iago, who persuaded me to change my mind, as doubtless was your intention.'

During his confession last night, he'd admitted not just to killing, but also to loving, and the guilt he felt because of the carnal desire that was part of that love. The priest had advised him to send Cristin back to the village, and Llywelyn suspected his mother was behind *that*, too. But that was a penance he wasn't ready to pay, not just yet.

And neither had it helped to speak to Iago about his weakening vocation that had once seemed so clear and so strong. Now it appeared not just to be weakening, but in danger of crumbling to dust altogether. The priest had had little counsel to offer him, practical or spiritual, except to pray harder still!

Behind him, he heard the creaking of the bed and Llywelyn's flesh recoiled, as if the talons of a hawk had reached out and gripped him. A wounded hawk now, one that no longer had the power of flight or the ability to prey on those weaker than itself.

'So, here I am,' he said through gritted teeth. 'My ears tell me the tyrant has awoken?'

'Llywelyn!' Tangwystl rose from her stool, her eyes flashing, as if she was addressing the child he'd once been, not the man he was now. 'If you cannot see him civilly then do not see him at all.'

Her fingers curled around his arm. 'But the priest says your father is dying, and if you do *not* see him, it is *your* soul that will be imperilled not his, for Cadwgan has made his peace with God now.'

Cristin had risen, too, her eyes earnestly willing him to do as his mother commanded. Shaking Tangwystl's hand away Llywelyn turned towards the bed. He was here so he might as well get it over and done with. As for his father's soul, that was nothing to do with him. Cadwgan was beyond even prayer. On the day of his judgement, he alone would have to seek atonement for his sins.

'The priest may have absolved him here on earth,' he threw the words over his shoulder, 'but I do not, and if that means peril for my soul, so be it. It is enough that I am here.'

The curtain that enclosed the bed was moving now, the creature behind it stirring, like a monstrous beast awaking in its cave. And then it spoke. 'Llywelyn…is that you… my son?'

Llywelyn's feet froze on the spot and it was left to his mother to draw the curtain aside. And there, in front of him, was Cadwgan, leaning up on one elbow, his eyes blinking in the sudden light.

His face was criss-crossed with scars, the cheeks sunken, the mouth drooping. But the thick hair was as black as ever, even if his beard was grey, and the dark eyes, though dimmed, were still forbidding beneath the bushy brows.

Llywelyn's gaze shifted, looked past the bed, as all the years of fear and hate and recrimination closed like a fist around his throat. 'What do you want?' he said to the wall. 'If I can grant it I will.'

A forefinger lifted and beckoned. 'Come…closer. I cannot…hear you.'

Sweat beading his brow, Llywelyn walked forward until he stood a pace away from the bed, near enough to sense that, despite the weak and broken body, Cadwgan still had the power to compel.

'What do you want?' he asked again, curtly, his mouth filled with loathing. 'What comforts do you lack?'

'I wanted to see…my son.' His father slumped back on the bed, his chest heaving. Once it had been as hard as an oaken barrel but now it was little more than a concave shell. 'And I lack for nothing…except…'

Llywelyn forced himself to look at the ruined man before him. It seemed every bone in Cadwgan's once strong body had been destroyed. The big hands were gnarled where they'd been broken and, beneath the coverlet, it was evident his legs and feet had suffered the same treatment.

'Except what?'

His father stared up at him and, as their eyes held, bitter memories flowed between them. 'So…you hate me as much as you ever did!' He gave a thin chuckle. 'I expected nothing less.'

'What do you want of me?' Llywelyn asked a third time, his voice quivering with that hate. 'Speak!'

'Simply your forgiveness…but I know you will not give it. And I know, too, that you will not believe me when I say I regret…so much.'

'It is too late for regret.'

'Then I will beg instead a promise, and hope that you will find it in your heart to grant it.'

'A promise?'

The head on the pillow nodded feebly, as if every effort to move or speak weakened him. 'Before I die, I wish…'

But, even as Llywelyn's ears strained to hear the dimming voice, it faded away. His father's eyes rolled in their sockets, and spittle began to form at the corner of his mouth.

'Tangwystl! Wife!'

Cadwgan's call brought Tangwystl to the bedside at once. Dropping to her knees, she placed her hand on his forehead and began to murmur soothingly, as if to a child. Cristin came forward, too, with a cup of ale, holding it to Cadwgan's lips.

His presence forgotten, Llywelyn stepped backwards,

out of the way. He watched, his face impassive, as Cadwgan moaned, his hand gripping that of his wife. A hand that had so often struck her in violence. Tangwystl's face was impassive, too, and he saw, as if a sheet of lightning had lit the room, that she'd not forgotten nor forgiven any of it. Yet, she refused to turn her back on him now that he needed her.

'Why, for God's sake!' he asked, suddenly needing to understand the incomprehensible. 'Why are you doing all this for him?'

His mother turned and glared at him. 'Why? Because if I did not, who would? You? Rhianon?'

'No.'

'Well then, since no one else will, I must.'

Cadwgan was crying now, tears oozing out between his eyelids and running in little rivulets into his sunken cheeks.

'Has he lost his wits as well as his strength?' Llywelyn asked, in contempt to hide the pity that, despite his will, rose up to choke him.

'At times he is himself, but those times are becoming less and less. He has lost *everything*, Llywelyn, his name, his valour, his strength, his pride. All he has is me, his wife—and *that* is why I do this.'

Tangwystl turned her head away again. 'The past is the past and, for him, there is little future left. Every dying soul deserves care and compassion, and the shame is on *you*, not him, if you cannot give either.'

Llywelyn could bear it no longer. Spinning on his heel, he lurched through the door and out into the passageway, pulling it shut behind him. He leaned back against the wall, a roaring in his ears, and a rumbling like thunder filling his head.

The door opened again at once. He didn't need to look to see who stepped through it, for he knew that it was Cristin.

'I thought you wouldn't have gone away,' she said, closing the door softly again. 'You couldn't, not now you have seen him.'

Llywelyn didn't even question why she'd followed him, why she was always there, seen or unseen, bidden or not. He never had to call to her, as Cadwgan had called to Tangwystl, because she came anyway, as she'd come last night, as she did now. Soundlessly and surely, whenever he needed her, even when he didn't *want* to need her.

'I hadn't expected to see him like that,' he said, the sight of it still vivid behind his eyes. 'Not so utterly helpless! How it must gall him!'

'But you saw him that first day, in the strong room? Surely you realised the extent of the injuries?'

'Yes, I did. But… I'd fought a battle, seen men die and didn't see anything clearly at all.'

Except her. He'd seen *her* with vivid clarity when he'd opened that door, when it was all over. The tattered gown, the white face, the blood in her hair, the half-starved body… the beauty that shone through it all, nevertheless.

'And now that you have seen him clearly?'

'I can't help but pity him!' Llywelyn spat the word out like a foul taste on his tongue. '*Him* of all men!'

She moved a step closer, her face filling his vision like the sun on a grey day. 'But how could you *not* pity him?'

'Because he doesn't *deserve* it, despite what my mother thinks!' He shook his head. '*Myn diawl*, Cristin, have you forgotten how he is, *what* he is?'

'What he *was*. He is no longer that man, Llywelyn, can't you see that?'

Llywelyn gave a bitter laugh. 'No, but I can see that he has fooled not only my mother, but you too.'

'Whatever he has done, he is still your father.'

'He was *never* that, Cristin. Not to me, nor my sister Rhianon, nor to Rhodri. Just as he was never a husband to his wife.'

'Yet now he *is* a husband, reconciled with his wife at last, and it doesn't matter how that has come about.' Cristin's argument came softly, persuasively. 'She says she does it because she must, that it is her marital duty, but it brings her a sort of comfort, too, to do it.'

Llywelyn turned his head away. 'It would have been more merciful for those men who attacked him to have spared her the task, rather than leave him like that, to die slowly, and in humiliation.'

'Most of the time, he is not lucid and does not realise. Or is asleep and forgets.'

'But what of his dreams, Cristin?' Through the door, reeking death oozed so thickly he could almost taste it. 'Cadwgan was a warrior. He would have chosen a quick and glorious end in battle rather than...*that* in there. Even I, who hate him, would have granted him that mercy, at least.'

There was a pause before she spoke again. 'Then...while he suffers so, while he lives, can you not show the same mercy and put your hate aside?'

'No, I cannot.' Llywelyn met her eyes. But *why* couldn't he find mercy, stop hating, even now, when Cadwgan lay on his deathbed? What sort of a man did that make him? Callous, unfeeling, worse even than his father? As she did, always, Cristin heard his thoughts as loudly as if he'd spoken them.

'But you haven't even tried to stop hating him, have you? Not once, through all these years?'

'How is it you can see so clearly into my soul, Cristin, when I cannot? How can you know my heart when it is hidden so deeply that even I can't find it?' He stared down at her, the torchlight flickering above their heads, licking like the flames of hell. '*Er mwyn Duw!* Why, after all the hurt I've caused you, do you not hate me, as I hate him in there?'

Cristin flinched at the bitter words, but the torment in his eyes was worse. He looked like a man stricken to the very depth of his soul. 'I could never hate you.'

His mouth curled. 'Then mayhap you should *learn*.'

'Why? Do you think that might stop me loving you?'

'Perhaps your love is misplaced.'

'No, it isn't.' Cristin moved a step closer. 'If so, it wouldn't have survived all these years.' She touched his arm, feeling the tension like iron beneath his sleeve. 'And, because I love you, I understand why you find it so hard to stop hating.'

'Do you? Enlighten me!'

The bitterness was cutting but she didn't let it disarm her. 'Those wounds Cadwgan inflicted on you haven't healed with the passing of time, have they? Not the inner ones. The ones that go deeper than the skin that cannot be healed until they are seen.'

He gave a bitter laugh. 'If you think *I* need your compassion now, or your healing, like Cadwgan needs my mother, you are mistaken.'

'Am I?' Cristin shook her head. 'I know you too well to believe that.'

He gave a grim smile. 'Yet only a week ago, you claimed to hardly know me at all.'

'I was wrong. I see now that you are not so very different from the boy who came to me for comfort when your father punished you, even though you'd done nothing to warrant it. The boy who showed his pain to no one but me, who suffered to save others and yet didn't speak of it.'

His gaze sharpened. 'What do you mean?'

She longed to take him in her arms, just as she'd done with that hurting, weeping boy all those years ago. 'Do you think I have forgotten how you tried to protect your mother and your sister, even the servants of your house, from your father's wrath?'

'For all the good it did!'

'Perhaps you couldn't always prevent him hurting others but at least you *tried*, Llywelyn!' Cristin closed her fingers tighter on his sleeve. 'I was your sister's maid. I knew each and every time you stood between her and your father's fist.'

'And still failed to stop him!' His head turned towards the door. 'I should have killed him, years ago.'

'That would have made you as bad as he was.'

'It might have been a small price to pay. One I almost *did* pay, once.' His eyes came back to hers, their brilliant blue dimmed and bleak. 'As soon as I reached manhood, when I *was* old enough and I *was* strong enough…then, I *did* go to kill him, Cristin.'

Cristin gasped, the sound loud in the quiet corridor but he didn't seem to hear it, as he went on, his eyes bleaker still.

'I could have challenged him, in the hall, in front of the whole household, but I didn't. I waited until he was alone, in his chamber, just the two of us. No witnesses, no intervention, because I meant it to be a fight to the death… either him or me…and it almost *was* to the death.'

He stopped and his chest heaved as he drew a breath. 'I'd taken my knife, and I would have used it, too, had he not fallen on his knees—not in supplication, but laughing, mocking me, *daring* me to do it! And the worst of it was…'

'What?'

'I couldn't do it.' The shake of his head was savage. 'Not even while he was there, helpless before me, taunting me. He knew I was too much of a coward to use that knife.'

'It wasn't *cowardly* to stay your hand.' Cristin touched her palm to his cheek, found it cold, taut, a muscle below the skin jumping erratically. 'It was *noble*.'

'Noble?' He jerked away from her touch. 'You don't understand! There I was, with my knife poised, ready, eager even, to kill my kin, as *he'd* killed *his* kin. At that moment I was exactly like *him*...just as he'd always *wanted* me to be!'

'But you didn't use it! You didn't kill him!'

'For God's sake, Cristin!' He swore, loud and harsh. 'Even if I *failed* to kill him, I *wanted* to! The *thought* was there, and evil thoughts are judged alongside evil deeds on the day of reckoning.'

Llywelyn fell silent, his limbs shaking, his breath rasping, as if he'd actually just relived that terrible fight with his father, not in only memory, but in action. And as the quiet stretched out and the torches sputtered, Cristin saw a way by which she might reach him.

'Then why don't you do it now?'

His eyes narrowed. 'What?'

She took a deep breath and prayed that the risk she was taking was the right one. 'Why don't you kill him now, like you did Maelgwn yesterday? If you hate your father so much, why don't you take out your knife now, go back into that room and rid the world of him, make it less cruel by his absence from it?'

He shook his head, not savagely now, but as if dazed. 'Kill him now?'

Cristin nodded, her heart in her throat, not knowing if her words were wise or fatally foolish. All she had was trust and her deep-rooted belief that, whatever he'd thought he'd become, had been *forced* to become, he was wrong.

'He cannot defend himself, after all,' she went on. 'And, although your mother would protect him tooth and nail, you would be easing her burden. The Cwn Annwn will justify it as apt punishment and, in the monastery, you can pray for absolution and will surely be granted it for so righteous a vengeance.'

His eyes left hers and went to the door again. She saw him swallow but he didn't move. His hand didn't even lift to the knife at his belt. Just as she knew it wouldn't.

'But you *can't*, can you, Llywelyn, any more than you could before?' Cristin released a silent sigh of relief. 'You won't, nor ever could, no matter what he's done. You are not like him.'

'No... No, I'm not like him.' He turned his gaze back to her and it was bleaker than ever. 'But even if I *can* feel pity for him, don't ask me to forgive him, Cristin. For I can't, any more than I can forgive myself.'

'What is it you need forgiveness for? For hating him? For *wanting* to kill him, even though you can't bring yourself to actually do the deed?'

'For even worse. Cadwgan might have put the sword in my hand, but it is I myself that took the weapon up and wielded it.'

'But you cannot condemn yourself for that! You had no choice but to take up the sword.'

Above their heads, the torchlight flickered as a draught blew down the corridor, casting his features into shadows. 'That doesn't make the weight of it any lighter.'

'Perhaps that is because you have carried it alone, held it aloft with *your* hands only, not letting anyone else share the load.'

'Would *you* share it, then, Cristin?'

'You know I would…if you would let me.'

His eyes gleamed darker, burning intensely into hers. 'If you only knew how tempting that offer is, you might regret asking it.'

Cristin leaned closer, until their bodies almost touched. 'Never…'

He reached out, his fingertips brushing her jaw. The draught in the corridor blew stronger. Vaguely, it came to her that someone must have opened the door of the keep below. Sounds drifted upwards, the clash of pots from the kitchen as the midday meal was prepared. A curse as someone dropped something, the sound of the water bucket splashing into the well.

Cristin heard it all with a keenness of hearing and yet the sounds signified nothing. Her heart began to thud as she waited for his response to an invitation that didn't need clarification. They both knew what she was offering to give him.

'You said yesterday, on the *crug*, that war might well come soon…' When he still didn't respond, she offered again. 'Is that not reason for us to grasp every moment while we still can? Make them last forever, even when they are gone.'

His forehead lowered to rest upon hers, his breath soft on her face. 'Oh, Cristin…if only it were so simple.'

'It *is* simple, Llywelyn. I love you. You love me. And now is all the time we might have together.'

His brow touched hers. 'There is already talk about us…'

'I don't care about talk.'

His head moved lower and his mouth feathered over hers in a light kiss, his palm cupping her cheek. 'And your reputation…your good name?'

'Matters little.' Cristin pressed her lips to his. 'All that matters is we will be together.'

But the kiss went no further. Footsteps sounded and the large figure of Gwion ab Adda appeared at the top of the stairs.

'My lord...' The man coughed and, halting, waved a rolled-up parchment in the air. 'A message from Castell Abereinion.'

With a curse under his breath, Llywelyn nodded and bade the man wait. 'I must go, Cristin.' His hand dropped away from her face, his fingers leaving a trailing caress behind. 'Perhaps it is just as well...'

After a long and searing look into her eyes, he turned and strode away along the corridor. The two men descended the stairs and Cristin leaned back against the wall, where he had leaned, the touch of his mouth, for all its lightness, lingering on hers. Like her invitation lingered, not quite answered, neither rejected nor accepted.

She fisted her hands tightly in her midriff, trying to stem her trembling limbs, calm her rapid breaths. For she had done nothing less than offer herself up as his leman, his *gordderch*!

But it wasn't like that, was it? Not so cheap, not so shameful, not so damning. What they had went far beyond bed sport, far beyond lust and carnal desire, as he'd tried to convince her last night. She saw through that as clearly now as she saw into him.

Llywelyn's heart wasn't the cold and empty heart of the warrior, and never could be, no matter what he had to do in the name of war. And, if love lived, then surely there was room for peace, too, inwardly if not outwardly, for forgiveness, and compassion and joy. Could she help him find those things again, as she'd once helped to heal the hurt inflicted on his body and his mind by his sire?

And could she pretend to herself, as well as to Llywelyn, that she would survive that second parting when it came, as she had the first? Go on with her life afterwards alone, knowing that he would be just there, in that monastery over the hills? Fulfilling his vow behind those forbidding white walls, where the love of a woman could not reach, not even *her* love?

Chapter Eleven

Llywelyn put down his quill and, gathering the parchments together, placed them back in their box. His fingers were stained with ink and his eyes ached after working at the manuscript until it became blurred and distorted, and he began to make errors. Rolling his shoulders, feeling the creak of bone and sinew, he sat back in his chair and looked around the chamber.

And, in the hiss of rush lights and candle, loneliness descended like a heavy mantle. This had been his sister Rhianon's room and, later, Rhodri's. Now there was nothing of either of them to be sensed here, only empty memories, and he missed them, especially Rhianon, but also Rhodri, in a way. His brother hadn't always been brutal, and they'd been close as very young boys, yet when Rhodri was killed in battle, he hadn't even mourned him.

He missed his mother, even though she was here, living in his household. They had always been distant, and had grown even further apart over the years so that now it seemed that gulf would never heal, not while his father stood between them.

But most of all he missed Cristin, she who was the closest of all, just beyond that wall, in his old chamber. Yet, she might just as well have been a thousand leagues away. Was it only that morning that he'd gone to see his father? Mere hours since he'd stood with her in the passageway and kissed her? It seemed much longer...too long.

Llywelyn pushed himself out of his chair and paced over to the window. Outside, the night was calm, the castle's chapel, where Maelgwn's body had been laid, was shrouded in darkness, the abbey bell beyond the hills announcing Matins. The sound grated on his nerves now, when it never had before. From Compline to Prime, from eve to morn. Day and night, it rang and reminded him of what he'd vowed to be, and what he increasingly doubted he could *ever* be.

And now with Peredur's message, in a day or two he would have to put down his quill, take up the sword and kill once more, this time in battle.

Turning from the window, Llywelyn flung himself down on the bed, one arm over his eyes. The tolling stopped and silence weighed heavy as the minutes passed. And then a scratching came at the door, interspersed with pitiful miaowing.

Mwg! It seemed the cat had yet again escaped Cristin's chamber, the third or fourth time at least that it had disturbed him, though why it had to settle itself outside *his* chamber of a night was a mystery. Leaping off the bed, he flung open the door but wasn't quick enough to prevent Mwg darting between his legs into the room, where he disappeared under the bed.

'Drapia di, gath!' Going down on his hands and knees, Llywelyn reached in and, taking the cat by the scruff of its neck, hauled it out. 'I should have insisted you go to live in the stables after all!'

Chewing his lip, he wavered. He *could* let the cat remain tonight and take it back in the morning. The solution was as simple as that. But even so, he pushed it out of sight as surely as he'd sealed that oaken chest on the table and locked away the precious *Vita*.

Unlike Saint Padarn, *he* wasn't a saint and, while Cristin was under his roof, he never would be.

Tucking Mwg securely under one arm lest he wriggle free, Llywelyn went out into the passageway. He paused a moment to listen before knocking softly at Cristin's door. There was no answer and no sound from within. Doubtless, she was either asleep or, despite the lateness of the hour, waiting upon his mother, Cadwgan passing a bad night, perhaps, as he often did.

Quietly he lifted the latch, intending to drop Mwg inside and retreat. But as the door opened just a crack, he saw a candle shining within. And there was Cristin, standing next to the table at the far wall, dressed only in a shift, washing her hair in a basin.

She wasn't aware of his presence as she reached for a cloth, her hand groping the chair next to her until she found it. And she began to dry the damp locks, leaning forward so that they cascaded to below her knees like a tumbling red sunset.

Llywelyn held his breath, knowing he should go away, silently, so that she should never guess he'd been there. But he couldn't move and, worse, he didn't want to. And then, as if she sensed his presence, she straightened up and turned around.

In the soft light her countenance was not one of surprise but of expectation. Beneath the pale shift she wore, he could see the swell of her small breasts, the shape of her body, slender rather than thin now, as she'd been when he'd first seen her the night of his return.

She looked like an angel that had stepped out of an alcove to welcome him—or chastise him for his lust! Clean. Good. Pure. A soul without stain that called to him even though she'd yet not uttered a word.

A call he couldn't resist. Stepping over the threshold, Llywelyn let the cat out of his arms. It slunk into a corner and began to wash itself with relish, like a man dusting his palms after a task done well!

'I brought Mwg back. He was scratching at my door.'

Cristin's eyes slid from him to the cat and back to him. 'He escaped. I looked earlier but couldn't find him.' Beneath her shift, her breasts rose and fell a little quicker. 'Thank you for returning him.'

There was a moment of silence while he waited for her to tell him to leave. But she didn't say anything. Instead, she turned her back, the glorious cascade of her hair seeming not a sign of rejection at all, but of invitation.

An invitation Llywelyn couldn't resist either. So he closed the door and crossed the room to stand behind her. Burying his hands in the heavy tumbling locks, he lifted them to his face and breathed in rosewater and juniper and her own essence.

'That wasn't the only reason I came, Cristin.'

Her head tilted backwards a little, spilling yet more of that tantalising red mane into his hands. 'I know.'

'But I should not be here. It is late…and you are doubtless preparing for sleep.'

'I am not asleep yet.'

'No, you have been washing your hair.' Llywelyn breathed deeper, knew he should leave, stayed where he was. 'Tell me why it is this colour.'

'You have heard that story many times.'

'Tell me again.'

'My mother's mother was an Irish peasant girl called Maeve, with hair the colour of wildfire, given to her by the faery folk.' Cristin's head tilted back farther, its clean scent drifting into his nose. 'She was captured by a Viking chief who, bewitched by her, took her onto his ship bound for his kingdom far across the northern sea.'

Llywelyn let her hair play through his fingers as the story ensnared him like a spell. Yes, he had heard it many times, but not like this. Not murmured on a soft breath that held so much more beneath the words.

'But the ship never got there.' He took up the telling, his voice a murmur too. 'It went aground on the rocks at Llanrhystud.'

'All on board were drowned but Maeve fetched up safely on the shore, where my grandfather found her.'

'He fell in love with her at first sight.' Llywelyn lifted a lock of hair to his lips, kissed it. It was wet, too, like that other woman's hair had been, though tasting not of sea water but of sweet and heady herbs. 'And he married her.'

'Yes.'

But that was where the tale turned to fantasy. He could never marry Cristin as her grandfather had married Maeve. Peasants married where and as they liked, and, even if the permission of their lord was needed, their union was too unimportant to think about, let alone deny.

Those men born noble had no such freedom. Even if *he* were to remain a lord and not enter the cloister, his prince would choose for him a bride of his own station, one who would bring alliance, wealth, heirs…but not love. How could he love any other bride when he loved this one woman who could *never* be his bride?

'If I were a poet—' he pushed the unfairness of that reality far away and let himself live the fantasy, at least for a little while '—I would compose a song about the way your grandmother, and your mother in turn, ensnared countless men with their beauty.'

'No, not countless men. Only *one* man…for my mother, for her mother…and for me.'

'And for me, too, only one woman.' Relinquishing her hair, Llywelyn wound his arms around her waist and, gathering her close, placed his lips to her temple. 'Tell me to leave, Cristin…' he urged, yet softly, half hoping the answer was *stay*, half praying it would be go.

'No, I won't… I don't want you to leave.'

Dipping his head, he kissed her neck at the spot where her pulse beat. 'If I stay, I will want to lie with you.'

She turned in his arms, still clutching the cloth she'd been drying her hair with. 'Then lie with me, Llywelyn!'

Llywelyn cupped her face in his hands. 'Tell me to leave!' he urged again, resenting the words, even though he had to say them. '*Tell me*, Cristin!'

'No.' Her eyes were bright, her lips already waiting. 'If you leave, it will be by *your* will, not mine.'

He stared down at her, her hair a blaze of colour before his eyes. Beyond the window, the stars shone, blinding him as surely as quicklime. And as the moon slipped out from behind a stray cloud and the summer breeze drifted in and wrapped around them, he knew his bewitchment was complete.

'I have no will left to me,' he said, lowering his head until their mouths all but touched. 'Not tonight.'

Cristin dropped the drying cloth and curled her hands into Llywelyn's tunic. Arching her body into his, she lifted her face, ready for his kiss. When it came, it wasn't gentle but passionate, desperate, a kiss that stopped her breath and stole her heart from her breast.

Beneath his tunic, she could feel *his* heart thundering, its beating so loud that she could almost hear it. On her face, his hands were warm, the ink that had dried on his fingers pungent, heady. Against her belly, his body was hard, his manhood urgent, even though she sensed restraint in him still.

'Lie with me tonight, Llywelyn,' she whispered through their kiss. 'Like we did before...'

He lifted his head and his gaze was stormy, at odds with the calmness of the night without. She tightened her fingers in the folds of his tunic, pulling him closer still. For it *was* like the last time, almost exactly. He was here now but tomorrow he might be gone, never to come back. 'The morrow will come all too soon.'

Llywelyn laid his forehead upon hers, his breath quick and shallow, his body quivering. And finally he said the words she longed to hear. 'Then we must make the night last as long as we can.'

A pause, as if they stood suddenly on the edge of a precipice, and then Cristin felt herself swept up into his arms. He carried her over to the bed and laid her down, damp hair and all, upon the coverlet. Dropping down beside her, he leaned on his elbow, his gaze still stormy but with a different sort of tempest now.

'But *this* night will not be like that one in the stable at Llanbadarn, Cristin. Tonight I want to *look* at you.'

His hand went to the neckline of her shift, his fingers softly tracing along it, beneath the linen. He slipped it off one shoulder and then the other, baring her throat, her breasts.

'I want to see your skin, so soft, so pale...like cream...'

The skin Llywelyn was praising began to shiver as he pushed the shift lower, down over her belly to her hips. She raised herself up a little to help him, her limbs weak, her mouth dry, her face aflame.

'I want to see your body, its perfection…though it is slender still.'

He paused, his jaw clenching, and Cristin heard his thoughts as surely as if he'd spoken them out loud. How the villagers had starved under the Normans, and worse.

'Would you have me round and rosy, then, like Dyddgu the laundress?' she teased, making the moment light again.

He smiled, shook his head, his hand stroking over her flesh, her ribs, the swell of her abdomen, his touch and his gaze exploring her in a way he had never done before.

'I would have you in *any* shape or form.' Llywelyn's eyes lifted to hers, dark and serious. 'For you are beautiful, Cristin.'

He was beautiful, too, and Cristin wanted to look at him as he was looking at her. As if he knew her wants, he went up onto his knees and peeled her shift down over her hips and legs and away. Taking her hands, he drew her up to kneel, too, the nakedness of her body thus exposed feeling strange, a little daunting…and yet so wonderful.

'I want you to see me, too, Cristin, all of me, as I am.'

'As do I…'

She undid the belt at his hips and, as his clothing fell loose, ran her hands up beneath, discovering the smooth expanse of his chest, finding his heartbeat strong and fast below. He gave a sharp intake of breath as she trailed her fingers downward, over the hard rib cage, the taut muscles of his abdomen, to where his hose was fastened at his waist.

Reaching for the hem of his tunic, Cristin pulled it upwards. He lifted his arms to allow the garment to come off over his head, leaving his upper body bare. They looked at each other for a long moment without speaking, the candle-light flickering over their flesh. Before, in that dark stable, they'd loved each other fully clothed, hands fumbling in the dark, eyes seeing nothing, only the sense of touch and taste bringing them together.

'We never saw each other before…not like this,' she said.

'No.' He shook his head, a smile still hovering on his mouth. 'And there is yet more to see.'

Lying flat on his back, he pushed the hose, braies and footwear from him in one swift movement, and then he was naked before her, his manhood erect, his limbs long and straight, his black hair upon the pillow gleaming like the ink with which he wrote on his parchment.

When young, Llywelyn had been slight, but that lean-ness now was a hardness, formed and honed to a warrior's strength. A strength that robbed her of breath as he brought her down on top of him, his arms coming about her and his legs entwining with hers. Flesh met with flesh, the warmth of him seeping deep into her soul, into her heart. And, as their gazes locked and held, Cristin placed her lips lightly to his, the overwhelming intensity of that love rising up to stop her breath in her throat.

'I love you so much.'

Llywelyn shifted, rolled her beneath him, trapping her in a delicious cage that she never wanted to break free of. The bed settled and the world stilled with expectation.

'I know and, no matter what happens tomorrow or there-after, Cristin, I love you too. I always have and I always will.'

Then he joined his body with hers, filling her completely, making her forget about *all* the tomorrows. Cristin wrapped her limbs about him, relishing the weight of him, the feel of him, the scent of him, the taste of him as he buried himself deep inside her.

As he loved her with his body, his hands, his mouth, it *wasn't* like before, just as he'd said it wouldn't be. They'd been so young that last time, desperate, excited, overeager in their innocence. Now they seemed to possess an ageless knowledge of the other that had always been there, a knowing that went beyond learning and experience and had always, would always, exist.

As if Llywelyn had read her mind, he whispered through a kiss. 'You will be a part of me, Cristin, until the day I die.'

Cristin's joy faltered a little. It was as if they were already saying goodbye! She held him tighter as he moved faster and deeper inside her. Her eyes filled, and part of her heart broke even as her body arched and a wave of exquisite bliss swept through her. She cried out his name, heard him cry out, too, felt him withdraw, quickly and with urgency. Then a warm wetness seeped across her belly and his limbs went slack and his head came to rest upon her breast.

Llywelyn could have stayed there forever, in Cristin's arms, in this bed, in perfect and peaceful communion, listening to her heartbeat beneath his ear. But pushing himself up and away, he tended to the practicalities.

Then, he gathered her to him once more. Her flesh was still hot and damp from their lovemaking, and her hair was as tangled as the bedding beneath them. Gently, he began to thread his fingers through the strands, teasing them out until they lay smooth again over her shoulder and breast.

Through the window, the night air came in, cooler now, bathing the skin of his naked shoulders, Cristin's soft sleepy breathing caressing his chest. Closing his eyes, letting the silence of the secret hours claim him for a while at least, Llywelyn started to drift into sleep.

'Why did you do that?'

Cristin's quiet question brought him back with a little jolt. 'Disentangle your hair?'

'No. Why did you take your…release like that?' By the light of the guttering candle, he saw her frown. 'The last time it was otherwise.'

He cringed. The necessary means he'd adopted almost spoiled the beauty that lay over them, like an invisible blanket snuffing out a pure flame. 'The last time I was careless…clumsy…without experience,' he said. 'I could have got you with child.'

She was silent a little moment, her fingertips tracing a line along his collarbone. 'And since then, you have known other women…and gained experience?'

Llywelyn shook his head and the doubt that had clouded her gaze vanished. 'But I have learned much about the world of men. When I told you a warrior is driven only by the lust for life and the fear of death, it is true, Cristin.'

'But not for you?'

'No…although there have been times when, in the presence of death, I was sorely tempted to clutch at life too. War makes a man want to live every moment that is granted to him.'

'Like this moment?'

'Yes…and no.' Llywelyn touched his fingertips to her cheek. 'This is so much more than that, Cristin. It is everything.'

'We were both so young the last time, weren't we? I didn't even consider that I might get with child.' Her gaze dimmed a little. 'But afterwards, when you'd left and I went to Castell Abereinion, shut in with all that loneliness, at first, I feared that I *had*.'

'Tell me your fears, Cristin,' he urged, gently. 'Did my sister know about us?'

'No, I don't think so. And that was the worst of it. I couldn't tell her, for all her kindness and tolerance. She thought—and I let her believe—that it was the sea, the wolves, the *morloi*, the isolation, that worried me.'

'But it wasn't?'

She shook her head. 'No, though those things were un-settling. But there was no priest there, no church even, to confess or seek counsel. And because I had to keep it se-cret, my fear grew until Lady Rhianon thought I was los-ing my wits. So she sent me home.'

Llywelyn brushed back a strand of hair from her face. 'And when you arrived back here, I left and went south to Cantref Mawr.'

She sighed, her breath tickling his throat. 'There was no babe in any case and so my worries were baseless. But when you didn't come to see me before you left, nor when you passed by here the year after, on the way to Aberein-ion for the christening of your sister's firstborn... I hated you then.'

'You had good cause to hate me.' He didn't add he'd hated himself far more. 'I didn't know you would come back here when you did, and that time I came this way again...it was too hard to come and see you, to say good-bye.'

Her gaze searched his. 'Yet soon, we will have to say goodbye all over again.'

Llywelyn turned onto his back and stared upwards, the knowledge of that parting already too painful to bear. The candles had burned low, the torches, too, beginning to hiss and die, the moonlight slanting in through the window taking their place and bathing the room in blue instead of gold.

Cristin turned with him, placed her head in the crook of his shoulder, her palm flat on his breast. 'It was only later, when you'd gone to fight for the Lord Rhys, that I realised I'd *wanted* to have your babe. If we'd never come together again, at least I would have had something of you.'

The shadows in the room turned darker suddenly and, instead of the blue of the night, the blackness of recrimination seemed to reach out from every corner, as, after a long pause, she went on.

'As it is, you had no need to be careful just now…when we joined. I have had no monthly courses since the pestilence came, two winters ago. And so there will *be* no babe, Llywelyn. Not now, perhaps not ever.'

Cristin seemed suddenly much older than he was, though she was a whole summer younger. She seemed wiser, more experienced and far worldlier, as if all the things she'd borne these past years had coated her with invisible armour in order to survive them.

'I'm sorry,' was all he had to offer, gathering her closer, his heart raging at his inability to take all that burden from her, a burden he'd placed there.

'Don't be.' She pressed a kiss to his flesh. 'It is for the best.'

The words held neither bitterness nor accusation, only common sense and acceptance. But she didn't need to accuse him—Llywelyn did it for her, albeit silently. What good would it do to speak out loud now, when he would leave her in a few short hours, mayhap never to return?

But as always, he didn't need to speak, for she read his mind, his conscience, with accuracy.

'After all, if you are killed in battle or enclosed in a monastery, how could I bring a child into the world, to raise it without a father? How could we ever marry, you being my lord, and I your bondswoman?'

Llywelyn stared up at the ceiling, his arm around her, his fingers in her hair, counting every breath she breathed. And, just when he thought she'd fallen asleep, she spoke again.

'Other women would doubtless marry elsewhere, to give a bastard a name. Someone lowly from the village…or one of your lower-ranking soldiers, old Iorwerth Foel mayhap?'

The prospect, and the bitter reality of what she was saying, tore him in two. 'For pity's sake, Cristin!'

'You think I will make this coming parting easy for you, like I did the last time?' She gave a soft, so sad little laugh. 'No, I have grown up since then. I'm not an innocent, fearful girl anymore, Llywelyn. I'm a woman, one who has lived through terrible things.'

'I know you have,' he said. 'And I wish I'd been here to help you through some of those things, spared you them, and not caused you even more pain.'

'You are here now and that is what matters.' Her head shifted where it rested against his shoulder, then settled again. 'It is not only warriors who clutch at life so fiercely. I also need to live for the moment, *this* moment. I don't want any other man, ever. I want *you*, only you.'

They lay in silence then, no more words passing between them, since everything had been said. Finally, he sensed the flutter of her eyelashes, sensed the moment she fell asleep in his arms, although he lay awake long into the night.

The hours passed and the candles went out, and through the open window the stars shone like jewels against the blue-black sky. And, on his breast, Cristin's hair lay dark and heavy, its thick strands ensnaring him in unbreakable bonds.

How could he leave her now? How could he let her go again after this night? Whether she got with child or not, whether they could ever marry or not, it made no difference. She was his—no other man's—and he was hers. It had always been that way and it always would be, until the day they died—and perhaps even beyond.

Chapter Twelve

Cristin opened her eyes to see sunlight creeping in long, bright fingers across the floor, turning the rushes from brown to gold. Llywelyn's arms had fallen slack in the night but, as she stirred, they enfolded her once more. She snuggled closer, pressed her palm to his chest, felt his heartbeat below, strong and a little rapid.

And then, as he jolted awake and his eyes found hers and locked on, she knew from the quick glint of anguish in them that he'd been dreaming. Not of her and of love—as *she'd* been dreaming of love and of him—but of killing, and of Maelgwn.

Cristin touched his cheek, his jaw, the little bump in his nose that enhanced his beauty rather than marring it, and then placed her lips to his. She felt his body, which had tensed, relax again. He sighed and smiled before he kissed her, and she knew the nightmare had receded.

'The morning has come quickly,' she said, wrapping her arms about his neck, knowing there was no need to speak about the dark dreams of his sleep. But if *he* needed to speak of them, she was here to listen.

He moved over her, his flesh hard and warm, as sunbeams reached the bed, dappling their naked bodies with gold. 'And come too soon,' he whispered, his lips brushing hers through the words.

'It is late.' Cristin heard no conviction, either in her voice or her heart. 'Your parents will want me.'

'Let them wait.'

A cock crowed from the village, a second joining in. 'My duties...' she protested, her half-hearted tone bringing a blush of shame to her cheeks, while her arms closed tighter and her fingers buried themselves into hair.

'They can wait too.' His blue eyes darkened. 'I cannot.'

Despite that, their lovemaking was slow and languorous, as if they had the whole day long to lie in each other's arms, pretending there was nothing outside these four walls to concern them, less still call them.

The room became filled with their breaths, murmured words, sighs of pleasure and moans of ecstasy so keen it was almost agony. The world outside, barred by door and window, receded just as Llywelyn's nightmare had done, at least for a while.

This time, when the moment of release came, even as he started to withdraw, Cristin held him fast. 'No, let us be complete, together. Don't leave me now.'

A hesitation and then he shook his head, a sound like a sob issuing from him. 'I won't.'

As he spent himself inside her, their eyes held and their cries of fulfilment were as one. And, in the moment, she might almost have believed that leaving and parting were just words, after all, and that it would be impossible to sever this bonding, not now, not ever.

Afterwards, they lay satiated, their limbs entwined amidst rumpled bedclothes. Llywelyn's head rested on her breast and, as the sun rose higher and the cockcrows ceased, something settled. A kind of certainty of a love that had never withered, not once over all the years, and never would, no matter what happened.

Llywelyn shifted then, turning onto his side, stretching his arms above his head, his body arching as he stretched his spine too. And his gaze, brilliantly blue now in the bright daylight, was sober as he spoke and the severing began.

'Tomorrow I will have to ride for Blaenporth, with Peredur.'

'I know already.' Cristin's stomach hollowed and filled up with foreboding. 'What else would that message from Abereinion have meant?'

'But today—' he touched his fingertips to her cheek '—is for us, and tonight too.'

She grasped those hours he was offering her like a rope thrown to a soul drowning. He was here, with her, in this bed, and he loved her. She was as sure of his love now as she was of her own, and tomorrow—as terrible as it might be—was far away still.

'And what do you suggest we do with these hours that we have?' She placed her hand over his heart, felt the steady drum quicken, felt her own do the same. 'We cannot spend all that time in bed…can we?'

'Cristin!'

She and Llywelyn stilled as one entity as the answer came from outside, and in its wake, other sounds that Cristin hadn't noticed until then. The daily noise of the castle from down below, in the hall, outside in the bailey and up on the ramparts. Animals being fed, water being drawn from the well, the bark of a dog, a gruff exchange of voices as the night guard was changed to the day watch.

'Cristin, where are you?'

Tangwystl! Out in the corridor, her voice shrill with impatience and displeasure. Cristin wanted to scream with fury that this precious time should be snatched away, so quickly, so cruelly. But instead, she leapt up out of the bed as if the mattress had suddenly sprouted thorns instead of straw. Dragging on her shift and kirtle, she scooped her hair up into a knot and tucked it into a coif, then sat on a chair to pull on her stockings.

'Don't forget these.'

She looked up to find Llywelyn sitting on the edge of the bed, naked and unashamed of the fact, holding out her shoes.

'How can you sit there so unperturbed!' she said, jumping up and snatching her shoes, while her pulse raced all over again at the sight of his naked body. A whole day had many hours, and her duties would soon be done, especially if she did them with haste. 'Any moment now, we shall be discovered!'

His eyes danced and a note of mischief entered his voice. 'In that case, you'd best go before I make your shame complete.'

Out in the corridor the sound of footsteps came and the door latch rattled, followed by silence, as if the person without was listening hard, before the feet receded. The door of the adjacent chamber closed with a bang, indicating that her mistress was far from pleased.

Llywelyn's tone went from mischievous to ironic. 'While you slept, I got up and bolted it…just in case.'

'That was…prudent,' she said.

But they had gone far beyond prudency now. Anyone who'd looked for her last night, or had chanced to pass by her door and stopped to listen, would surely have heard them.

Once she was fully dressed, shoes and all, Llywelyn got

up, still naked, and opened the door for her, stepping behind it out of sight, so that he wouldn't been seen.

Cristin walked to the threshold but before she could step over it, he caught her around the waist and, drawing her close, kissed her so deeply she couldn't breathe.

'Stop!' Reluctantly, she extracted herself from his hold and, planting her hands flat on his chest, pushed him away. 'You mustn't…someone will see!'

'Who?' His brows lifted and his eyes twinkled. 'There is no one else here, behind the door…only we.'

It was as if time had gone backwards, and they were reckless and defiant children again, hiding their secret love in corners, behind doors—except they weren't. 'I must go,' she said, shaking her head, feeling his heart quicken beneath her palms, her own quickening in reply. 'Your mother will surely be cursing me by now!'

He nodded, and his eyes danced even merrier. 'I can almost hear her tutting from here.'

So could Cristin! Patience was not one of Tangwystl's virtues, only where her husband was concerned, when it was endless. But there would be no little explaining to do, not just about her tardiness that morning but the fact her door was locked against her mistress.

'And you must be gone from my chamber at once,' she said, sternly, fighting the urge to giggle again, despite the situation, even despite the fact he would be riding out to wage war soon. She pushed that thought away swiftly, before it spoiled all the other thoughts. 'And with your clothes on!'

Llywelyn brushed his thumb over her mouth, his gaze darkening, growing serious with intent. 'Very well, but only until tonight…when I shall take them off again, and yours too.'

It took all her will to walk away, to leave him there, arms folded and a smile of promise hovering on his mouth. And it took even more strength to close the door behind her, deprive her eyes of all his beauty, her body of his body, her heart of his heart, even for a short while.

She knocked on Tangwystl's door and entered, her feet so light they hardly seemed to touch the floor. For Llywelyn had kissed her, not in a farewell, but in a pledge of what was to come that night, and perhaps other nights too.

'You are making a habit of being tardy, Cristin! I thought more of you.'

Even Tangwystl's sharp reprimand didn't banish her joy, though she bowed her head. 'Forgive me, *meistres*, I slept hardly a wink during the night.'

Her daring defence elicited a tut from Tangwystl and Cristin had to turn away and hide a smile as she remembered Llywelyn's accurate prediction. And as she began to busy herself with the duties that awaited, a small seed of hope started to grow inside her.

If Llywelyn loved her as she loved him, would he not decide to stay here now, as lord of Ystrad Meurig? On his return from the battle—and he *must* return—would he turn from the way of the monk and accept the way of the warrior, after all? But as soon as it had sprung to life, her hope faltered a little.

For, even if he *did* remain in the world, could there really be any place in *his* world for *her*? Whatever his decision, nothing would change for her, and it would be as it had always been. He was a lord of noble birth and she was naught but his bondswoman and his mother's maidservant, and as such, could never be his wife, only his bedfellow.

Her joy faded with her hope. The warm sunshine outside the window cooled, bringing a cloud over her heart.

Their love—strong, durable, eternal—was as futile now as it had always been, and nothing could ever change that.

The arrival of Peredur ab Eilyr in the afternoon brought two things with it and Llywelyn cursed both—the war and the curtailment of his time with Cristin. Tomorrow he would have to ride and lay siege—but today he had to make a confession.

'It was too dark at first to see who it was, and even if I had seen, it was too late. Your brother came so quickly at me, I had no choice but to defend myself.' The explanation, although true, only seemed to make the act even worse. 'I'm sorry.'

'Don't be.' Peredur's voice was harsh, though below it, regret echoed. 'Maelgwn chose his own fate and his life was never going to end well or peacefully.'

They were standing in the little chapel off the great hall where Maelgwn lay on a makeshift bier, his body shrouded under a blanket, his face exposed. Llywelyn remembered how that face had looked in life, the day of his sister's wedding. Then it had been young, handsome, though cruelty had spoiled the comely veneer even then.

Now there was no facade of youth or beauty. It was as if all the years of his misdeeds had been scored into the skin, aging him before his time. The mark of Cristin's fingernails was still on Maelgwn's sunken cheek, inflicted that day she'd tried to defend herself, and his parents, adding to his misdeeds.

'If nothing else, you have spared him the traitor's death he would have faced had Rhys taken him alive.' His kinsman's eyes met his. 'And he would have dispatched you without hesitation had you not defended yourself.'

'I thank you for that, though it is little comfort. He is... was your brother.'

'Those foster ties did not bind us together at all. Instead, they rent us far apart.'

Llywelyn nodded. He knew the history as well as anyone. 'Do you wish him to be buried here, in that case?'

'Thank you for the offer, but no.' Peredur responded with the last words Llywelyn had expected. 'I will have his body laid to rest alongside our father, Eilyr. Perhaps, in the life beyond this, Maelgwn will find both mercy *and* reconciliation.'

A silence fell and the quiet of the little chapel was tainted by the sounds of activity from without—the sharpening of weapons and burnishing of shields. The ring of iron on anvil as horses were reshod. The shouts and bravado of men, some of it forced, some not.

'Can you spare two men and a cart, to carry the body to Llanbadarn tomorrow?' His kinsman's request broke through all those other sounds, turning introspection to practicalities. 'God alone knows how long this siege will last, or whether I will return from it alive, so I would rather arrange the burial now.'

Llywelyn nodded. It was the least he could do. 'Of course, and gladly.'

Death seemed to surround him on all sides, in front of him, the already dead, and outside, those who might very soon fall victim to death, too—as might *he* also. Before, that had never mattered but now Cristin was in his life, *was* his life, and he was very reluctant to relinquish it.

'With luck, Blaenporth will fall quickly, and without too much bloodshed.' Peredur went on, turning the talk again to the business of taking the two castles that still held out against Rhys. 'But I fear that Aberteifi, when the time comes, will be a massacre.'

Aberteifi was a formidable stronghold, and one that its castellan, Robert Fitz Stephen, would not give up easily. The smaller Blaenporth was still held for Roger de Clare, even though he was a hostage.

'Rhys won't rest until he has recovered every turf of grass that belonged to his forefathers, and more if he can get it.' Llywelyn replied, recalling the Prince's words as they'd ridden to the Roman road. 'Even so, the Flemings at Blaenporth will not hand it over willingly.'

His half-Flemish brother-in-law knew that better than anyone. Llywelyn had never seen Peredur's infamous Flemish father, Letard, though tales of his harsh and cruel rule in Dyfed were still spoken of, thirty years after his death.

'It is strange,' he said, after a moment of silence, 'that, as the sons of such brutal warriors, we both abhor war.'

'Perhaps not *so* strange, Llywelyn, but whether we abhor it or not, war will go on.' Peredur looked at him thoughtfully. 'I know of your wish to take up the religious life, but Rhys will not release you until his goal, and our freedom, are won, no matter how long it takes to win them.'

Llywelyn met the steady grey gaze. He and his kinsman had become close during the past years of bitter fighting, more like birth brothers now than kin by marriage, but he'd never told him about Cristin.

Now that omission sat uneasy on his shoulders and, before he'd even thought up the words, they were coming out of his mouth. 'There is a woman...'

Peredur's brows lifted. 'I see.' There was a pause when it seemed that the older man saw everything. 'And you love her?'

Llywelyn looked towards the window behind the bier, where dust motes and candle smoke hung in a haze. 'Yes.'

To his relief, his brother-in-law didn't ask her name. 'That complicates matters further still, *fy mrawd*.' He gave a heavy sigh. 'Leaving Rhianon to fight this war, knowing I might be killed and never see her again, was the hardest thing I've ever had to do.'

Llywelyn put his own burden aside, at least for a moment, and listened to Peredur talk about *his* love. There was nothing more he could—or would—reveal about Cristin anyway, not even to this man who was his friend. What could he say? That she was a servant and he a lord bound, sooner or later, for the monastery, and therefore his love was as futile as it was forbidden.

'I never thought, once upon a time, that I would ever marry, but now I can't imagine existing without her.' The grey eyes softened. 'Knowing that my wife is there, waiting for me, is what helps me face every battle. I would die for her sake and her safety, even more than for the freedom of our country.'

Silence followed that statement and, as one, the two men turned to stare at the bier, each lost in their thoughts. Not thoughts of war, or battles, but of the women they loved, lived for and would die for if need be.

And, as he looked into the unknown, Llywelyn knew *he* would die for Cristin too. Dying for her, to keep her safe and free, would be far easier than living without her. To exist behind those hallowed white walls beyond the hills, to know she was little more than a league away, yet to not be able to see her, touch her, lie with her...

The bells from the abbey church took up, floating across the hills and in through the window, breaking into the sombre moment. Peredur straightened up, rolled his shoulders, shaking the introspection from him as a hound shakes water from his coat.

'The hour of Nonce already! I'll take my men on to Ystrad Fflur tonight and camp there, and not eat into your resources here.'

Llywelyn roused himself too. 'I will join you tomorrow, with thirty of my men, and perhaps Abbot Enoc will give us his blessing for an easy victory and a swift return to our homes…and to our loved ones.'

His brother-in-law clasped his forearm. 'We might not have the chance to talk close like this again, therefore, I will leave you with a word of advice, *fy mrawd*, for what it is worth.'

'What is it?'

'There is more than one path in life for every man and more than one way to God. This woman you love has entered your life for a reason, as Rhianon entered mine.' His kinsman looked one last time upon the face of his dead brother. 'So think carefully, Llywelyn, about the paths ahead of you before you step forward, for there may be no going back.'

Peredur left the chapel but Llywelyn remained long afterwards, staring down at Maelgwn, trying not to breathe in the stench of decay. Outside, the golden afternoon slowly slipped into evening, and quiet fell around the castle as men put down their tools and weapons and went in to supper. The serenity that followed was so profound it was impossible to think that Wales was at war at all.

Iago ab Dafydd entered and, with a whispered greeting, came to stand beside the bier, to pray and keep vigil. *He* should keep vigil, too, and pray for forgiveness, for killing done and killing yet to come. Once, even a week ago, he would have done so, but now…how *could* he kneel, and pray and lie—to God and to himself—when he'd begun to doubt the foundations of his entire vocation?

So Llywelyn didn't kneel. Instead, with a nod to Iago, he turned and walked away. His footsteps might be uncertain, his path dark and indistinct, split into myriad other paths that writhed like so many serpents before him. But one lay clear, gleaming as bright and as sharp as a river under moonlight, and he followed it without having to think at all.

The path that led to Cristin.

When the Compline bell at the abbey had ceased tolling, Cristin took off the green kirtle she'd worn while doing her chores that day and put on the fine blue gown. Changing her coif for a clean one, she then placed the shutters across the window and doused the lights. As she passed by Mwg, asleep on a stool, she put out a hand and stroked his fur. His spine was still bony but he wasn't so thin as before, and at times he seemed almost like a kitten again. But he wasn't, any more than she was the girl she'd been when Llywelyn had given her the cat all those years before.

Crossing to the door, she went out through it, shutting it quietly behind her. It was but a step to Llywelyn's chamber and she entered without knocking, knowing he was inside, waiting for the sun to sink, for the night to come, as she was.

He was sitting at the table, wearing only a shirt, the sleeves rolled up to his elbows. Thin woollen hose encased his long legs, and his feet were bare upon the rushes. He was working on the translation of the *Vita Sancti Paterni*, though the candle on the table had burned so low it was a wonder he could see what he was writing.

As she closed the door softly, he didn't turn in his seat, nor rise to his feet, but his hand stilled on the parchment, and his head lifted swiftly. It was a warm night, even for early summer, and a breeze drifted in through the open window, caressing his hair and rippling his shirt so that it touched his body, tantalisingly hinting at the beauty of line and limb below the linen.

Cristin went to stand next to him, her hands already eager to peel away those concealing clothes and feast her eyes on the man beneath them. Instead, her gaze fell upon the parchment and she bent her head better to see what sacred writing Llywelyn was etching so carefully with his quill.

But it wasn't writing—it was a drawing, in the margin at the bottom of the page. Her heart gave a leap, because the image was of a young woman with eyes of brown and hair the colour of fire tumbling down about her face.

'Is…is that me?' she gasped, her voice a-quiver with awe.

He nodded and the fingers of his left hand found hers, locked gently, his gaze lifting to hers. 'I'll have to erase it, of course, eventually, but tonight…as I worked and waited… I needed to see you.'

Cristin's stomach fluttered. 'Do I really look like that?'

'No. My pen, nor these colours, least of all the little skill I possess, could ever really capture your radiance, the fire in your hair…the autumn of your eyes…'

Llywelyn had jested once about being a poet, and she could well imagine him besting even the greatest of the court *beirdd*. 'How will you erase it now that it is done?' she asked.

'By scratching it out with the edge of a blade.'

He put down the quill and took up his knife, touching the edge of it to the drawing, as if he would scrape it away now. 'If I do it very lightly, in ages to come, someone looking closely might yet be able to see it, if only like a ghostly shadow…and they might wonder who had drawn it…and why.'

The knife clattered down upon the table and Llywelyn sprang to his feet, pulling her to him. 'But not yet.' He dipped his head, found her lips, his hand sweeping the coif from her head. '*O f'anwylyd*, I have missed you this day long.'

'And I you,' she breathed, as he led her over to the bed and there began to unbraid her hair with tender fingers, teasing it out around her shoulders. Slowly, he stripped the kirtle and shift from her body, then with more haste pulled his shirt over his head. A long-awaited storm seemed to break then as he removed her shoes and stockings and struggled out of his hose.

Finally, they were both naked and on the bed, their limbs entwined in an urgent tangle, as he joined with her. Cristin clung to him, her soul cleaving to his soul, as he loved her as never before. It was pleasure and pain, savage and gentle, powerful and exquisite, as if all the other times they'd lain together, from the first youthful experience to the intense reunion of the previous night, had all merged into one perfect joining.

She dug her nails into the flesh of his back, the rippling of his muscle, the hardness of bone, the smoothness of his skin, setting her senses aflame. And all the time, as he drove into her body, into her soul, his heart thundered in time with hers, the beat so perfect that it brought tears to her eyes.

It was as if he was loving her for the very last time and, since it might well be, Cristin loved him back with the same selfish and selfless passion. At the culmination, their union was so complete, so beautiful, that she cried out loud, and

Llywelyn's harsh yell as he spilled his seed deep inside her was even louder.

So loud that surely Tangwystl two chambers away would hear. So abandoned that their cries would surely fly through the open window to the ears of anyone below in the bailey, soar upwards again to the ears of the guards up on the ramparts.

But Cristin didn't care anymore who heard and who gossiped, who judged and condemned. There was no shame, no regret, no recrimination or excuses. There was only love, as there had always been, and only this moment, which might never come again, to cling to and hold in her heart forever.

Chapter Thirteen

The next morning there was no call from the corridor or rattle of the door latch as the bell of Ystrad Fflur sounded the hour of Prime. Tangwystl didn't need to search nor to wonder, as she'd done yesterday, since she must know full well where her maid was.

Lying with her son, in his bed, in his arms, as his *gordderch*—his lover.

Gordderch! It was an ugly word, one of shame, ridicule, contempt. And yet, here in the half-light of the hour just before dawn, with no sun yet, still the world was beautiful and she cared nothing for words.

If one loved a man more than life itself, and that man loved her in return, surely names, even the most despicable of them, meant nothing. Did it really matter, then, if that man was a lord and she a servant?

As if he sensed her thoughts, Llywelyn's eyes opened and, taking her hand, he turned it and placed his lips to her palm. Cristin's heart swelled with joy but, at the edges, the new day was tainted with dread. This morning, when the light was full, he would be going to war, and he might never return.

'How long have you been awake?'

'Not long.' She shook her head, though, in truth, she had awoken well before, when the dread had shaken her from sleep. The night, the precious hours, had gone too quickly, in the blink of an eye, it seemed.

'What hour is it?'

'Prime,' she replied. 'The abbey bell has only just tolled.'

His gaze clouded and he gathered her into his arms, resting his chin on her head. During the night, instead of sleep, they'd loved and talked so as to make the hours longer than they really were, and now there seemed nothing left to say.

Except one thing. And now that the time for departing had arrived, too soon, too quickly, despite all their attempts to delay it, Cristin needed to say the words that both of them must surely be thinking.

'If you don't return from Blaenporth…'

He turned onto his back, his jaw clenching. 'A warrior never knows if he will return or not, Cristin. It is always best not to know.'

Cristin didn't want to know either, but she *needed* to know, and there were things she needed to *say*, now, before it was too late to ever say them. 'But you are not a warrior, are you? Not in your deepest soul. In there…' She touched his breast just over his heart. 'There, you are a monk.'

His head turned on the pillow and he met her eyes. 'Not even that—not yet.'

'No, not yet,' she repeated. But whether he were killed in battle, or enclosed behind the walls of a monastery, her world would end either way. 'But the things we did last night are not things a monk would do, are they?'

He smiled but there was no laughter in his eyes. 'No, they are not.'

'Then does that not prove that you are not meant to be

a monk at all?' This was madness but she couldn't stop herself. 'That you do not belong in the cloister either, but here in the world?'

His expression grew grim and he turned his head away, stared up at the ceiling. A long silence passed before he answered, so long that Cristin thought he might never answer.

'I don't know what it proves or disproves,' he spoke at last. 'But the night I killed Maelgwn…do you know what I felt, Cristin?'

She swallowed, the strange question sending a sudden shiver down her spine. 'Yes,' she said, 'I saw it in your face when you came into the room.'

'You only saw part of it, the outer horror that a man can't hide when he has committed such violence.'

'So, what else did you feel…in here?' Cristin pressed her palm harder, until the slow and steady thud of his heart echoed in her heart too. 'Tell me.'

'Relief.' His head turned and his eyes met hers. 'Gladness even, that he could do no more harm to you, to anyone, that I'd rid the world of him.'

'And that was wrong?'

'Whether it was wrong or not, it shouldn't have *been*, Cristin. I'd just committed the worst of sins, I'd spilled blood in a church, and yet that shame mattered less than the relief I felt.'

His eyes closed and she saw his nostrils flare as he inhaled deeply. 'Even the guilt I felt standing at the bier yesterday with Peredur wasn't sufficient to dispel that relief… or the knowledge that I would do it all again.'

Then he turned onto his side again, facing her, and his fingers began to thread through the tangles of her hair. 'But I cannot—I *must* not—go on killing men in the name of war, or even by chance, in a moment of surprise, as I did Maelgwn.'

'But Peredur forgave you. He holds no blame towards you.'

'No, and I am grateful for that. But it is easier to forgive someone else for a terrible deed than it is to forgive yourself.'

Cristin searched his eyes, the bleakness in them chilling her soul. 'You told me that a warrior thinks only of lust and death. Is that really true?'

'For some, it is. For me… I think only of all the women I rob of their husbands, the mothers I rob of their sons, with just a stroke of my sword or a thrust of my knife, sometimes even with my bare hands.'

Untwining his fingers from her hair, he held his hand up in front of his face, as if he could still see the blood there. 'It sickens me to my soul because I can never undo those acts, nor give life back where I have taken it, but at least in the cloister I will never have to commit violence again.'

'But your hands have not always wrought violence and brought death. I have seen what *else* they have done.' Cristin laced her fingers between his. 'The manuscript, the story of Padarn the peacemaker, the beautiful drawings…'

'Yet no matter what I write or draw, the ink will never wash them clean.'

Her heart shuddered. 'You are not responsible for everything that is bad in the world, Llywelyn! You might have had to fight wars but so have countless other men. If Rhodri hadn't died and you hadn't had to take his place…'

'But Rhodri *did* die, and I *did* take his place, since there was no one else. There is no alternative for a lord but to fight…or to lay down his sword altogether.'

Cristin stared at their hands locked tightly between them.

'Many warriors take up the habit at the end of their life, make amends for their lives of violence on the point of their deaths, but not when they have years yet to live.'

'That is between every man and his conscience.'

She felt her argument flounder. *He* was the clever one, not she. *He* was the scribe and the poet chained up within the warrior's armour. She couldn't even read—but suddenly, she could *think*, and more clearly than she'd ever seemed able to before.

'But conscience is different to conviction, is it not?'

He nodded. 'Yes.'

'If it weren't for your father, would you be so set upon a religious life? If he had been kind, not cruel…and if your mother had been loving, not indifferent, if you had grown up in a safe and happy home, and not one filled with fear and danger, would you have pursued this vocation of yours, all these years?'

Llywelyn, too, had been staring at their two hands, still joined between them. Now their eyes met. 'Perhaps not… but I will never know that.'

Cristin felt her way carefully, sifting through her words, searching for the right ones. 'Then, if there is doubt in your heart, Llywelyn, any doubt at all, however small, might that mean that your vocation is not a true one, after all?'

His gaze grew turbulent, as if her argument, as weak as it was, had stirred up a storm inside him. 'It is too late for me to examine that now, Cristin, as it is too late to undo all the violence I have done. It must stop, before I become like Cadwgan, like Rhodri, before even killing ceases to matter.'

'It would *always* matter to you, Llywelyn.' She shook her head. 'You are not cold-hearted and pitiless, nor ever could be. The things you have done *had* to be done. Everyone, man and woman, has to do and feel things they would sooner not, at times.'

He looked at her almost with sadness, as if she still failed to understand him, though now she understood with terrible clarity. 'And every man and every woman has to pay the price, sooner or later. Each has to face their conscience and accept the proper penalty.'

'But not everyone seals themselves up in a monastery or nunnery. They stay and pay their penalty in the world, and go on living, nonetheless. They don't live a lie but face themselves, and the truth.'

'Truth?' His shoulders heaved as he let out a sigh. 'Since I returned here, saw *you* again, I can't tell what is true and what isn't anymore, Cristin.'

Cristin took a deep breath too. 'I know what is true. My love for you and yours for me. That is why I'm asking you to question this conviction of yours. And if it is sound, if it is what you really want, I will accept it and...'

Her voice trailed off, unwilling to say the words *let you go*. What power did she have after all to hold him?

His eyes narrowed. 'And if it proves false?'

'Then we are free to love each other, without fear, without shame, for as long as we live.'

'Are you saying that we continue like this? That you share my bed, be my *gordderch*, knowing, even were I *not* to become a monk but remained as lord here, that I could never make you my wife?'

Cristin felt her heart twist. 'Whether we are wed or not, I don't care, as long as we are together.'

'No, Cristin! They can call me what they will, but I will not let them shame and slander you.'

'There *is* no shame in this, in us.' Cristin squeezed his

hand tighter. 'Love can transcend everything, so the priest says. Is God *himself* not love?'

He moved suddenly, rolling her beneath him, his body coming over hers. '*Myn Mair*! You are tying me in knots with your arguing! When did you grow so versed in words, *ddynes*?'

It was a jest and yet it was not, for his eyes blazed with anguish. Cristin wrapped her arms around his neck, burying her fingers in the black hair and drawing his head down.

'A woman in love finds the words somehow.'

'I don't know which would be the hardest to bear. To be in the world and see you shamed, or to be in the cloister and not see you at all, ever again.' A muscle clenched in his jaw. 'And were you to marry anyone else...'

Cristin's breath caught as she felt his resolve weaken. 'Would it pain you so much if I *were* to wed another, knowing that I could never love *him*, because I love *you*?'

He gave a grimace. 'It would cast me into hell to see another man take you as his wife, to know that he will bed you, whether you loved him or not.'

'Monks are not supposed to care about such worldly things.' Cristin tilted her mouth up so that it hovered close to his. 'Monks are not even supposed to harbour such thoughts, nor covet what other men have.'

'That is why they don hair shirts and lash scourges across their shoulders and prostrate themselves before the altar night after night.'

'That sounds like hell anyway...'

He nodded, slowly, his gaze sober. 'It *will* be hell, Cristin...'

Cristin swallowed, the seriousness of his words like a terrible foreboding. 'Then if the monastery is hell,' she urged softly, 'is it not better to renounce it? Stay here, in the world, with me?'

* * *

Llywelyn stared down at Cristin. In the morning light her eyes looked more green now than hazel, their beauty holding him even tighter than her arms did. Her flesh was warm beneath his, her heartbeat strong and sure, and, at the back of *his* eyes, tears of frustration burned like brimstone.

'Do you think that, since I can never marry you, I could go on like *this*? Making you appear wanton in the eyes of the world, to hear people call you so, which they will?' He shook his head. 'You are worth far more than that!'

Her fingertips touched his lips. 'Do you *think* me wanton, to lie here with you, like this?'

'Dear God, Cristin, of course I do not!'

She placed her mouth where her fingertips had been. 'Then I *am* not, and our love is as clean and as pure as it is true.'

Her lips parted, sought his, but he withheld the kiss she was demanding of him. If he kissed her now, he would never be able to leave this bed. If he joined his body with hers again, he wouldn't even want to *try* to leave.

As always, she knew what he needed, and offered it 'Kiss me...'

But his men would be assembling, Gwion ab Adda having roused them at dawn, as per his orders. His stallion would be saddled and waiting for him, his shield burnished bright, the teeth of the Cwn Annwn bared and eager for the hunt.

'Grist annwyl!' He took her mouth then, deeply, desperately, only lifting his head again when they were both breathless and gasping. 'Of all the men who would be proud to be loved by you,' he ground out, 'why must you choose the one most unworthy of it?'

'Because we don't choose love, it chooses us.' She

shifted beneath him, her legs wrapping around his. 'Stay, Llywelyn…a little while longer at least.'

'I cannot…'

'Why not? Because your men are waiting for you? Because the war is waiting?' Her head lifted off the pillow, her mouth seeking and finding his once more. 'Let it wait…'

Llywelyn groaned and kissed her again, more desperately than before, his loins burning to join with her, as if there would never be any more parting, now or ever. But what right had he to love her like this, knowing he must leave her, not just for this battle, but for the cloister when the time came? What right, when he could never truly make her his, decently, with his ring and his name as well as with his heart, which had always been hers?

'Enough!' Pushing himself upward, he leapt from the bed, turning his back on her, resting his elbows on his knees. A moment later she rose, too, and came to kneel behind him. Her arms wrapped around his shoulders and her cheek rested against his.

'Llywelyn…?'

He stared in front of him, at her blue gown and pale linen shift, lying crumpled on the floor where he'd thrown them. Next to them, her coif, its snowy whiteness catching the first rays of the sun that were creeping slowly across the floor.

'You are asking too much of me, Cristin.'

'Of which man am I asking too much? The warrior lord…or the monk?'

Llywelyn took a deep breath. 'Of both, since neither can give you what you deserve.'

She leaned closer, her hair cascading down over his back, her arms folding around him. 'I will take it anyway, from either one of you.'

'Lord Llywelyn!'

Cristin's arms slackened again, and a chill descended as her hair fell away, leaving his skin with a final caress, like a farewell. 'It is your body servant, come to dress you.'

He nodded. 'Yes.'

The knock came again, louder this time. From the bailey below, through the open window, the sounds of preparation, unheard until then, now came loudly—the ring of hooves as horses were led out of stables, the sharper ring of steel as swords and shields were counted and chain mail donned.

Cristin leaned forward, touched her lips to his ear. 'Send him away. If you have to go, then *I* will be the one to gird you for battle.'

Llywelyn hesitated and, naked as he was, went to the door and opened it just a crack, so that his man shouldn't see into the room. Issuing orders, he sent him away, and when he turned back, Cristin had dressed in her shift and was at the table against the wall, pouring water from the ewer into the basin.

He crossed over to stand behind her, lifting her hair to his face, breathing deep, as if her essence was the very air he needed to live, which it was. 'He didn't see you.'

She shrugged but didn't turn to him. 'It matters not whether he did or didn't.'

The noise from the bailey below grew louder still and, with a sigh, Llywelyn washed and dried himself quickly, as Cristin went to his coffer and took out his armour.

Without words, she began to dress him, placing each piece on his body as if she'd done it a hundred times before. But before each item of clothing went on, she touched her lips to his flesh with the lightest of kisses, each and every one piercing far below the skin and into his very soul.

When she came to his leather gambeson, her hands faltered, as if it was one item she didn't know what to do with. So he helped her, their fingers working together to tie the jerkin securely around his waist. She faltered again when it was time to belt his sword at his hip, so prising it out of her fingers, he did it himself.

Finally, she placed his cloak around his shoulders, securing it at his throat with its heavy bronze clasp. Only his gauntlets and helmet remained, and the shield in the corner, where the Cwn Annwn waited, bathed in sunlight.

It was then, when he was about to reach for the shield, she gave a little sob and laid her forehead against his chest. 'Promise me you'll come back!'

Llywelyn clasped her tightly to him, buried his fingers in her hair, breathed in its meadow-sweet scent until he'd filled his lungs with it, with her, once more. 'That is one thing I cannot promise, Cristin,' he said. 'The future is in God's hands now.'

She looked up at him, her eyes clouded with anguish, and a host of words hidden in the shadows of those deep hazel-green depths. 'Then I will pray to Him.'

As she said it, Llywelyn felt a choke in his throat. He might never see her again, never hold her, kiss her, lie with her. It was too much to contemplate and he shook the thought from his head. Cupping her face between his palms, he dipped his head and kissed her, long and deep and—as the thought pushed its way back—perhaps for the last time.

'He will hear you, I promise, but His will is already ordained, even so,' he said, feeling his heart break in his breast, knowing that hers was breaking too. 'Goodbye, Cristin, God keep you always.'

Before he changed his mind and stepped off the path he had to follow, Llywelyn let her go. Donning his gauntlets, he picked up his helmet and shield and strode to the door.

Opening it, he almost tripped over Mwg, as the cat darted over the threshold.

But for once, as he closed the door with a final look back, he didn't curse the creature. The cat had always been a link between them, and more so now, as they parted, perhaps forever.

Cristin stooped and picked Mwg up. Cradling him in her arms, she listened to Llywelyn's footsteps stride along the corridor and down the stairs to be swallowed up in the noise from the bailey. She didn't go over to the window to watch him ride away at the head of his men. Instead, Mwg still clutched to her breast, she sat down on the bed, the blanket cold now where before it had been warmed by their two bodies.

Outside, the gates creaked open, men calling out good fortune and a safe return to their comrades. The jingle of bits, the sound of shields and weapons, of leather and of steel, the thudding of hooves, seemed deafening, but she made herself listen until it had all died away and the gates swung closed again.

Then she rose and, letting Mwg out of her arms, tied her coif around her hair. Unlike he usually did, the cat didn't dart away, after mice, or in pursuit of a she-cat on heat. Instead, he swarmed around her legs, as he had done so many times around Llywelyn's, as she went around the room, collecting discarded clothing and making the bed as neatly as she could.

Finally, Cristin crossed over to the table where Llywelyn worked on the manuscript. Her face, portrayed in bold colours at the margin, looked so out of place beside the elegant writing and saintly miracles, and yet it seemed to belong there all the same.

The eyes stared up at her, seeing her as she saw herself—
a woman who loved a man openly and honestly in front of
all the world. The image might be erased one day, or perhaps it would just fade over time, but for now, it was there.

Her love for the man who'd drawn it would never fade,
but now she accepted it was impossible, just as he'd said
it was, although not quite in the same way as he'd meant
it. And so, in the short space of time until he returned—
which he must!—she had to learn to hide it, deny it, pretend it *had* faded.

For, as she girded him in his armour, she'd realised, truly
realised for the first time ever, what that armour meant.
She'd felt the weight and strength and roughness of it. She'd
scented the sweat and the blood that had coated it during
numerous battles. She'd seen the tear in one side of the
gambeson, where some blade had pierced the thick leather,
which had been stitched back together.

Llywelyn had survived so many battles. He'd come out
victorious and safe even though he'd hated waging them.
But what if his luck ran out during this battle? Or if not
this one, the next one, or the one after that? What if the
skill that had enabled him to win and not lose, that kept
him alive all these years, finally deserted him?

She'd even seen it in his eyes as he'd bid her farewell,
telling her his fate was now in God's hands. Did he think
that would bring her comfort? Or did he sense, too, that a
warrior's luck couldn't hold forever? Was he ready to accept whatever that fate was to be, and so he'd advised her,
wisely, to be ready to accept it too?

Cristin began to shake and she leaned forward, her palms
flat on the table, her fingers clutching the parchment, creas-
ing it, so that her face disappeared. She stared down at her
hands. They were soft and pale, not calloused and red-

dened like the hands of the other servants, though they had been once.

She traced the veins beneath her skin to where they vanished under the cuff of her blue kirtle, the lady's kirtle that Llywelyn had given her, the gift of a gown that had sealed her position as being apart, above, privileged.

Yes, she was privileged but not in the way Dyddgu and old Gronow Gof and all the others thought. She was privileged because she loved and because she was loved in return. Love could change everything. It could do wonderful and unheard-of things. It could be as simple as the taking off of an old kirtle and the putting on of a new one, the drawing of a face on parchment. It could be so powerful that it could alter worlds, as it had altered hers.

Could it do more still? Could it decide a man's fate? Could it turn defeat into victory, and death into life? And could she use *her* love as surety to ensure that it could and it would?

Cristin took a deep breath and pushed herself up straight. She might lack Llywelyn's conviction, and her faith might be simpler, one of habit than anything else. But neither was she afraid to barter with his God. Smoothing the parchment out, she traced a finger over the face—her face—that he'd drawn there, so carefully, so beautifully, so lovingly.

And then, Mwg still at her heels, she crossed to the *priedieu* in the corner where Llywelyn did his daily devotions and, dropping to her knees, she began to pray.

Chapter Fourteen

⁓⁓⁓⁓⁓

Later that morning, Cristin stood with those who were left in the castle and watched Maelgwn's shrouded body being lifted onto a cart, bound for burial at Llanbadarn. And, suddenly, as it rumbled out through the gates, two men-at-arms going with it, she felt something lift from her, and in its place something else descend upon her.

He'd burned her village, killed people she'd known and loved, starved and mistreated those he'd left alive. Everyone, including she, had walked in terror lest his vicious eye fall upon them, which it had upon her in the end, that day he'd come for Llywelyn's parents.

Maelgwn's death, however terrible, was a mercy for everyone, but it had also caused Llywelyn to examine his conscience, question his vocation, even if he did claim it was too late. That startling admission of his feelings in that church, where blood had been spilled at his hands, and how that mattered less to him than her safety, should have made her want to sing out loud with joy and with pride.

But as she turned away, leaving no prayers behind her, Cristin's steps were as heavy as her heart. For whatever his decision proved to be in the end, *her* vow was made. And

should he stay in the world and not retreat to the cloister—
which surely was not where he belonged—her vow would
be even harder to keep.

When she went to wait upon her mistress, she found
Tangwystl up, dressed and standing at the window, looking out, doubtless having watched the death cart depart
too. In the bed, Cadwgan still slept even though the sun
was high, but the atmosphere in the room was so cold that
icicles could have hung from the rafters.

When Tangwystl turned slowly around, the blue eyes
were like steel, her tone even sharper and the words painfully to the point. 'I am aware where you have spent this
last night, and the one before, too, but I never expected
such…wantonness from *you*, Cristin.'

Cristin felt her face flame. It was as if Tangwystl had been
listening through the wall, but she held the other woman's
accusing glare. 'It is not what you suppose.'

'Is it not?' The haughty chin tilted. 'You must know he
can never marry you, surely! Even if Llywelyn were not set
on the religious life, you are too far beneath him.'

The truth cut cruelly. 'I know that and I have no such
ambitions, *meistres*.'

'You mean you are content to share his bed, like a common harlot?' Tangwystl tutted, pursed her thin lips. 'There
will be talk among the castle folk.'

'There is already talk.'

'And you care not?'

'No.' Cristin shook her head. 'I love him. I have *always*
loved him.'

'I know you have.' Tangwystl's tone softened and her
eyes became troubled. 'But you are headed for sorrow, Cristin. Whatever path Llywelyn chooses eventually, the end-

ing will be the same for you.' She crossed to sit on a chair, as if suddenly weary. 'Bring me some wine, child.'

Cristin handed her a cup of wine, noticing how the hands that received it shook. She was replacing the jug on the side table when Tangwystl's next words sent a shock of fear to her heart.

'He may be killed, of course, like Rhodri was…or injured and left as helpless as Cadwgan.'

The jug clattered onto the tabletop, though thankfully still upright. 'Then we must both pray that he will not be.'

Tangwystl nodded. 'Yes, we must pray…yet it still might not be enough. You would be better off not loving him, *forwyn*, nor any man who has to fight in wars. The loss and the suffering are too hard to bear.'

'Yet *you* have borne it.'

'I have had no choice but to bear it.' Tangwystl drank from her cup, her blue eyes—Llywelyn's eyes—sad behind its rim. 'And I would not wish to see *you* bear it too.'

Cristin picked up a discarded night shift and folded it carefully into a coffer. She was rolling a pair of stockings when Tangwystl spoke once more.

'Or are you determined to bear that burden, whatever advice I give you?'

Placing the stockings in the coffer and shutting the lid, Cristin turned around. 'My love for your son, even if it *is* hopeless, is not a burden, *meistres*. It is an honour, even if I am not worthy of it because he is a lord and I am a peasant.'

'That matters naught to Llywelyn, and I don't know whether to admire him for that or curse him for it.' Tangwystl put her cup down and gestured. 'Fix my hair now, Cristin. Lord Cadwgan will be awake soon.'

As she plaited the silver hair, Cristin knew she should have curbed her tongue. But how could she have said otherwise, dissembled and denied her feelings? She'd already denied so much, on her knees there in Llywelyn's chamber, and to deny her love, too, would be the worst sacrifice of all.

She was tying the binding at the bottom of the plait when Tangwystl turned her head, her tone tinged with regret.

'Forgive me my harsh tones, child. If things were different, I would give you *both my* blessing.' The thin mouth quivered. 'I have been unfortunate to have found no love in my marriage, only sadness and fear. I would not, therefore, forbid *you* the chance of love, should it come.'

Cristin swallowed back the lump that rose to her throat, the unexpected gift of understanding, of approval, touching her deeply. But it was a bittersweet gift since nothing could come of it. Her decision, and her vow, had already been made, and there was no taking it back.

Stooping, she took the bony hands into her own and squeezed them gently. This woman had become the closest thing she had to a mother since the death of her own, but until today, their differences in status had always stood between them, a barrier that was impossible to cross.

'It is good to know that you would give me your blessing…but I won't need it now.'

'What do you mean?'

Cristin took a deep breath. 'This morning, after Llywelyn left, I prayed hard and for a long time. Not for guidance, or a blessing, or forgiveness, but for steadfastness and strength of heart.'

Tangwystl frowned. 'To bear the slander and condemnation of your liaison? For it will be so, Cristin, from many quarters, if not from me.'

'No. For the will to resist and deny my love, to hide it, not just from Llywelyn, but from everyone.' The words of her dawn prayer rose up to choke her. 'Because if God brings him back safe and well, I have vowed, on my knees before the holy cross, that I will give him up.'

'Oh, Cristin.'

Her mistress's gaze swam with tears, the first Cristin had ever seen there. 'You would make my son a worthy wife indeed, were circumstances otherwise.'

Cristin blinked as tears swam in her eyes too. 'But circumstances are not otherwise, are they?'

'No, though I wish they *were*. I truly do, Cristin. You are more than a servant to me, and to my family. You belong and always have and, for sheltering my husband and me, for saving our lives at the risk of your own, we are forever in your debt.'

'You owe me nothing.' Cristin shook her head. 'I did what I did willingly and would do so again.'

'I know, *forwyn*.' The hands in hers squeezed back and a new understanding passed between them, when, for once, they were not mistress and servant, but only two women.

'This blue kirtle you wear was my daughter, Rhianon's, wasn't it? Too fine for a bondswoman yet my son thought it fitting for you.' Tangwystl's shoulders lifted and dropped. 'Yes, perhaps it *is* fitting that you should wear it. Perhaps it is fitting also that you should love Llywelyn—and that he should love you. Who am I to judge you? I, who know nothing of a man's love?'

'Yet Lord Cadwgan loves you. I know he does.'

'It has come too late for me to return it.' She smiled sadly. 'I love my children, of course, but I cannot show them. Like you, I have hidden my feelings away until now even I cannot find them. That is Cadwgan's doing.'

'Perhaps your children know it anyway?'

'Perhaps.' Tangwystl withdrew her hands and folded them in her lap. Her head turned to the window and her voice went out through it and far away. 'When they were very young, I tried to protect them, you know. They don't remember. Perhaps they were too young to remember...or perhaps they chose not to.'

Cristin's heart missed a beat but she said nothing, silently willing her mistress to go on, to speak of something that was clearly very painful. And, after a moment, she did.

'In the beginning, I managed it, giving them to servants to hurry them away and hide somewhere, drawing his anger to me, not to them. But when they got older, and Rhodri changed so, and Llywelyn and Rhianon seemed to deliberately provoke Cadwgan, it got harder and harder.'

She paused and the bony hands tightened in her lap. 'The more they incited his anger, the worse he took it out on me, as well as on them. And in the end, I stopped trying. I failed them, Cristin. Yet how *could* I save them from him when I couldn't even save myself?'

'And that is why you cannot tell them you love them, because you feel ashamed of failing them?'

Tangwystl nodded and met her eyes. 'Yes.'

Cristin took her hands again, feeling them like ice now in hers. 'Perhaps it is time to tell them why you failed... and that you love them. They deserve to know.'

'Yes...they do. And, God willing, I will find the moment to tell them both, before it is too late.' Her mistress's eyes swam all over again. 'Does Llywelyn know of your vow to give him up, Cristin?'

'No.'

'It is for the best, though I know you won't understand that now, not yet. I would rather him stay here, as lord, than see him become a monk. But if he will not remain, I would have him alive in a monastery, not dead in battle—and so must you.'

Cristin nodded. Yes, it was best, and yes, that is what she must do. Be thankful to have him alive and safe, *wherever* he was. Hide her love and her sorrow, and if her sacrifice was enough, if God brought him back safe and whole, keep her vow forever.

The moment of closeness passed, a solemn quiet ensued. Tangwystl moved to sit where she always sat, at the side of the husband she could not love, thinking perhaps of how and when to tell her children how much she loved them, how sorry she was that she had failed them.

Cristin turned back to her duties. She, too, would have to think on how to tell Llywelyn of her vow, how to say that she was sorry too. And, lest she not find the strength when that moment came to tell him, it must be soon, as soon he returned. If he returned…

It was brutal, it was bloody, it was terrifying but most of all it was sickening. The firing of the wooden walls of Castell Blaenporth, the dodging of arrows, boiling water, filth and other missiles launched at them by the defenders. The cries and screams of burning men and horses. The ramming of the flaming gates and the roaring headlong charge into the fray within.

Then the suffocating confines of the bailey, the blinding, choking smoke that blotted out the sky and stung his eyes. The slashing and thrusting of swords, men falling around him, his own and the enemy, the pitiless slaughter on both sides.

It went on and on until it became like a nightmare with no end. At Llywelyn's flank, old Iorwerth Foel—who'd danced so spritely with Cristin on May Day—gave a strangled shriek and then dropped like a stone, an arrow through his neck. The vision of the May Pole, Cristin dancing around it, laughing with sheer joy, cut like lightning through the carnage for an instant.

Almost an instant too long. The thud of an axe split his shield in two, cleaving through the heads of the Cwn Annwn as if they were nothing but flesh. There came a sharp slice of pain as the blade continued downward, slicing through the sleeve of his tunic into the skin of his forearm.

Llywelyn gasped, twisted, thrust his sword blindly but accurately, and closed his ears and his heart to the sound of death, even as he dealt it. Desperately, without thinking, less still feeling, he kept on engaging, evading, striking, parrying, his left arm hanging useless, his body undefended now that he had no shield. His sword arm flayed wildly, without skill, in this direction and that, making contact, often missing, sometimes maiming...sometimes killing.

The heat was stifling, as if they fought in hell, not on earth, and, everywhere, the rancid metallic stench of blood grew stronger and stronger. Llywelyn's feet began to slip and struggle for purchase as bodies began to pile up on the ground, Flemish *and* Welsh. His eyes streamed with smoke and sweat, his breath became a rasping sobbing and, with every engagement, his weapon grew heavier and heavier in his hand.

A piercing yell sounded behind him and instinctively he spun around, swinging his sword in an arc, attacking his assailant and defending himself at the same time. The man, without helmet and his face a blur, made no sound at all as the blade connected, and he crumpled as if boneless into a heap.

And then, abruptly, it was all over...

An awful quiet descended and, suddenly conscious of the pain in his left arm, the blood-soaked sleeve that clung to his skin, Llywelyn fell to his knees, driving his sword point into the ground and leaning his forehead upon its gleaming hilt.

For a long moment, he just knelt amid the dead and the dying, and simply breathed air deep into his lungs, since he could do nothing else. The aftershock of battle was always the same, draining a man of strength, leaving nothing but an empty aching void, and an unbearable sense of remorse.

Slowly, inevitably, the aftermath began—the checking of who was dead and who alive, the hasty binding of wounds, the pouring of water into parched mouths. Llywelyn lifted his head, and his heart froze in horror. Right in front of him lay the man he'd just slain, the mouth slack and strangely amazed, blood oozing into a grey beard and pillowing the thick head of darker hair in a ghastly crimson halo.

The old Fleming looked so like Cadwgan that for a moment he thought it actually *was* his father lying there. Vomit rose into his mouth and, turning to one side, he retched, his shoulders heaving, his ribs feeling as if they would crack beneath his armour.

Then, his stomach empty and the taste of bile thick on his tongue, he looked again. It wasn't Cadwgan, of course, but the similarity to how his father had been once, before the assault that had left him a wreck, was startling. Even the eyes, black and piercing, looked up at him as his father's had done so often, with brutal intent, their expression frozen for all eternity at the moment of death.

Grasping his sword hilt, Llywelyn leaned forward over the body and passed his palm over those eyes, closing them forever. And then he pushed himself to his feet and looked around him at the scene of death and destruction. And as he looked, he wished he could close his own eyes, too, but he couldn't.

The sun was barely cresting the mountains to the east when Llywelyn took his men—what was left of them—out of Castell Blaenporth the next day and led them homeward.

More than a quarter of his force was dead, while many others were wounded and had remained behind to be treated and sent home later. So only eight men rode with him out into the new day.

The horse he sat on was a Flemish one, his own stallion having perished on a spear point in the charge through the gates yesterday. A bandage covered his left arm from elbow to wrist, so he rode one-handed, the cutaway sleeve flapping in the breeze. His shield probably still lay in two halves on the red earth of the bailey, the Cwn Annwn rent asunder forever.

At Llanbedr, where the charred remains of an enemy castle heralded yet another Welsh victory, they turned northeast and followed the course of the Teifi River. The soft bubbling of the water was soothing, the darting of dragonflies across its surface a reminder that there was vivid and eager life, and not just futile and pointless death, to be had in the world—for some, at least.

At Rhydfendigaid, he sent his men onwards the short distance to Ystrad Meurig, and he himself turned southeast, for the abbey of Ystrad Fflur. The valley in front of him opened up into wide green fields, its gentle hillsides blooming with colour, as befitted its name—the Vale of Flowers. Passing in through the West Gate, Llywelyn left his borrowed mount there and went on foot to the abbey church.

It was the hour of Terce. The sound of plainsong seemed to come not from the choir, but from heaven itself, and a beautiful sense of tranquillity hung over the walls of the cloister. He entered through the arched doorway and walked up the lofty nave, his feet almost soundless on the tiled floor. And the sacred psalm that filled the church filled him, too, with a peace and a certainty he hadn't known in a long, long time.

* * *

'Good afternoon, Cristin! I see you're wearing your blue kirtle again today! Put it on for the return of your lord, have you?'

The spiteful remark greeted Cristin as she entered the laundry, as she did most days, with Lord Cadwgan's soiled bedding to be washed. Unlike the last time they'd sparred, however, she didn't retaliate in kind. After all, her lord hadn't returned…yet.

'All warriors who come back from a battle deserve a fitting welcome, Dyddgu. How is it that *you* haven't made an effort?'

The woman's jaw dropped and then the spite was back, more eloquent than ever. 'Flaunting about with your hair loose like that, tempting the eyes of men who should know better than to look!'

'At least *I've* got hair to flaunt!' With a pointed look at the thin brown strands of hair that poked out from beneath the laundress's coif, Cristin dropped the dirty linen at her feet. Then, with a sour smile, she turned and marched back out through the door. There were far more important things to worry about today than malice.

Tangwystl had told her already what news the men had brought back with them yesterday, amid tears of joy for the victory, relief for the survivors and regret for the dreadful losses. Cristin had shared all those feelings, but her eyes had been dry, even though she'd wanted to weep too.

But she couldn't weep because if she did, she might never stop, and only she and Tangwystl had known why. There could only be one reason, after all, for Llywelyn's strange departure at the ford of Rhydfendigaid, where he'd sent his men home and he himself had turned south, for

Ystrad Fflur. He'd put down his sword and taken up his monk's habit at last.

And even though she knew it, there was a little part of her heart that still rebelled against the vow she'd imposed on it. A little part that longed to take that prayer back, pretend it had never been prayed at all, there on her knees at Llywelyn's *prie-dieu*, in the room where they'd lain together for the last time.

Because now it had been answered.

Going into the hall, she sought out some of the men who'd returned, who were sitting at table even though the midday meal had ended, discussing the battle, as seasoned soldiers always did. They looked up in surprise as she cleared her throat.

'Did Lord Llywelyn say nothing more to you yesterday, when he left you?'

One of them, recovering quicker than the others from the bluntness of her query, got to his feet. 'No, maiden. Only that he was going to the abbey.'

'And the wound he sustained…it wasn't mortal, and was tended to properly?'

The man nodded. 'It wasn't mortal, no, but deep enough even so, and the arm will take some time to heal.'

'And other than that…he was well?'

This time there was only a shrug. Cristin nodded her thanks and turned away. As she retreated, a whistle followed her, then a stifled snigger and finally a curt *'Taw!'* from the soldier who'd answered her questions, clearly the leader of the group.

Perhaps he thought it prudent to hush the lewdness, in case their lord *did* return, after all, and celebrate a glorious, if costly, victory in the bed of his *gordderch*! But she knew better than them, and her knowledge needed no more questions, no more answers.

Outside, the sky was so blue it hurt the eyes. The abbey bell had long tolled Nonce, and the afternoon was ebbing slowly into an evening that promised to be drowsy. Her duties were done until evening, and there seemed no purpose to her day, only to fall into bed at the end of it, where she would clutch Mwg tightly to her breast and try to endure the breaking of the heart within.

So as she'd done every afternoon since Llywelyn had ridden out, she went to the *crug*. Now, however, there was no expectation, no uncertainty, no dread and no hope. There was nothing at all.

She didn't notice the flowers along the way, nor the birds nor the bees nor the butterflies. Instead, her gaze was downcast and her feet were like lead as they dragged her onwards through the yellowing grass.

Climbing to the top of the mound, Cristin sat and stared southward, towards the abbey, hidden behind the hills. Around her, the blue speedwell waved in the gentle breeze, the buttercups gloriously bright in the sunshine, but for once, she didn't notice them either.

The hours passed, the warmth of the day receded and, in the stillness, she prayed again for the will to go on living, knowing that Llywelyn was so close and yet a world apart. The strength to stop herself wanting what she could never have and had vowed to give up. The determination to keep her vow even though it didn't really need to be kept in the way she'd envisaged.

Llywelyn had come back alive but she didn't have to give him up in return for his life. He'd given *her* up instead and had entered the monastery without even saying goodbye.

The weight of that pressed down upon her, bringing her

existence full circle and her world to an end. Bowing her head, Cristin wrapped her arms about her updrawn knees. The blue kirtle she wore seemed to suffocate her, the rich material crushing her bones, squeezing the breath from her lungs, grounding her heart to little pieces.

Tonight she would take it off and never put it on again. It would lie in the bottom of her coffer, to rot into forgotten strands of her love, one that could never have survived, no matter how hard and how long it had been fought for.

The sound of a startled blackbird nearby brought Cristin's head up again. She blinked against the sun to the west, lower now in the sky, and a gust of wind caught her hair and blew it across her face. Quickly, she pushed it back to see a man coming towards her at a run.

He was on foot, long legs scything through the tall grass, leaping over the small rocks and shallow ditches that characterised this neglected pastureland. He wore no cloak, his head was bare and his left arm hung strangely loose at his side. He wore no monk's habit either, but she knew that was because it didn't happen that quickly.

A novice had to earn his place first, through his devotion, his abstinence, the divesting of all his worldly goods and the trappings of his secular life. Perhaps, before he did all that, Llywelyn had come to say goodbye, after all.

Cristin felt her heart leap into renewed life but, even as the breath piled up into her throat, her heart sank again. Balling her hands in her lap, she dug her fingernails into her palms and waited as he bounded up the *crug*.

The joy on his face, the brightness of his eyes, the beautiful smile, almost undid her as he knelt before her and pulled her into his arms. He was so warm, so alive, so *necessary*, that she nearly weakened at once. But somehow, she held herself still, kept herself apart, willed herself to not clutch him to her breast and never let go.

It seemed an age before he went still, too, his body freezing as if winter had suddenly swept in, and his arms dropped slowly away. He drew back and looked at her, his chest heaving, as he recovered his breath. Then his eyes clouded like a blue sky suddenly turning to grey, and his face, so full of joy an instant before, became a mask of bewilderment.

'Cristin…?'

Cristin steeled herself to hear his goodbye, for that was surely why he'd come, to tell her he had made his decision to follow his vocation. He'd even made it easier for her in doing so, though he didn't know that, of course. So it was for *him* to speak first.

And when he did, perhaps it would be easier, too, to return his farewell, to wish him well in his new life of enclosure within the walls of Ystrad Fflur, and pretend that *her* life hadn't ended at all.

Chapter Fifteen

Llywelyn sat back on his heels and stared at Cristin. She was so still, so remote, reluctant to look at him let alone embrace him, as he had her. It was like that first time, when they'd met in the village after seven years apart, but so much worse.

A terrible taste of fear rose into his mouth. Reaching out his good arm, he touched her cheek, found it as smooth and as cold as marble. Her lips were pressed firmly together, and her hands were clenched so tightly that the knuckles shone white.

'Cristin...?' he said again. 'Why don't you speak?'

Her gaze dropped to his left sleeve. 'You are wounded...'

Llywelyn shook his head. 'It is nothing, a glancing blow from an axe.' That wasn't what he wanted her to speak of, and the deflection wounded him more than any blade could. 'My shield was shattered.'

'Then the Cwn Annwn...?'

'Lie where I have left them, in the bailey of Blaenporth.'

She paled but made no reply, and her silence sent a chill down his spine. He'd been absent less than a week, and yet an eternity seemed to have passed since the morning he'd left her in his chamber. And, in the interim, the closeness they'd shared, the love they'd given each other, had apparently fallen into abeyance, as if it had never existed at all.

'I had thought that you would be gladder to see me.'

Even as he voiced it, Llywelyn cringed at the complaint. That was the sort of thing a spurned and impetuous youth would say, and even in their childhood, their love had been more mature, more honest, than that.

'I am glad to see you returned safe, of course.'

Her response was cruelly trite, but the lack of feeling behind the words was belied by the anguish in her eyes. Eyes that darted away from his and came slowly back. Eyes that were surely hiding a secret as they dropped to her lap then, and refused to look at him at all.

'What's amiss, Cristin?' Llywelyn forced himself to patience, certain now that something was very wrong indeed. 'What happened while I was gone?'

'Nothing happened. Everyone at the castle is well.' She turned her head away, stared southward, towards the abbey he'd ridden from that morning after passing the night in the pilgrims' hostel. 'As you came here on foot, I presume you have been to the castle already?'

Twisting his body, Llywelyn sat down, crossing his legs and resting his elbows on his knees, struggling to make sense of this. 'Yes, I've been to the castle before coming here.' He plucked a sprig of blue speedwell from the ground, as the distance between them grew wider still. 'I went to see my parents.'

The flower blurred as he looked down at it and a hot sensation rose behind his eyes. God forbid! Was he going to weep? He'd cried often here, as a boy, when he'd sought solace in Cristin's arms after one of his father's beatings. And she'd always given it, unstintingly, but now…

'I needed to see my father,' he added, the memories swamping him, all the more poignant because they were so at odds with the aloof woman who sat beside him.

She turned towards him but her eyes were still guarded, her tone without inflection. 'Why now and not before?'

'Because of the battle, partly, at least.' Llywelyn picked another sprig, wound the delicate trailing stem around the first, starting to form a string to help him string his words together too. 'It was terrible, Cristin. We lost so many men, killed so many of the enemy…'

His words faltered and she supplied them, a note of concern at least replacing some of the coolness in her tone. 'Worse than other battles you have fought?'

He nodded. 'I have fought Flemings before, but not like these. They were determined to hold the castle or else perish in the attempt.'

'And…*did* they perish, all of them?'

'No, a small few were merely wounded. We expected them to fight to the death, but some surrendered in the end.'

'And they were dispatched?'

Llywelyn glanced up. There was no horror in her question, nor on her face, as there had been when he'd retaken Castell Ystrad Meurig and his *penteulu* had put the garrison to the sword.

'Not that either,' he said, pausing in the work of winding flower around flower. 'Peredur and I were in agreement that they be allowed to go free.'

Her head turned away again. 'That was noble.'

He went on, wondering if she was even listening to him, let alone hearing. 'Noble, or foolish—since they live to fight us another day—it nevertheless taught me something, Cristin, something that I long needed to learn.'

'And what was that?'

'That, although there are wars, the men that wage them can still retain compassion, extend mercy and fight with honour, no matter how terrible the battle. Even in war, good is able to exist alongside bad, transcend and conquer the evils of the world. *You* told me that, did you not?'

'Did I?'

'You *know* you did.' Llywelyn's fingers fumbled as he plucked and wound another sprig of blue speedwell onto the string, breaking the fragile bloom, so he had to reach for another to take its place. 'Do you understand what I am trying to tell you, Cristin?'

'Yes. At the battle of Blaenporth, you learned the meaning of compassion, mercy and honour.' Her voice softened then. 'But you didn't really need to learn those things, Llywelyn. You live by them already, and always have.'

'I have always *tried* to.'

'I know. Gronw Gof told me that it was Gwion ab Adda, not you, who ordered the execution of the surviving Normans when Ystrad Meurig was taken. You would have spared *them* also, had you been able to…would you not?'

Llywelyn nodded, glad that she'd known the truth all along, even though she'd never told him she knew. 'Yes, I would have spared them.' There was a pause and, during it, the distance between them started to close at last. 'But something else happened at Blaenporth too…' he continued, since there was more yet that she had to know. 'I killed an old man…'

She met his eyes and Llywelyn resisted the urge to reach out and close that gap a little bit more.

'A man so like Cadwgan that, for a moment of madness, I thought it actually *was* him.' As he took another bloom from the ground, his hand brushed hers, and he sensed her fingers flinch. But at least there *was* feeling there, warmth despite the cold veneer. 'And when I saw that man's face and thought of Cadwgan, something happened to me...or rather was given to me.'

'What?'

'A gift...the gift of clear sight.' Llywelyn felt hope fill his heart, driving out some of the chill. 'And I know now that I must see into my soul, as deep as I can. Banish hate and find forgiveness instead, for others, for the enemy... and for myself, too, no matter what I have to do, even for the things I would rather *not* do.'

Her gaze was searching his now, deeply, although uncertainty still lingered in the hazel-green depths, as if he'd been away too long and had come back a stranger to her, as he had before.

'So, before I came here to you, I went to talk with my father.'

'Then you have stopped hating him...and forgiven him?'

'Not yet...but at least I am ready to try.'

'I think he will be glad.'

Despite the fear and dread that were piled up in his throat, Llywelyn smiled at the irony of what had passed between him and Cadwgan earlier, while his mother sat quietly at the window and hid her tears from him.

'Do you remember that day I went to see him, when he tried to ask something of me, and I turned away instead of listening?'

'Yes.'

'Well, he asked it of me today. He wishes to end his life as a monk, so that he can truly repent and find salvation!'

Cristin's mouth dropped open and she stared at him in astonishment, a host of feeling transforming her face, betraying things that surely she'd been harbouring inside all along.

'And will you grant him that wish?'

'Yes, and gladly.'

Her eyes lowered to the flowers in his lap and there was a moment of silence, as if they were both thinking only of those tiny blue speedwell with their small spear-shaped leaves. And then, from saying nothing or at best very little, her next words streamed out of her like a river in spate.

'Your mother will grieve sorely to lose *both* of you to the cloister. She will be comforted, of course, for the sake of her husband's soul…but she would rather see *you* remain as lord of Ystrad Meurig…and as her son.'

'And she *will*, Cristin, since I am not *going* to the cloister.' Llywelyn turned onto his knees to face her, crushing the fragile rope of flowers beneath him in his excitement. 'I am remaining here…in the world…with you.'

'But I thought…' Her eyes flared wide. 'I thought when you went to the abbey and didn't come back with your men…'

'That I'd put on the monk's habit?' He shook his head. 'No, I didn't, and I never will, even though that means I will have to go on fighting until this war is ended.'

'But… I don't understand…'

'Neither did I…but I do now. I must accept who and what I am and the life I must live. I am a lord, with responsibilities, to a house and to people who depend on me. I have a duty to my family, to my tenants, to my country. But far more important, even than *all* of that, I have a duty to *you*, Cristin…my love.'

Llywelyn paused, dragged in a breath. 'I have been a coward all these years, in pursuit of an escape, not a vocation. Not a coward in battle—' he touched his breast, his fingers trembling '—but here, in my heart. The religious life I sought wasn't one of faith, but a hiding away from the world, an abhorrence of fear and cruelty because I'd had little experience of anything else. You said that, too, didn't you?'

She made no response and, quickly, desperately, he went on. 'So, I rode to the abbey to tell Abbot Enoc that I would not be joining his brethren there, now, or ever. I knew the truth of that before Blaenporth even, but couldn't speak it, just in case...'

Cristin's gaze became wary, almost fearful. 'In case you didn't come back?'

Llywelyn nodded. 'You were right when you asked if I was seeking a sanctuary from the world because of my father's violence, the fear that I would end up like him, and not because of any true conviction at all.'

'Perhaps you would have seen that for yourself, in time, but I am happy you are reconciled with your father...and with yourself, at last. I truly am, Llywelyn.'

The remark was complete and yet it was not with a note of finality in it that widened the distance between them even more.

'And is that *all* you are happy about, Cristin?' He reached out, tried to take her hands in his, but she'd balled them in her lap now, and all he could do was lay his hands over them. 'Is my reconciliation all you *care* about?'

She gave a little shrug, the movement so dismissive it sent a shudder through him, but her reply was even worse.

'Is there more?'

'Yes, there is, much more!' Llywelyn sensed her move further away than ever, though she'd not actually moved at all. 'The true reason I will never enter the cloister is because I love you, Cristin, and I cannot live my life, anywhere, or at all, if you are not in it, with me. I will even go on being a warrior, for as long as I must, if you are by my side, always and forever.'

Her face paled and her eyes lowered, so that it was impossible now to read their expression. 'Oh.'

'Oh?' Letting go of her, he sat back on his heels, feeling the earth beneath him falling away and himself sinking into an abyss of despair. 'Is that all you have to say? Have you not heard anything I have said?'

'Yes, I heard, but…' There was a little tremble of her mouth before she went on. 'We have known each other since childhood, so perhaps that is why you *think* you cannot live without me.'

Llywelyn's heart plummeted lower still, his eyes raking her downcast face, trying to see into *her* heart. A heart he'd thought she'd given to him but which, for some unfathomable reason, she had decided to take back.

'I don't *think*, Cristin, I know! Or I thought I did.' He forced the question out through gritted teeth, on a breath that shook, dreading the answer he might hear. 'Have you really stopped loving me, then? After all these years, has your love finally died, in the space of a few days?'

Her gaze still didn't meet his. 'I admit there has been more than friendship between us always, and a sort of love, yes…but we must forget that now.'

'Forget?' Llywelyn felt the blood drain from his face. '*Dduw annwyl*, Cristin, *why*?'

She shook her head, the gesture seeming strangely helpless. 'Because we must remember who and what we are, and in future behave in the way we *should*, like master and servant.'

'I don't believe you mean that! You *cannot* mean it!' Twisting and rising onto his knees again, Llywelyn took her hands in his at last, gripping them so tightly that he knew he must be hurting her.

But for once, and for the first time ever since the day they'd first met, it was *she* who was hurting him, inflicting pain far worse than he'd ever suffered from his father. For *this* pain went far deeper than skin and bone, and pierced straight down into the centre of his heart. 'For God's sake, Cristin…tell me that you do not!'

Cristin winced as Llywelyn's fingers wrung hers, the wreath of blue speedwell forgotten now and crushed into the ground. His eyes blazed bright with bewilderment and disbelief, but the harder she tried to pull away, the tighter he held on.

'Let go of me…*please*!'

'No, not until you tell me *why* we should forget, why you even *want* to forget!'

She looked away, the anguish on his face unbearable. 'Because we *must*!'

'That is no explanation at all! Something has happened here, hasn't it, between my leaving and my returning? Tell me what it is!'

The landscape began to blur. 'It is just that…what you said is true…we cannot be together…it is impossible…'

'You are baffling me, Cristin.' He shook his head. 'We *love* each other—or at least I *thought* we did. God knows *I* still love *you*!'

'He knows that only too well, that is the problem.'

His fingers tightened even more. 'Stop talking in riddles, for pity's sake!'

The tears pricked hotter behind Cristin's eyes and she blinked them back. She had to be stronger now than she'd ever been. 'Very well.' She turned to look at him, feeling her heart begin to crack. 'I will speak plain but you need to let go of me first.'

Llywelyn hesitated, as if he thought she might bolt like a hare the moment he did as she bade him. But with a nod, he released her and sat back, his hands fisting on his thighs.

'I am waiting, Cristin.'

Cristin stared, not into his face, but at his wounded left arm, the sleeve cut away and stained red. And the words she had to say seemed harder than ever, when it should be easy to say them. For she'd said them to herself over and over this past week until she knew each and every word by rote. But once they were said to him, out loud and with conviction, it would be impossible to take them back.

'The morning you left, you said a warrior never knows if he will return from a battle or if he will not.'

'What of that?' Llywelyn's tone was impatient. 'I *have* returned.'

Forcing herself to breathe and speak plainly, as he'd asked, Cristin went on, digging her fingernails hard into her palms. 'Yes, you have returned. I prayed that you would come back safe and my prayers have been answered.'

'With God's mercy.' There was hurt and accusation now in his tone, as well as impatience 'Then what is it? Tell me!'

'Because I did *more* than pray…' The breaking of her heart made her voice shake. 'I made a bargain with God, and sealed it with a vow.'

'A vow?'

Cristin nodded, forced her eyes to remain locked with his, as she broke *his* heart too. 'When I placed the armour upon your body, I understood what battle was, what Blaenporth would be, what it might mean.'

His brow furrowed, not with confusion, but with a dawning understanding. 'You had never seen me ride to war before?'

'No.' The tears were too strong to hold back any longer, and so she let them come at last. 'And the fear that you might not return, that you would die there, became unthinkable...unbearable.'

'Cristin... I didn't die. I am here, alive, with you...'

'But I didn't know then, when I made my vow, that you would renounce the way of the monk.'

'Then the fault is mine, for not renouncing it sooner.' He lifted a hand, touched her sleeve, tentatively, as if he thought she was losing her wits, not knowing she'd lost far more. 'I love you, Cristin, and I know your love hasn't died. You do love me. You *do*...don't you?'

'Yes... I love you.' The tears spilled faster, heavier. 'But it's...it's too late now.'

He leaned forward, cupping her face, his thumbs brushing the tears from her cheeks. Though her eyes were swimming in grief, in *his* eyes, Cristin saw something she'd never seen there before, not even when he'd suffered the worst of Cadwgan's attacks. Terror.

'Cristin...for heaven's sake, what's wrong?'

'I prayed to God to bring you back safe and alive, and in return...' The words faltered but she forced them out, piecemeal, as each one choked her. 'In return... I swore... to give you up.'

Llywelyn's expression froze and his hands dropped to his sides. 'Give me up...?'

'When you'd left...' she went on, nodding helplessly. 'I knelt at your *prie-dieu*...for hours... I was so afraid that you might die in that battle...that it would be *God's* will, just as you said. And so, I made a pact with Him.'

'Oh, Cristin!'

Slowly, he rubbed his palms over his face, as if he dreamt a terrible dream. His hair fell over his brow, glinting like jet in the sunlight, but there *was* no sun really, only a dark and gloomy prospect that turned day into night.

A silence stretched out, futile and terrible because there was no hope at the end of it. Llywelyn picked up the blue speedwell he'd been threading together, staring down at them, as if he wondered who had wound them so prettily together, and who it was that had all but crushed them.

When he spoke again, a long moment later, his voice was bleaker than she'd ever heard it. 'Then what are we to do, Cristin?'

'Nothing.' Cristin shook her head, feeling a pain close around her brow. 'It is for the best, really, there was never any hope for us, was there?' The truth sounded crueller than ever since it was *she* who spoke it. 'You might not be a monk now but you are still a lord and I am still a servant.'

'Servant?' His head lifted and his eyes flashed. 'It matters not to me *what* you are, nor what *I* am. Those are just accidents of birth. We *love* each other, Cristin.'

'But there is no *place* for our love! You yourself said I was too good to be your *gordderch*…and so I vowed that I would *not* be that…even though I was prepared to share your bed, despite what anyone thought or said…'

She heard his breath catch. 'What did you say?'

Cristin swallowed down more tears as the words poured out of her now in a flood of despair. 'I promised that if you chose the religious life, I would accept it and be happy for you, and that I would not lie with you as your *gordderch* ever again.'

'My *gordderch*…?'

Llywelyn repeated the word as if he'd never heard it before, as if he didn't understand it, when they both understood it only too well.

'I vowed that if you came back safe and alive, I would be content,' she went on, more quickly now, desperate to get to the end, and not have to speak anymore. 'And I thought I *could* be, that I would be able to bear it.'

Suddenly, he jerked up onto his knees, as if a bolt of lightning had come out of the sky. His hands closed around her upper arms and his eyes were no longer bleak but burned bright, eagerly and with hope.

'What *exactly* did you promise, Cristin? What *exactly* were the words of your vow?'

She stared at him. 'I have just told you—'

'No, no!' He shook his head. 'What were the *words*, just as you said them, just as you meant them?'

Cristin didn't have to struggle to remember the words. They'd been inscribed on her soul from the moment she'd said them. 'Dear Lord, bring him back and I'll never be his *gordderch* again.'

A smile lit on his mouth. *'My gordderch?'*

She nodded, her heart twisting with confusion now as well as misery. 'I vowed I would not share your bed as your...'

But the word died on her lips as Llywelyn began to laugh. *'Gordderch!'* His forehead came down to rest upon hers. 'Oh, Cristin, *f'anwylyd.'*

Cristin drew her head back, stared in disbelief. Had her grief actually sent her mad? For surely his eyes should be like hers, empty except for sorrow and pain, not filled with mirth and joy. And yet, that is what she saw.

'What have I said wrong?'

Llywelyn laughed louder. 'Nothing wrong at all, but only right! You don't have to break your vow at all, Cristin, don't you realise? No, of course you can't, because I haven't asked you yet.'

'Asked me what?'

'To be my wife, of course!'

Cristin gasped. 'Your...wife?' Even as the hope surged, it sank. 'But how can that be?'

'How can it *not* be, *'nghariad i*?'

She shook her head again, but her mind wouldn't clear. It was as if she was asleep and dreaming all this, curled up in her bed and not sitting here on the *crug* at all.

'But...if you wed, when you wed, it will be to a lady of your own standing, surely...'

'By whose command?'

'That of the Lord Rhys...of your father...'

'For the former, that is for *me* to settle, but as I am remaining in Rhys's service, come war or peace, I think he will not object. And as for my father...'

Llywelyn's face sobered then and, releasing her, he opened the pouch at his belt, taking out something round and shiny. 'Cadwgan has given us his blessing already. That was the other reason I went to the castle first, before coming here—to ask his permission for our marriage.'

Cristin stared down as he held out his palm. On it was a gold ring set with a ruby, a ring she recognised. 'This is your mother's ring...'

'And now yours, with her blessing, too, and her love— though she said that both were already yours. What did she mean?'

She smiled then, albeit with a tremor on her lips, remembering the talk in Tangwystl's chamber. 'It was a conversation we had...the day you rode away.'

Llywelyn didn't ask any more about that emotional hour she'd shared with his mother, but Cristin had a feeling he would do so later. For now it seemed he had a far more important question, one that could wait no longer.

'So...will you give me your answer, Cristin?' His hands closed eagerly over hers, the ring pressed between their palms. 'Will you be my wife?'

Uncertainty rose up once more, wrapping like a fog around the trembling joy that had begun to bubble inside her. 'But...are you *sure*? Is it possible...and right?' She searched his eyes, since the answer was beyond her. 'Or are we trying to trick God with our words because we *want* it to be right?'

'It *is* right.' His gaze grew serious. 'I would never imperil your soul, Cristin, nor my own. God doesn't need definitions of words, not when He can see into the hearts and souls of men and women.'

'And can He see into ours?'

He nodded. 'Especially into ours and with clarity. He knows *our* truth, and we will be blessed in this marriage, and in our love, I promise you.'

Cristin hesitated, not daring to believe, even now. But if Llywelyn had said so, it *must* be so. She looked down at the ring again, saw the tremble of his hand, felt herself tremble, too, as she met his waiting gaze.

'Yes.' The word was a whisper, so quiet, that she wasn't even sure she'd said it. So she repeated it, louder this time, her voice startling her as it rang out into the stillness of the day. 'Yes, I will be your wife!'

Llywelyn slipped the ring onto her finger and sealed his troth with a kiss, a deep kiss that did indeed make everything right. Then he pulled her to him, his arms, despite his wound, wrapping so tightly around her that she could hardly breathe.

'I knew you'd be here, waiting for me...as you've always

waited.' His shoulders heaved as he drew a deep breath. 'But, *o nefoedd*, Cristin, for a terrifying moment, I really thought I'd lost you.'

'I'm sorry.'

'No, I'm the one who is sorry, for not coming to my senses years ago.' He drew his head back and the solemn moment, and with it all fear and doubt, vanished as his gaze twinkled merrier even than the blue speedwell. 'And now I would like, more than anything, to lay you down here, on our *crug*, and join with you. But I won't, not until the priest has married us properly.'

Cristin wound her arms around his neck and teased him, her heart quaking at the thought that they nearly *had* lost each other, for a little while.

'You mean, we must abstain until our wedding night? That I must keep my vow, until then at least, to not be your *gordderch*?'

Llywelyn shook his head, his smile dazzling. 'You were never that, Cristin, and well you know it.'

'Yes, I know it.'

His gaze as dazzling as his smile now, he released her and took up the half-crushed wreath. Threading fresh flowers into it, his long fingers quick and deft, he formed it into a circle and secured the two ends together.

'That crown that Rhys honoured you with on May Day was pretty, Cristin, but sorely insufficient.'

'How so?' Cristin asked, tears threatening once more, this time ones of joy and so much love that she wondered how her heart could contain it.

Llywelyn placed the crown of flowers on her head, a little lopsided at first, as his wounded arm hindered him, his wry grimace making her love him all the more.

'Because no flower, however beautiful, could match your

beauty.' Cradling her face in his hands, he looked deep into her eyes. 'You were a May Queen then, but now you are, and always will be, *my* queen, Cristin Gwalltcoch.'

Epilogue

Before the altar in the church of Llanbadarn, Cristin wore a crown once more. Not a May Queen's crown, nor a simple chain of blue speedwell, but a bridal wreath. Her wedding gown was a pale saffron, made of fine silk, with a silver girdle at her waist that matched the silver slippers on her feet.

She'd never been dressed so richly—but then she'd never been the bride of a lord before!

Instead of the priest incumbent, Llywelyn's uncle, Edwin ab Ieuaf, married them, despite his blindness. In fact, he seemed to see deep into her soul as his gentle hands read her face, made the sign of the cross on her forehead and he smiled down at her.

Their vows already said at the church door, Llywelyn slipped the ring onto her finger once more, as he had on the *crug*. When he dipped his head and kissed her, it felt like it was the first time he'd done so. But when his lips left hers, the love in his eyes was the same as had always been there.

They walked hand in hand down the nave, beneath the gilded saints and angels on the vaulted ceiling. Above the door, Padarn himself, his golden staff in his hand, bestowed his blessing as they left his holy church and walked out into a new life.

Outside in the sunlight, Cristin found herself welcomed, not just into a new life as Llywelyn's wife, but into the bosom of a new family. This day of union was a reunion for the houses of Eilyr and Cadwgan, too, separated by long years of war, and by longer, more personal battles.

Her former mistress, Rhianon, was the first to embrace her. 'I am so happy for you, Cristin, and for Llywelyn!'

Returning the embrace a little shyly, Cristin recalled that terrible night in her mistress's bed at Abereinion, when she'd sobbed in terror and begged to be sent home. It was clear that Rhianon remembered it, too, for her eyes, so like her brother's, danced kindly.

'Just to reassure you, it is only the month of August, and there are no *morloi* yet at Abereinion to spoil your wedding feast tonight!'

'Oh, *meistres*…'

Cristin bit her lip, her response born of instinct and habit, but Rhianon burst out laughing and shook her head. 'We are no longer mistress and servant, Cristin! It is Rhianon you must call me now, or if you like…*chwaer.*'

Sister! Her mind reeled at the change in her world. No, there would be no duties or orders, no cajoling or scolding. No simple kirtles and linen coifs, but fine gowns and silken veils. And no gossip or slander! But even with all those blessings, her new position would take some getting used to all the same.

'Yes, I would like that very much…*chwaer.*'

'And we have a fine new hall at Abereinion now, with comfortable bedchambers—the best of which will be yours and Llywelyn's tonight.' Rhianon's head tilted shrewdly and her gaze narrowed into a mischievous gleam. 'I always suspected there was more than just friendship between you and my brother, when we were all children together.'

Cristin saw the answer even before she asked the tentative question. 'And…do you approve?'

'I do, very much. And I am looking forward to hearing *much* more about it later! I am also looking forward to introducing you to my children, your nephew and nieces.'

'Will they still be awake when we arrive at your home?'

'Oh, yes!' Her former mistress gave a rueful sigh. 'They will be far too excited to go to bed. All three of them run rings around Esyllt, who replaced you as my maid, in a way they would never dare with *me,* the imps!'

But the remark was not stern and Rhianon's eyes were soft as she glanced over to the far side of the churchyard, where Peredur stood at the graveside of his father and his brother. A merciful rest that had finally laid their turbulent past to rest too.

'We will speak more later, Cristin, just you and me.' Taking her hands, she squeezed them warmly. 'We have a lot to catch up on.'

With a kiss on her cheek, her new sister left her and went over to join her husband. There she threaded her arm through Peredur's and leaned against his shoulder, her dark head contrasting with his golden one, as he bent and pressed his lips to her hair.

Cristin smiled as she remembered how reluctant Rhianon—wed and widowed once before—had been to marry Peredur. But it was clear that this second marriage, far different to the first, was blessed with love and trust, a union so strong that not even war could sever it.

Like *her* marriage was! She turned, impatient now with longing, to look for *her* husband. As she did, she glanced up at the hill opposite where the walls of the burned-out castle of Llanbadarn were just visible, stark against the sky. Not yet rebuilt, it was a grim reminder that the war wasn't over, for all the peace that reigned here in this ancient churchyard.

The stable where she'd lain with Llywelyn all those years ago would be burned down, too, no doubt, but it also would be rebuilt, just as their love had been rebuilt and consecrated in marriage here today.

Turning again, her eyes found Llywelyn, talking in the shadow of the porch with his mother and his uncle. As if he sensed her need of him, he bowed and left them and made his way towards her, his gaze sparkling brighter than the rich blue tunic he wore.

Taking her elbow, he led her around the side of the church and into the shade of the east wall. Just like he'd led her around to the lee of the church at Ystrad Meurig that night of his return—and yet not like that at all. Then, they'd been strangers…now they were as one and would never be strangers again.

'So, wife, we are alone at last.' He lifted a lock of her hair, left unbound as befitted a new bride, and touched it to his lips. 'Are you happy?'

Cristin nodded. 'Do you need to ask it?'

'No, as neither do you need to ask it of me.' Drawing her into his arms, he kissed her, rather more passionately than the reverent kiss he'd bestowed at the altar. 'I will be happier still tonight when you are in my bed and we truly become husband and wife at last.'

Cristin drew back and, planting her palms on his chest, teased him. 'But tonight we will be under your sister's roof, in fine new chambers, I'll have you know. And your mother will doubtless not be sleeping far away, to say nothing of your nieces and nephew! Dare we?'

'Oh, yes, we dare, Cristin. I have waited two months already to lie with you. I cannot wait for you any longer.'

The words, light though they were, brought a moment of solemnity in their wake. Llywelyn's father had died, in the infirmary of Ystrad Fflur, a fortnight after the battle for Blaenporth, sooner than expected, and before he could become a monk as he'd wished. So they had delayed their wedding, not just until a lull had come in the fighting, but also until Cadwgan's soul had departed for another realm.

Cristin touched her fingertips to her husband's mouth, traced the curve of his lips, brought his smile back again. 'Do you think your father found peace at last, even though he didn't live long enough to take the habit?'

'Yes, I believe so. The brethren there interceded day and night for his soul.' Taking her hand, Llywelyn enfolded it in his. 'And I am glad, before he died, that I gave him my forgiveness at last.'

Cadwgan's wasn't the only death. Mwg had also died, around the same time, peacefully, curled up on Llywelyn's bed. It had felt as if, now she and Llywelyn were finally together, the cat had no reason to remain. She'd wept, of course, as they'd buried him on the *crug*, beneath the blue speedwell, which had died, too, but would return next spring, as it always did.

Some days later a grey kitten with amber eyes had appeared, curled up in the same spot. Clearly, one of Mwg's many offspring, it had stayed and, although Mwg Fach— as they'd called him—could never take the old tom's place, he'd already wriggled his way into their hearts.

'Tangwystl has made the right choice in going to live at Abereinion.' Llywelyn's voice broke into her thoughts. 'She, too, has found peace in this reconciliation with my sister.'

Cristin curled her fingers tighter around his. 'And reconciliation with *you* also.'

He nodded. 'Rhianon and I understand everything now, the extent of her fear of my father, the love she has always had for us, the guilt because she couldn't shield us from him.'

'I'm glad she found the courage to tell you the truth at last.'

His smile returned, wide and beautiful. 'I think she has always had courage, more than she realised, more than we, her children, realised. And now being with her grandchildren has brought her a contentment I've never seen in her before.'

'I am happy for her, though you will miss her, as will I.' Cristin paused before asking him what she'd asked herself countless times during these two months of waiting. 'And you…? You have no regrets at the choice you have made?'

'Cristin or the cloister? No, no regrets at all, *'nghariad i.*' The blue gaze darkened, not just with desire. *'Nefoedd,* I cannot wait for this day to end, and the night to come, when we can be alone.'

Cristin's stomach gave a little flutter. Something else had happened after Blaenporth too. Her monthly courses had returned and one day soon, God willing, she would be a mother as well as a wife. Perhaps she would be made a mother-to-be this very night!

'Nor can I,' she whispered, as his head lowered and his breath mingled with hers and stirred desire. His arm went around her, a hand entwining in her hair, dislodging her wreath of flowers and her bridal veil, which floated on the breeze to the ground.

'Whatever wonders await us in the next world, Cristin, I have finally found heaven here on earth with you, *f'anwylyd*, my lady…my wife.'

As his mouth took hers, in a promise of the fulfilment to come later, when they would join once more, flesh and heart and soul. Cristin didn't care about the wonders of the next world. This one was wonder enough for her.

'As have I found heaven with *you*. My lord, my love… my husband.'

* * * * *

If you enjoyed this story,
be sure to read Lissa Morgan's
other great historical romances

The Welsh Lord's Convenient Bride
An Alliance with His Enemy Princess

Or find out how it all began with the first book in
The Warriors of Wales duet

The Warrior's Reluctant Wife

Historical Note

In August 1165, the Lord Rhys, and nearly all the other princes of Wales, united to face the army of Henry II near the Berwyn Mountain range, a campaign that was meant to put down Welsh resistance once and for all. But apart from some skirmishes, there was no great battle, and the King was defeated within a few short weeks, more by the Welsh terrain and unseasonable weather than by force of arms.

Henry never again campaigned in Wales, but instead vented his spleen on his Welsh hostages, including the blinding of Rhys's young son, Maredudd, and two sons of Prince Owain ap Gruffudd of Gwynedd. In November that year, Rhys took Castell Aberteifi—Cardigan—and thus re-established in its entirety the Kingdom of Deheubarth, which he ruled until his death in 1197.

For the purposes of this book I have used the term 'Norman,' but in reality, by the middle of the twelfth century, the family on the English throne was Angevin, and the 'enemy' is more accurately, though not in a contemporary sense, described as 'Anglo-Norman.' Roger de Clare and Walter de Clifford were Marcher lords descended from men who had come over with William the Conqueror in 1066, so they would very much have considered themselves Norman. The Welsh would have called them 'the French,' as the English were called 'the Saxons.'

Roger de Clare's fate after the fall of Llanbadarn Castle is not documented. He might have been captured and held for ransom, as depicted here, or he might have fled Ceredigion. Either way, he seems to have relinquished his ambitions in Wales by the end of 1165 and concerned himself with his estates in England and Normandy. The fate of the murderous Gwallter ap Llywarch is not known.

According to legend, Llanbadarn Church was founded by Saint Padarn in the sixth century—the Golden Age of the Welsh Saints. Before the Norman Conquest it was a Celtic church—a *clas*—and under Bishop Sulien, and his sons Rhigyfarch and Ieuan, was a centre of religion, learning and the compiling of manuscripts, including the *Vita Sancti Paterni*. With the coming of the Normans to Ceredigion in the early eleven hundreds, the *clas* was ousted, a Benedictine cell was established and the site was gifted to the monastery of St Peter's in Gloucester.

Llanbadarn came back under the care of native clergy during the Welsh resurgences of 1136, 1156 and 1164, though it never regained its former status. The copying of manuscripts thereafter was done in other holy places, including at the Cistercian Abbey of Ystrad Fflur—Strata Florida. The Cistercians were sympathetic to and supportive of the cause of the Welsh princes, and frequently suffered the wrath of the English kings as a result. Several members of the royal family of Deheubarth were buried at Ystrad Fflur, though the Lord Rhys himself was laid to rest in Eglwys Gadeiriol Tyddewi—Saint David's Cathedral.

The Medieval period was warlike and brutal, yet it was also an age of deep religious faith. Many warriors ended their days in monasteries, in order to ensure the salvation of their souls after a lifetime of violence. Some men—like Llywelyn intended to do—even laid down their swords in their prime and donned a monk's habit instead, perhaps out of a religious calling or a distaste for war, or—like Cadell ap Gruffudd—because they'd sustained injuries serious enough to warrant their retreat from political and military life.

The *crug* at Ystrad Meurig was long thought to have been the site of the original Norman motte and bailey castle, the remains of which lie a quarter of a mile to the west. But it might indeed have been a place where earlier kings held assemblies and audiences, where they could see and be seen by their people. There are *crugiau* all over Wales, and they often occur in place names, such as Grug Hywel— Hywel's Crug. I like to think that Cristin's and Llywelyn's *crug* was one such special place.

I am grateful to Ymddiriedolaeth Ystrad Fflur—Strata Florida Trust—for their welcome, help and inspiration in the writing of this book.